DYING ALIVE

BASED ON A TRUE STORY

jono comiskey

LUCIDBOOKS

Dying to Live
Based on a True Story

Copyright © 2019 by Jono Comiskey

Published by Lucid Books in Houston, TX
www.LucidBooksPublishing.com

ISBN-10: 1-63296-326-4
ISBN-13: 978-1-63296-326-0
eISBN-10: 1-63296-299-3
eISBN-13: 978-1-63296-299-7

Scripture quotations are taken from the New King James Version®. Copyright © 1982 by Thomas Nelson. Used by permission. All rights reserved.

Special Sales: Most Lucid Books titles are available in special quantity discounts. Custom imprinting or excerpting can also be done to fit special needs. Contact Lucid Books at Info@LucidBooksPublishing.com.

Table of Contents

Introduction

Some lives are unremarkable and make little or no impression on the world around them, but some leave a lasting impact that must be shared.

I have been a counselor for many years, yet I have never come across a story quite like the one you are about to read—four lives inexplicably connected across space and time who face unusual triumphs and tragedies. Together, they can change the world, but opposed, they will advance the agenda of hell itself.

In the end, they face a decision. Three must die so one can live. This is their story.

Chapter 1

Officer Smith

The orange glow outside the window seemed unnatural as he forced his eyes to open. He couldn't move, and just breathing seemed like an impossible task. He tried to focus, but his thoughts were too blurry to make any tangible sense of what was happening. Drifting in and out of consciousness, he heard pieces of a frantic conversation going on outside.

"There's a cop trapped inside, and the engine is on fire!"

The voices were getting clearer, and the realization of his situation started to set in.

"Try to break the glass."

"Do you have anything to put out the fire?"

There was an obvious fear in their tone. The heat from the flames was making its way into the cabin. The smell of melting plastic was noxious, but he could not get his body to respond. The taste of metal filled his mouth, and he knew he was swallowing blood. As he pieced together his predicament, he began to understand that the car would be engulfed in flames at any moment, yet he could not get his body to move. He could barely breathe, let alone get out of the car.

"He's not moving. If we don't do something, he'll die."

"Oh, my God! What if he is already dead? What will I do? I have killed a cop!"

"Stop freaking out! I need you to focus and help me put this fire out."

"What the heck, man! I just took my eyes off the road for a minute. I think I must have fallen asleep or something. Why didn't I pull over earlier? Oh God! Oh God! Oh God! Please don't let him die!"

Thud! Thud! The whole vehicle shook as they tried to kick in the glass. "It's not working. Get me a tire wrench or something to break the glass. We've gotta get him out, now!"

Traffic had come to a standstill. Onlookers could not take their eyes off the scene unfolding before them. The officer's cruiser had rolled several times and was perched upside down on top of an embankment. Flames were starting to envelop the whole front end. Everyone watching had seen enough scenes like this in the movies to know a large explosion was imminent. The two men trying to get the officer out were surely in the blast radius if the fire could not be extinguished.

A local bowling team returning from a nearby competition was caught up in the traffic jam. Several of the team members were standing outside the bus, visibly shaken by the horrific scene unfolding in front of them.

"Do something, Harold!" yelled a petite African American woman to her husband, who appeared to have probably been an athlete at some point, but those days were long past.

"There's nothing I can do!"

"Help them put out the fire or he's gonna burn to death."

"What do you expect me to do? Spit on the fire?"

"Use the water in the coolers or something."

That last comment kicked the man's 300-pound frame into gear, and he moved in a fashion that defied his size. Grabbing the first cooler, he yelled at a buddy to bring the other 10-gallon container. Fortunately, they had filled them up before leaving, and both were almost completely full. As the two men reached the car, they could feel the heat of the flames from 10 feet away.

"I don't think we can get close enough to the fire."

"We can get close enough to throw the water on it." Harold took the lid off the cooler and picked it up, one arm shielding his face and the other holding the bottom of the cooler. He targeted what he thought was the heart of the blaze and threw the open cooler in that general direction. The water lapped up the flames, causing them to die out for a moment, but they burst back into life almost immediately.

"Quick! Give me the other cooler." Again, Harold demonstrated athleticism more reminiscent of a time when he could chase down a quarterback than his current exploits as bowling team captain. He launched the second cooler at the same spot and whispered a prayer of desperation, "Lord, this is the last of our water, please put out this fire and save this officer."

The flames sputtered and were unable to catch hold again. Harold, his buddy, and the two men trying to break the glass started throwing fistfuls of dirt on the remnants of the blaze. Within 30 seconds, the fire was completely out. Harold spoke again. "There's blood all over the window."

"Help is on its way!" shouted a mom carrying her baby, who seemed to be sleeping through the commotion.

"He may not make it given the amount of blood he's lost. That crash could have torn someone apart. I can't even see his legs, but I think they're trapped under the dashboard."

"Oh, God! Don't say that! Please, don't say that!" cried the young man whose truck had veered across three lanes of the highway and collided with the unsuspecting cruiser. His mind was now stuck replaying the event that was making a constant loop in his head.

"Don't worry. The ambulance is coming. I bet he'll be all right." Harold intuitively realized that empowering a blame game at this point would only hinder the rescue attempt. "Tell Betty to get over here," he yelled to his wife, who relayed the message into the bus. Betty, a retired ER nurse, emerged and ran to the scene.

"What is his condition?" Her years of training kicked in right away.

"We don't know," the less hysterical of the initial two helpers offered his best guess. "We think he's trapped, and there's a lot of blood inside the car."

"Can you break a window? I need to check his vitals."

Harold found a large rock and smashed the driver's side back window with one blow. Glass shattered everywhere, but Betty forced herself into a position where she could check his vitals.

"His breathing is very shallow. He's not getting enough oxygen," she said out of instinct rather than trying to inform the helpless, would-be rescuers, but they all nodded nonetheless.

The officer tried desperately to breathe, but something was blocking his airway. As Betty probed his throat, she could feel teeth that had been knocked out of his gums. They became dislodged from somewhere deep within his throat, and he coughed to life. Betty had inadvertently bought him some time. After completing her confined examination, she asked how long the ambulance would take.

"They said less than 10 minutes, and that was at least five minutes ago." The mother with the baby looked at her watch to verify the statement.

Betty continued in nurse mode. "His legs are trapped under the dashboard, and my guess is that they are broken. He's likely sustained internal injuries and is at risk of bleeding to death if he doesn't get proper medical attention in time." Harold pushed his palms together and signaled to the team on the bus to pray. The officer needed a miracle, and Harold wanted to make sure they did everything possible to make that happen.

Inside the car, Officer Smith knew he was going into shock. His body felt mangled, and although the fire had been extinguished, he knew he was not even close to being in the clear. He couldn't formulate words, so he was left to process his thoughts internally. *I don't want to die like this. I am too young to die. Please, Lord, don't let me die.*

It seemed like an eternity before the EMS arrived, and it was even longer before they got Smith freed from his metal prison. The medical team worked to keep him alive while the rest of the crew tediously cut through the compressed body of the car. It was a battle between time and potentially causing further injury. Eventually, enough of the car was peeled back, and they transferred Smith to the ambulance.

An issue over insurance reimbursement caused the ambulance crew to make an almost fatal mistake. They took their patient over difficult roads on an almost 50-mile journey to a hospital in the neighboring county. It was not equipped to provide the treatment needed to save his life.

"Why did you bring him here?" the irate ER doctor yelled at the ambulance crew who were giving him the rundown of the injuries.

"Dispatch told us to bring him here."

"But Knox County has a level one trauma center with the resources to treat this man. You guys are unbelievable! You have put this man's life in extreme danger just so you can file an extra $1,000 with the insurance company. Now I have to Lifestar him, and it will be on your conscience if he doesn't make it."

The EMS crew didn't offer a rebuttal, knowing they had gambled the officer's life to satisfy their employer's desire to get more money. They made Officer Smith as comfortable as possible and stabilized his condition until the helicopter arrived. When it finally got to the University of Tennessee Medical Center, the operating room was already prepped, and Officer Smith was rushed into surgery.

Seven of Smith's ribs were crushed, and both legs were broken in multiple places. Significant internal lacerations and possible terminal blood loss were the highest priority. His broken jaw, teeth, and nose would have to wait until there was proof he was going to make it.

That was far from a foregone conclusion. Each of the doctors knew it would be a long and, quite likely, fruitless night.

Chapter 2

Scott

He waited until his dealer was alone and then made his way to the usual exchange point—the alley behind the strip-center housing. It was the last of the businesses to survive the economic roller coaster this area had endured. The more parasitic a business, the more resilient it became. The pawn shop, the payday loan shop, the smoke shop, and of course, the adult store—it seemed more than appropriate that their backyards offered the next step in exploiting human weaknesses.

The back of the strip center was narrow, which is why the garbage truck hated doing pickups there. Despite complaints from the out-of-state landlord, and although the bills were paid, albeit late, the trash collectors always waited to do the pickup until the Goodwill two blocks away complained about the smell. The worst of the trash in the dumpster must have been at least six weeks old. Rats and cockroaches fought over the feast left for them to devour. The local police often ignored this place for no reason other than the smell, but it invited the lowest of the low to its haven. Those who profited from others' weaknesses found here that one man's trash could quite literally be the source of another man's treasure.

Hiding in a crowd was hard for him due to his intimidating look and physique. Pumping his body full of steroids and only God knows what else had prematurely aged him. However, even in his worst state, he could still out-fight and out-muscle most other men. He was approaching the one man in town who could solve his all-consuming problem. Stealth was not his goal, and he did not care that, as usual, he stood out like a sore thumb.

"What do you want, Scott? I told you, I am done with you. So get out of my sight, or I'll force you out."

"Look, Sean, I'm not leaving until you give me the drugs. I need a fix, and I'll do whatever I need to get it."

The dealer seemed to interpret from his former client's body language that he meant business. He had dealt with all sorts of desperate individuals, and he knew the dangers it brought. He pulled out his 9-millimeter Glock.

"I will blow you away, and there's nobody in the world who will even care. So get lost, man!"

"I'm not here to beg. I need my fix, and I said I'm going to do whatever I need to get it."

"Look, asshole, you already owe me money for the last two times I fixed you up."

Scott was about 20 feet away, moving with a menacing gait. The dealer knew he had only a few seconds to decide if today would be a day he killed someone.

"You're a dead man, Scott, if you come any closer!"

Drugs cause their victims to make illogical choices. The worst drugs cause choices that often get their addicts killed. This victim had crossed that line, and his dealer knew it. Lucky for Scott, Sean was not willing to take the heat or the interruption to business that a corpse brings. He grabbed a crowbar that he kept close by, and as the addict lunged toward him, he unleashed a blow that was designed to cause maximum damage.

The crowbar crashed into Scott's head, and his scull caved in under the force of the forged metal, but he did not stop advancing. He was a man possessed, and his dealer now regretted not using his gun. Scott shook off the searing pain in his head and drew on all his instincts as a seasoned street fighter to quickly reduce to a defenseless lump the one who moments ago was breathing threats. Hit after hit rained down on the dealer's head and torso. Like a rabid pit bull, Scott didn't stop until he heard the crack of the man's radius as the guy held up his forearm for protection. Convinced he could now take whatever he needed, Scott extracted all the drugs from the concealed places he had seen Sean hide them in the past. He was only moments away from the relief for which he had caused such great harm. As he turned his back on the now almost unconscious source, a thought of whether the man would live or die never entered his mind. He had fewer morals than the amoral. He had only one thought—himself.

Chapter 3

Joey

The mountain air of Tennessee offered an allure that no adventurous seven-year-old boy could resist. In most ways, Joey was a typical boy who loved the outdoors. As soon as he was liberated from the bondages of school and chores, he longed to venture up the well-worn path from his back door to his favorite vantage point about halfway up the mountain on which his parents had chosen to build their home.

His mom had long ago stopped fighting him over going alone on the trek he would take religiously at every opportunity that presented itself. Instead, she often packed him a lunch since he would usually lose himself in the adventure and forget to come home and eat.

Squirrels, deer, hawks, and many other wild creatures played their part in the adventures that only a young boy can conjure. However, he never felt like the adventure was complete until his meanderings brought him to that most special place—the place that allowed him to see the whole world. It was where eagles felt more at home than people, where the clouds would roll in when a storm approached, making him feel like he could step out and walk on top of the dark gray canopy covering the world below. It was a place where his inner Viking could be summoned, where battles raged until he vanquished the imagined foe, and where a little boy's thoughts of God could be given context in creation and beauty. Above all else, solitude and the unspoken desire for connection to something greater separated this boy from other adventurers his age.

"Don't stay up there all day," Mom shouted in vain when Joey was almost already out of sight.

"Okay, Mom" was the preprogrammed response no matter what the intention. It was not a lie, just a healthy understanding that this passionate half-Cherokee woman was not to be disrespected.

"I hope I see a skunk today," his little brain prioritized out loud as he cast his next battle. "A skunk would beat a raccoon. Yes, I think it would beat a raccoon." He didn't like the ambiguity, but since there was no way of knowing short of actually having them fight, he would have to rest on his limited life experiences to draw his conclusions.

The path turned into quite a hike at certain points as dirt turned into rock and rock into boulders. Joey imagined Indians scaling the mountain face on the hunt for food. The Viking within didn't like being relegated to second fiddle to a dark-haired Indian, and he made his feelings known to Joey.

"A Viking would beat an Indian." The Viking voice seemed quite happy with itself until the Indian responded.

"No, an Indian is faster and smarter, so he would win."

"Vikings are the strongest people in the whole world, so he would win for sure." The inner battle raged for quite a while until both parties—the Indian and the Viking—realized an unrecognizable bug carrying its prey on its back had absorbed their host's attention. No conclusion would be made about who could beat whom today.

The bigger boulders protruding from the mountain face offered great footing for the young adventurer. Joey could probably have climbed with a blindfold on since his feet knew exactly where to place themselves as he rose higher and higher above his home and the world below. At just the right point, the steep face leveled off in a mini-plateau that had just enough room for a vigorous Cherokee rain dance or for Thor the Viking god to stomp his foot and call down thunder from heaven, depending on who was in the ascendancy in their battle when he reached the stopping point.

Joey didn't realize how hungry he was until he stopped. He was always glad that his mom packed an extra sandwich with the perfect amount of peanut butter and jelly. She seemed to intuitively know that the jelly had to be running out the sides in order for it to taste just right.

Once the bounty was consumed, there was only one thing left to do. The adventurer lay flat on the stone and gazed at the sky above. Clouds morphed into a variety of everyday items—from cars to crayons—that were all iden-tified and appropriately categorized. As his warrior battles were finished for another day and his scientific work completed, he was free to ponder and communicate with the One—the Creator—who was responsible for providing all the wonderful things he loved so much.

"Why do skunks smell so bad?"

"Why do baby deer have spots, but grown-up deer don't?"

"Why do snakes not like people, but dogs do?"

"Why is the grass green, and why is the sky blue?"

There seemed to be no end to the questions, and the only thing that would end the conversation that brought so much delight to both the one asking and the One asked was the lowering of the sun and with it the cooling of the air. Downward Joey would go at twice the speed he had ascended, too fast for primitives and demigods to battle and too fast for bugs to catch his attention, but never too fast for the quiet whisper of the Creator: "Come back soon, young explorer."

Chapter 4

Diesel

The cold, hard floor of a nine-by-seven cell met the beast of a man, aptly named Diesel, as he climbed down from the top bunk. The words from chapter three of the apostle John's Gospel still resonated in his soul. His thoughts went to the song on the radio that had earlier echoed the prayer, "Word of God, speak!" Now, perhaps for the first time in his long, hard life, he had heard the living Word not just speak but call *his* name.

"Diesel, you have loved darkness instead of light because your deeds are evil. Diesel, you must be born again. Unless you believe and trust in Me, you will die in the darkness of your sins."

Jesus, the Word that became flesh, spoke, and a life that had seen more than 40 years of hardship and abuse responded to the call of his Savior. Diesel somehow intuitively knew that although Jesus knew his sin, He refused to identify him by it. Instead, that same Savior spoke of redemption, hope, and deliverance from a life of bondage—of purpose yet unfulfilled. Diesel's tears soaked the coarse prison floor as he identified and confessed years of sin. An hour passed as he laid his soul bare. He didn't care that his cellmate, Spencer Coon, could hear, for he was the hardened criminal who had introduced him to the Bible just a few months before. Spencer had demonstrated how to live a Christ-centered life while incarcerated. He had listened to the ridicule of his cellmate while all the time secretly praying for Diesel's eyes to be opened.

Spencer saw the big man fall to his knees, and he watched his body heave in sighs of repentance. He knew the Holy Spirit had shifted the boundaries of hell to yield control of his fellow inmate. The powers of hell were forced to retreat and look for a new soul to torment. It was a holy moment, and Spencer bowed his head in quiet prayer and appreciation for the miracle he felt privileged to be watching.

Chapter 5

Officer Smith

Richard and his wife, Ann, stared at their son's body lying motionless in front of them on the critical care bed. Their eyes, like the rest of their bodies, were weary from enduring the worst night they had ever experienced. Initially, they were told he could not have survived the crash, only to find out he was admitted to the ER in critical condition. Living in the anxiety of not knowing if their son, broken beyond recognition, would make it through another day was physically, mentally, and emotionally exhausting. The only signs of life were the beeping of the heart monitor and the sound of the respirator artificially keeping him alive.

The doctor walked into the room and subconsciously didn't look at Ann to avoid staring into the pain of a mother's soul without being able to bring solace. He directed his comments to Richard.

"Your son is in very critical condition," he said before pausing for what seemed like an eternity. "He has sustained more than 60 broken bones, and his body has suffered significant blood loss. I don't want to give you false hope. His head hit the windshield, causing significant swelling on the brain. Most of his teeth were knocked out. Almost all his ribs were broken, and some of them splintered inside, causing internal bleeding and a punctured lung. His knee caps were shattered. His shins and several bones in his feet and hands were also broken. Right now, the machines are keeping him alive, and we have done all we can to give him a chance to survive. If he makes it through the next 24 hours, his chances will improve, but even then, the odds are stacked against him. I don't often say this, but if you believe in prayer, this would be a good time to exercise that belief."

The words penetrated Ann's heart in a way that only a mother can understand. Immediately, she thought of the scripture about Mary and how she was told that her beloved baby Jesus would cause her such pain later in life. Ann knew that her son was not being crucified for the sins of the world, but her pain was compounded by the unnecessary and undeserved cost to her child, and she finally broke down, sobbing.

Richard was numb. He could not process what he had just heard, and though he instinctively reached down to hold his wife, he offered no conscious comfort, for what little he had in reserve had been pulled out like a rug underneath him by the doctor's hopeless words. Being a pastor did not make these tragedies any easier. In fact, the unspoken expectation that God will take care of your children while you go about His business hung over his heart like a snake waiting to strike its cornered prey. Richard could keep that snake at bay as long as the machines kept beeping, but his faith seemed unable to defend itself if the unspeakable were to happen. A lifeless prayer left his lips, almost without his permission.

"Please help us, God."

That night had all the elements of the valley of the shadow of death, but as the sun came up the next morning, Richard knew his lifeless prayer had found its way to the giver of life. The doctor looked straight at Ann, and for the first time in almost 48 hours, a glimmer of hope rested on the face of this aged surgeon.

"Well, he made it longer than we expected, and his vitals have stabilized. He is by no means out of the woods, but the odds have shifted some in his favor. As the swelling goes down, we will need to address some of the less critical injuries. However, his condition is as good as we could have hoped, given the severity of his injuries."

He stopped short of offering a full lifeline of hope, but Richard and Ann felt like they had been given their son back—back from the dead a second time. Richard was deep in thought as he turned to his bride of 30 years.

"All night, I kept thinking about his battle with cancer and how it nearly destroyed us watching him fight to stay alive. He was only a teenager and should have been thinking about girls and football, not about dying. I kept asking God why He would let him live only to take him away now. Something kept telling me everything would be okay, but I…I…I just felt so helpless. I felt like my prayers were just dropping to the floor. When the doctor said the worst is over, the knot in my stomach loosened its grip, and I'm almost afraid to say this, but I feel like he's going to make it."

Ann had supported her husband's call to the ministry. Richard was not a natural student, but he worked harder than his fellow seminary students to get his degree despite being older than all the others. His call came a little later in life, and his ministry was to the mountain folk of Tennessee. With six mouths to feed, he couldn't survive on the modest stipend he received from his denomination. The only way he could make ends meet was to sell insurance during the day and see to the business of pastoring his flock in the evenings and on weekends. Ann played her part in that call and willingly paid the price of raising a family almost singlehandedly. She believed in him and in their Lord, but there were some things the human soul was never designed to experience, and losing a child was one of them.

"I don't know…" Her voice trailed off as she stared at the machine telling her that her son was still alive. Her emotions were raw, and she wasn't used to sharing her weaknesses with her husband. Her role was to support him while he supported their church family and their community, but she couldn't be strong anymore. "I just don't know if I can take this. My heart is broken looking at him with all the wires and tubes. I can't even recognize his face. Why would God let this happen to us? The cancer was hard enough, but at least I could talk to him, hold him." She was spent. The anger wanted to say more, but her soul would not allow that indulgence. Rest could not come soon enough for them both.

Chapter 6

Scott

The drugs were wearing off, and Scott's instinctive drive for the next fix was interrupted by an excruciating pain in his skull. It felt like a metal ball with sharp points was slamming around inside his head. He had consumed the last of his prescription pain meds two days ago, but the need was not just recreational now, and relief was at the other end of the prescription pad. The only problem was that every doctor in a 50-mile radius knew him on a first-name basis, and they were close to posting his face at their front desks as well.

Being dependent on drugs made the addict a rare breed of desperation and resourcefulness. Scott often joked that he became the smartest man alive when it came time to getting a fix. It didn't matter if he needed cash or a favor. He found a way to extrapolate drugs from whatever equation that challenged him. Today, though, the pain restricted his ability to focus on sourcing his next fix, demanding his immediate attention.

If most men looked in the mirror and saw a concave shape on their head, they would feel instant fear. But Scott was not like most men. His death wish came second only to his habit, and in this life-threatening injury, he only saw an opportunity. "The ER won't turn me away with an injury like this. Thanks, Sean, for giving me a fix last night and writing me a prescription for today!"

Blood was caked all over the shirt he had worn for six days straight, and fresh blood was still oozing from his head. Driving was his only option to get to the hospital, and he almost passed out from the pain more than once. As he stumbled into the ER, one of the orderlies shoved a wheelchair under his legs right before he would have slumped to the ground.

"What happened this time, Scott? When are you going to learn?" The orderly knew Scott from high school but had become reacquainted with him in recent years with his frequent trips to the ER. Scott's real and imaginary conditions were well-known by all the staff. There was no doubt, though, that this trip was legitimate.

"I...I...I ran into," Scott winced as every word sent off a massive ringing pain in his head. He hadn't spoken since he woke up that morning and was caught off guard with the amount of pain he was experiencing. "A tire wrench," he eventually murmured loud enough for the orderly to hear and write it on his chart.

"We are busy today, Scott, so it may be a little while until you are seen. I will get you in triage and get that wound cleaned up. We will know more then."

"Just give me something for the pain, dude. I'm begging you." This was not rhetoric designed to get an expedited fix. Scott was desperate by this point to have his pain mitigated by whatever means necessary.

"You know it doesn't work like that. They'll give you something soon enough, though. Just hang in there a little while longer. If you drove yourself here, then you can handle another few minutes of waiting."

Scott shifted his focus to surviving the next few minutes. An addict can suck the life out of every part of his world while pursuing his addiction, but Scott had learned to control the urges for short periods of time. He now knew he would make it to his next fix, and that alone brought him the hope he needed to endure the pain.

Chapter 7

Diesel

Years of pain, guilt, shame, selfishness, pride, vulgarity, depravity, and much more rolled off his tongue in a confession that lasted the better part of an hour as this once enslaved soul found the true freedom that transcended the prison of bricks and bars. Diesel held nothing back as he sensed the washing of his soul every time he mentioned the next sin that came to his memory. All the way back to childhood, sin after sin revealed itself, and just as quickly as they were unveiled, they were banished by the cleansing blood of his newly found Savior, never to hold the power of his captivity again.

As Diesel rose from the floor, he felt like he was floating and had a sense of relief. No, it was more than that—it was true freedom. Turning to the man who was once the object of his ridicule, he saw him in a new light. The one who had appeared naïve and stupid was now his only source of understanding.

"Spencer, I have no idea what just happened."

Spencer was one of the cruelest and truly most evil criminals to have walked the halls of this infamous prison. The very cell where James Earl Ray was assigned to a lifetime of punishment for the tragic shooting of Dr. Martin Luther King Jr. was a fitting home for this killer. However, as Spencer was fond of saying, "When the dark gets darker, the light gets brighter." When Spencer arrived, the stench of hell that permeated those walls was not enough to stop heaven from once again trampling on the devil's trophies and stealing the unstealable for its own purposes. Though Spencer may never see the light of day, he knew his new convert would, and he vowed to make the most of every opportunity to continue to destroy the devil's works, both inside and outside of those prison walls.

Spencer chuckled as he answered his new protégé. "Well, Diesel, I know exactly what happened. You just died to your old way of life, and now you are a brand-new creation. Diesel was not unfamiliar with the terminology. He was raised in a Baptist home, and church attendance was obligatory every Wednesday and twice on Sunday, not to mention the many extra functions that seemed to occur with an uncanny frequency. He had even walked the aisle with many other boys and girls to get saved, but never had he felt this cleansing, this tangible sense of freedom from an unseen but very real burden.

"I never...I never...I just didn't know. I didn't understand. I...I..." His voice trailed off. He knew he was making no sense, but as he looked at Spencer, he saw a look of recognition that was born out of experience, not explanation. With eyes full of tears, he somehow knew Spencer was like a father who had all the answers he knew would be necessary, even if he couldn't yet form the questions.

"What do I do now?"

"Now you get to know whose you are and who you are. Something extraordinary has just happened, and I'm gonna help you get ready to be a freedom fighter. It's called discipleship."

Both men smiled, Diesel as much out of confusion as excitement yet knowing that this moment marked the start of the rest of his life. Somehow, it didn't matter that he would spend much of it in that very cell, because for now, that cell represented life and freedom, not death and incarceration as he had known it before.

Chapter 8

Joey

"Joey?"

His mom's tone had an unusual sense of excitement about it, and his seven-year-old intuition kicked in, realizing that something good might be on the other end of that summons.

"Yes, Mom."

"Come out of the basement, honey. I want to show you something."

Most of the time, his mom wore plain dresses suitable for keeping house, but today, she had on a beautiful yellow dress with a gentle floral pattern. It was the start of Easter celebrations, and the family's strong Christian heritage made it a highlight on their calendar. She had one hand stretched out to take hold of his small hand and the other behind her back. She had a sneaky grin on her face as her other hand revealed a shoebox. She took Joey's hand and put it firmly under the box as she held the other end.

"Go ahead and open it."

"What is it, Mommy?"

"Open it, silly, and you will see."

If he had been told *not* to open the box, the lid would have already been on the other side of the room, but he cautiously raised the edge of the lid and peeked inside. Seasonal traditions were the source of some strange practices, and Easter was no different. At this time every year, farmers would dye their chicks and sell them for the amusement of kids during the most holy event on the Christian calendar. Was that because children don't naturally gravitate to the more somber elements of a religious festival, or simply because parents want them to have good memories of important events? Whatever the case, the practice brought great joy to the homes of many small children, and Joey was no different. He marveled at the adorable and very spritely yellow and blue chicks his mom had just given him.

"One is for you, and one is for Kelly."

"Thank you! Thank you! Can I hold them?"

"Listen to me, Joey. You can hurt them if you play too rough with them. Look me in the eyes, Joey, as I want you to understand something." She waited much longer than it should have taken for this mesmerized little boy to look her directly in the eyes. "I am making you responsible for their well-being. Do you understand? You have to take care of them and keep them safe. Your brother is only three, and he doesn't know how to be gentle yet like you."

There was still a faint smile on her face, but Joey had no doubt that this admonishing left no wiggle room for interpretation. In his heart, he made a silent commitment to obey and then a verbal confirmation to ensure that he could turn away from his mom's steely gaze.

"Yes, Mommy, I understand. I promise to take good care of them both." With that, he was off to the basement yelling his brother's name to come and play with their new treasures.

Both boys played with their chicks for hours. Joey wanted the little blue chick but let his little brother have the prized pet. Joey's heart was very protective of his little brother, and although unusual for a young boy, he was quick to sacrifice for his benefit.

As dinner came and went, the distractions of the day meant the chicks got time alone for much-needed rest. The next morning, the two boys scampered down to the basement to see their chicks before Mom had a chance to prepare their pancakes. Not even the promise of chocolate chips with fresh whipped cream and strawberries could curb their enthusiasm to play with their blue and yellow friends.

Kelly got to the box first, and his expression instantly switched from joy to tears when he saw his little blue chick motionless in the corner of the box.

"You killed my chick, Joey." The child's pain needed a culprit to blame.

"No, I didn't. I swear, Kelly."

"I'm telling Mommy that you killed my chick."

The full implication of this unfortunate death was just hitting Joey, and fear entered his heart. His mom was never mean, but with four rambunctious boys to corral, she needed an iron hand to maintain control, and she used it liberally as needed. Her commissioning to ensure the safety of these fragile birds was still ringing in Joey's ears from the previous day, and he needed some time to get ready to give an answer for the impending interrogation.

"He's just resting, Kelly. He'll be all right in a little while. You can play with mine for a while until he wakes up."

Children have a way of compartmentalizing lies that allow them a form of escapism that adults can't obtain. Relief gripped Joey as Kelly stopped yelling. He picked up the survivor and obvious perpetrator of the dastardly act. Relief, however, quickly turned to an innocent prayer that would draw his Father in heaven to respond by the simplicity of the request.

"Father God, please make Kelly's chick come back to life." In a bid to gain more leverage in this honest but unorthodox supplication, he added a selfless offering. "You can take my chick instead. Just make him come back to life, please." As quickly as the almost silent words left his lips, he was exercising diversion tactics to give God time to work. Both boys went off to play Legos at Joey's behest.

Joey had nearly forgotten the lurking threat of a spanking if the chicks were not taken care of and was deep into a defense of his self-proclaimed title as Thor, king of the Vikings. Kelly offered more than a few rebuttals of that claim and staked a claim of his own to this virtuous endeavor when the birds wafted back into his thoughts.

"Let's go play with the chicks again."

"No, let's keep playing Vikings, Kelly. It is so much more fun."

Kelly was already at the door, his little but nimble legs swifter than his lack of balance suggested. He almost fell over as Joey dashed to the box to check on the status of the birds while brushing his little brother aside. He was amazed at what he saw as Kelly's face appeared at his right elbow. "How did you change them, Joey? How did you change them?"

Joey had no answer as he surveyed the little shoebox for clues. The once dead blue bird was now making his way from one end of the box to the other, while the yellow bird that had committed the crime now lay dead. Joey gasped. Even though his own bird had suffered the same fate as her blue sister, Joey knew one thing for sure. There is a God, and He listens to little boys' prayers.

Chapter 9

Scott

The triage nurse quickly prioritized Scott's wound as needing immediate attention. She ordered a scan to determine the extent of the damage, and the wound would need to be stitched up if surgery wasn't required.

The medication they gave him was nowhere near enough by his own estimation. Over the years, he had learned his body's tolerance and dosage requirements.

"I need real meds to help with the pain. I need morphine!"

The nurse was unimpressed. "Take it up with your doctor later. Right now, you're going in for a scan of that crushed skull of yours."

The staff had zero compassion for Scott. They knew why and how this had happened without getting any details from their patient. Even if the injury did not come from his own hand, it was still most definitely self-inflicted. At this point, they saw attending to Scott as a hindrance to taking care of those who deserved help.

The scans showed that his skull was crushed at the site of the blow, but miraculously, the brain was virtually undamaged. His thick skull had done its job. The medical staff marveled at the irony, but one young doctor in particular couldn't hold back his frustration.

"This idiot, who time and again self-destructs and no doubt has made life miserable for every poor soul who knows him, escapes with no long-term damage, while Officer Smith over there is struggling for his life after a freak accident while serving the community." As he turned to his colleagues, his expression sharpened, and an unexpected hint of anger filled his eyes. "I'm telling you, not believing in God has served me well as a doctor. I think I would go mad with the ironies we see every day."

The medical team approached Scott's bed to share the good news and then wheeled him off to the OR to have the wound cleaned up and closed. Anesthesia was a poor second to getting a fix, but it was far superior than the unthinkable position of not being able to keep his body's demands for drugs at bay. "Do what you gotta do. Just make sure I have sufficient meds in recovery. I need at least twice the normal dosage because of my size, and I have become desensitized to pain medication." They knew he was probably right, but his comfort was their last concern, and his selfish demands made them want to lower the dosage, not increase it.

"You will get the normal dosage of meds for your size, Scott."

"That won't be enough! It won't even take the edge off."

The same doctor couldn't help but speak up. "I don't care about your addiction, Scott. I don't even care about your well-being. I just care about discharging my duties to the best of my ability, and that is what you will get." His candor took his colleagues by surprise, but none disagreed with his statement.

"What's your name, Doc?"

"Johnson. Dr. Robert F. Johnson." An air of defiance filled his response.

"I don't care about your well-being either," Scott retorted, "and I sure as hell don't care about helping others, but let me tell you something. You don't want to piss me off. You don't want to have me as an enemy."

"You forget who controls your meds."

The young doctor turned away, unmoved by the threat of this gorilla-sized patient. He rested assured, knowing that his was the last word and that this patient was already paying for and regretting his outburst.

The hospital was old, and space was at a premium. The surgery was successful, and after recovery, the staff wheeled him into a room with a young police officer who was also in recovery. Dr. Johnson felt like the injustice of the officer's situation might speak to Scott. He should have reconsidered.

"I don't want to share a room."

Scott's selfishly predictable objection fell on the orderly's deaf ears.

"What kinda crap treatment are you serving up these days? I don't pay taxes to be put in a room with this kid."

The irony wasn't lost on himself, as he knew he had cost the county far more tax dollars than he could probably ever pay.

Dr. Johnson, who had heard Scott's tirade, walked over and chimed in. "That 'kid' is a decorated police officer who was injured while serving our community. You would do well to take a long look at a life worth saving."

Dr. Johnson seemed to rub Scott's nose in his predicament as much as teach him a lesson. "Oh, and by the way, Scott, he is sedated, not unconscious. Whatever you say can and will be used in evidence against you." He knew his last comment was unprofessional and over the line, but he didn't care. It was worth even the remote chance that young Officer Smith may have a positive effect on the drain on society Scott had become. The doctor kept this thought to himself: *The officer is in a medically induced coma and is nothing more than a prop at the moment.*

Chapter 10

Officer Smith

Six days had already gone by, and while the machines had kept all Officer Smith's vital functions intact, the doctors now wanted to bring him out of his medically induced coma. As his consciousness returned, the patient stirred, and he assessed his surroundings in a desperate attempt to grasp his strange circumstances. *Where is the light coming from? Why am I in someone else's house? What happened? Why can't I move my body?* Waves of semi-coherent questions hit his brain until his eyes could focus on his room, and he realized he was not in a house. As he started to verbalize a question, he felt something in his mouth and started to gag.

Nurses swept into the room as the machines started buzzing with activity. A quick injection brought some relief from the overstimulation, but he was still coherent enough to want answers to the most obvious of questions: *What the heck am I doing here?*

His eyes must have communicated his distress because one of the nurses started explaining in plain English what they were doing. Plain English withstanding, it still didn't explain why he was there, and more importantly, why his body felt like it was on fire. The nurse could see that his pain was intense and reached over to the morphine controls to dispense the maximum allowable dose. She knew his road ahead was going to be incredibly difficult and wanted to do as much as possible for her newly awakened patient.

As his heart rate slowed down, the words of the nurse started to penetrate his stressed thoughts. "Officer Smith, you have been in an accident. You are incredibly lucky to be alive." For some reason, those words stood out to him, and he knew they would be tested at some point in the future. Pain sensors all over his body were going into overdrive. He would have screamed if he could have.

Over the next few hours, the staff removed his tubes, and his clarity started to return. He wanted to shake somebody and ask how he ended up in this unfair situation. A kindhearted nurse felt she should give him an itemized litany of his injuries from the accident so he could come to grips with his situation as quickly as possible. However, one look at the pain and anxiety in his expression confirmed that a generic statement was a more humane answer at this moment.

However, the young officer could not come to terms with his predicament. The medical team was seeing the effects of his stress, physical pain, and mental anguish as he wrestled with how debilitating his accident had been. His vital signs were elevating, and a nurse injected a strong sedative to usher him back to sleep so his body could once again involuntarily work to keep him alive. As the drugs started pulling him back into a drowsy sleep, he subconsciously took note of the patient in the bed across from him who was acting like an irate wrestler and screaming that he wanted more meds.

For the next 24 hours, Smith drifted in and out of consciousness. It seemed like every waking moment involved some form of movement, and every movement involved more and more pain. As the conscious moments became more frequent, the doctors explained the full extent of his injuries. The circumstances of his accident along with the absolute bad luck of the timing etched anger onto his heart. A man can be forgiven for being angry while in pain, but how much suffering can a man endure in such a short life?

As his anger started to burn, his glare was met by a cold stare from across the room. He remembered he was sharing the room with an unusually large man, but he was in no mood for conversation and communicated as much with his demeanor. Unfortunately, the older, larger man took no notice and launched into a self-serving diatribe of complaints aimed at fueling the officer's already growing anger.

"So they tell me you were injured in the line of duty. Was it worth it?"

The sneer on Scott's face revealed the mocking intent of his question. Officer Smith ignored the opening remark, but that only encouraged his roommate to continue. "Dude, you are messed up. If you are anything to judge by, a career in law enforcement is for fools." Smith's continued lack of response caused another escalation in the man's attack. "You're an idiot, man! I would never allow myself to be used as a pawn in someone else's agenda. They don't care about you. They don't care what happens to you. The system is just going to toss you to the curb and let you rot now that they can no longer use you."

Officer Smith knew that these words were not true, but they hit home nonetheless. He did feel used, and he did feel rejected, just not by the police force. He didn't have a rebuttal or at least one he wanted to offer.

"Your tongue broke, too? I hear you broke almost every bone in you, bro. You are a real-life Humpty Dumpty, man. That's what I'm gonna call you now—Humpty. Officer Humpty."

"Go to hell, man." Smith's answer had real bite, but Scott was looking for something to break, and this young officer's resolve looked like the perfect candidate.

"Oh, I'm going there all right, and pretty soon is my guess." He pondered that statement for a moment, knowing it was the first thing he had said for quite a while that had an air of truth. "You better believe it. I am on a high-way to hell, but at least I am taking advantage of everything life has to offer along the way. God does not offer much in the way of living. No, dude. As the song says, 'Better to reign in hell than to serve in heaven.'"

Although Smith knew this man's words were just a taunt and that the beast across the room might as well be shoveling manure out of his mouth, the absence of any real living evidence in his short life suddenly haunted him. For as long as he could remember, he battled fear. He had been sexually abused as a young boy and never found the courage to tell his parents. His battle with cancer as a young teenager and the daily threat of impending death created a toxic mix of fear and anger. His unlikely successful high school football career was met with a dismal and fear-driven implosion in college. His desire to make his life worth something had led him to law enforcement, but now he was faced with the stark reality that his worst fear—that he had no significance—was still accusing him from the bed across the room. No matter who was delivering the sermon, the conclusion was the same. He was completely expendable. Though he had chosen not to go down the path of self-indulgence like his accuser, his reward was still hell on earth. Right then he decided, *If I am going to suffer hell, I might as well earn it.*

"Nurse! Nurse! Get this idiot out of my room."

The nurse had overheard much of the onslaught leveled at Officer Smith and was already calling the doctor to reconsider his experiment.

"You must leave the other patient alone, Scott." Her weak attempt was meant to distract rather than deter since she could see Dr. Johnson approaching.

Scott went on the offensive. His distraction across the room was no longer entertaining him, and he could feel the grip of withdrawal begin to call his name. His milder-than-hoped drugs were wearing off, and he was getting angrier by the minute. "Listen, nurse, I need more medication. You have to up the dosage. My pain is off the charts."

"We will do no such thing, Scott," Dr. Johnson responded as a couple of capable orderlies stood by his side. Scott was too distracted by the pain to start a fight, and his desperation always overruled his pride when drugs were involved.

"Listen, Doc, just a little more. I am in serious pain."

"No, Scott. I am not going to be part of feeding your habit. You have enough drugs in you to take care of the pain."

"You don't understand, Doc. My tolerance for meds is way higher than other people's, and my body mass is a lot more." Both of these were legitimate arguments, but Dr. Johnson's pride was not about to be overruled by the obnoxious desperation of this leech on society.

"No, Scott. No!"

"That's it, then? You won't give me anything? Well, I can take better care of myself on the street than you are doing." That revelation hammered home as he looked at the steely resolve of the doctor staring back at him. "Get me the hell out of here. I'm not gonna let you torture me."

Scott signed the release papers and left the building shouting a curse-filled rant. But the commotion of the last 10 minutes did nothing to remove Officer Smith's awareness of his new reality. It was at the forefront of his now very conscious thoughts. With the room empty, he addressed the One whom he clearly saw as the cause of his suffering.

"Why? Why? Why?" His parents' deity refused to answer, and his anger grew. "What did I do that was so wrong that you picked me to torture? You sent someone to take advantage of me when I was just a little boy and couldn't protect myself. You gave me cancer and took away my chance to have a family, and now you let some punk smash into my car and leave me a cripple. What the heck kind of God are you? Do you get some sick pleasure from this? My parents have dedicated their lives to serving you, and this is how you treat us? I will never believe in a God who punishes those He is supposed to love. You can't possibly love me and then treat me this way."

His rant continued as he unburdened more than a decade of anger. He was in pain in his body, heart, and soul, and he unleashed it all on the One he believed could have prevented it from happening.

"I wish you would have ended it all in that crash. I don't want to live if all I am going to do is go from one form of your punishment to another. I am done! From this moment on, I am separating myself from you. I reject your 'conditional' love. I reject the salvation my dad says you offer. I don't want anything to do with your sick sense of humor and your empty promises."

His final sentences caught the attention of an unnoticed, sinister figure outside his door. The figure was captivated by those words and silently made a pact to deliver this tortured soul from his obligation to his cruel God. Smith was his new protégé, and he would remain in the shadows of the hospital while he recovered. He would watch as Smith fed his anger and bitterness with reminders of the evil God he had rejected.

From that time on, he never left Officer Smith's presence.

Chapter 11

Diesel

In the months following his conversion, Diesel transformed from a life shrouded in bitterness, anger, and hate to a beacon of hope for everyone who had the fortune of crossing his path. However, his transformation came with a cost.

A group of six men stood in the corner of the yard. Although all were dressed in the standard issue prison denims, it was obvious who was in charge. Big Red was known for his penchant for violence as much as his head of bright red hair. Many things were available on the black market in prison, but red hair dye was not one of them, yet most would swear that Big Red's almost-orange mane was not natural. But no one ever felt the need to make him aware of their doubts.

The other five mostly nodded as Big Red pointed to the newly nicknamed Yard Preacher. "I am sick of listening to the crap spewing out of this asshole's mouth. I didn't like him when he was quiet, and I sure as hell don't like him when he talks. Cyril, I want you to get the message across for him to shut up with all this Jesus mess he's spewing. He's giving people false hope, and that's one of the most dangerous and anarchous things to get under control."

Cyril wasn't his real name, but just like others who fell under Big Red's protection, he didn't care to correct him. He was fairly sure *anarchous* was not the right use of that word or if, in fact, it was even a word, but he knew how to rephrase the statement so its intended recipient would grasp the idea behind the request.

"I'll let him know. Do you wanna give him a warning first?" This was an afterthought since he didn't expect this kind of clemency from his overseer.

"Hmm. You know what, Cyril? This fool is in luck. I'm feeling merciful today. Give him 24 hours to change his ways, or I will close his mouth permanently."

Diesel was telling his favorite story to a mildly interested inmate. As he skillfully unraveled the rise and fall of the prodigal son in the parable Jesus originally shared with His disciples, God's love and forgiveness became real to the young man standing beside him.

"Listen, son, all you have to do is put your trust in Jesus. He loves you and wants to forgive you of all your sins. Just think of it—complete forgiveness of everything you have ever done, being in right standing with God. The Bible calls that righteousness, and Jesus died on the cross so He could offer you His forgiveness and His righteousness. *Justification* is the term the Bible uses to say that our sins are taken away. Another way to think of it is *just as if I never sinned*. You have a lot of sins, right?"

Diesel got his name from his grandfather, who had seen him exhibit unusual strength as a young boy. The diesel engine was the workhorse of the farming community, and since Diesel could do more than his fair share of work, he was valued highly and nicknamed accordingly.

"Yes," his captive audience of one responded.

"Do you believe that you will be held accountable to God for those sins?"

"I never really thought about it."

"Well, the Bible says that you will. Are you willing to take the chance that you may be found guilty and receive the punishment for your sins, which is hell?"

"I never really thought about that either."

"Son, it's time you started to take these matters to heart. It's time you started to get serious with God. Don't you know that you can get shanked any time in this place? Have you not noticed the steady stream of body bags leaving here?"

As if on cue, Cyril interjected, "Sorry to interrupt your conversation, but your constant preaching is bothering others in the yard. You are formally being asked to refrain from having such deliberations within earshot of, well, everybody." Cyril had grown up in the hood, but his unusually high IQ caught the attention of some of his teachers, who felt he could be saved from a life on the streets. He was sent to a private school on a scholarship, but the treatment he received from his rich schoolmates made him certain he was not going to end up among the rich and the famous. He did go to law school and pass the bar, but then he became the lawyer for some local mobsters. He could have made a very nice life in the suburbs, but he gladly owned the prophecy spoken over him by his absentee father when he heard his estranged kid was leaving his old neighborhood: "They can never take the streets out of the boy no matter how far they take the boy out of the streets."

Diesel may have been zealous, but he was no fool. He knew Cyril's threat was real and that his life was on the line if he kept preaching. He was not one to back down from intimidation, but how much good could he do for his Savior if he were dead? Cyril broke the stream of thoughts racing through Diesel's head. "You have 24 hours to change, but either way, the preaching stops."

The young man who had taken in everything Diesel had just said moments ago was now faced with his own mortality and pending judgment. But he also had the opportunity to avoid the final onslaught of sin and forgiveness and conversion questions. He was captivated by the irony of the events unfolding before him, and Diesel knew it. As Cyril walked away, Diesel turned his attention to the one he was proselytizing to finish his line of questioning, but his mind was still processing the threat on his own life.

"What was I saying?"

"I need to go, Diesel. Thanks for the talk, man. I'll think about what you said and get back to you."

Diesel's eyes didn't even track the unusually hasty departure of his discussion partner. He was facing a dilemma. He had boldly told as many as would listen that his life was now God's, and that he would do whatever it took to help as many as he could understand the message of the cross—that he, like his Savior, would gladly lay down his life to help save as many lives as possible, that he would proclaim the gospel for the rest of his days, however many they may be. His shoulders slumped ever so slightly as he walked to a quiet part of the yard. Facing the fence, he put one hand on the cold metal and lowered his head in prayer.

"Father, you know me. I don't want to die now that I finally feel alive, but You know I am willing to die for You. I will do whatever will bring You the most glory. I just feel like my witness for these last few months wouldn't be worth much if I can be silenced by the threat of a disciple of darkness."

Diesel could not see it, but a tall figure towered over him and placed His large hand on his shoulder. He felt a rush of adrenaline fill his body, and his resolve was strengthened. "I can't back down, Lord. The testimony of Your great goodness is tied to my response, and as for me and my life, I choose Your goodness and glory."

He didn't walk over directly to Big Red and tell him his decision, but he did grab a group of three men hogging the weights and preach with refreshed vigor.

Chapter 12

Joey

Joey was out on his bike with his big brother Mark when they ran into the neighbor down the street. Karl was 13 and just a little older than Mark. Joey enjoyed playing with the bigger boys since he always wanted to learn how to do the cool tricks on his bike. Karl taught him how to ride without holding on to the handlebars and how to pop a wheelie. Mark was glad Karl didn't tell Joey to scram when they hung out. He knew his mom would be on his case to take care of his kid brother.

"I'm done, Karl. I gotta chop some wood for the fire before my dad gets back, or he'll kill me."

"Ah, come on, Mark. Just one more time around the neighborhood."

"Sorry, I've already pushed it too far. My dad will be home any minute, and I'd better at least be swinging the ax when he gets there."

"Suit yourself. Hey, Joey! You want to go around the neighborhood with me? I'll teach you how to jump over the ramp at old man Barns's yard."

What an invitation! A chance to learn how to do jumps! Joey thought Karl was the best at jumps. He seemed to make his bike stay in the air forever.

"Sure! Tell Mom I'll be home later, Mark."

"Don't be late for dinner, or Mom will be mad."

Joey had no intention of being late, but all his focus was on this world-class tutor with whom he had just acquired the rest of the afternoon without any interruptions. Joey felt like the day couldn't get any better as they rode off together down the street.

After about an hour of attempting jumps and finally landing his bike squarely on the ground a few times, Joey felt ready to give the ramp a proper attempt. He backed off the ramp about 50 feet and peddled full steam ahead. As he approached, a squirrel darted across the yard right in front of the ramp and right in front of his wheel. He instinctively jerked the handlebars to the right, causing his bike to collapse on itself and propel its driver over the handlebars to land face-first on the dirt ramp. Pain shot through Joey's whole body, and he could feel blood coming from his lip, but there was no way he was going to cry in front of Karl, even if everything in him wanted to.

"Joey, dude, are you okay? You ate it, but you saved the squirrel." Karl's attempt at distraction through humor seemed to work.

"I would have made the jump, Karl."

"For sure, Joey. I know you would've." Karl's form of comfort may have been different than his mom's, but Joey felt better nonetheless.

"We need to get you cleaned up before you go home so your mom doesn't freak out." Karl winked, and both boys shared a brotherly moment as Karl helped Joey up off the ground and handed him a tissue from his pocket. Karl pushed both bikes and walked alongside Joey for the short trip back to his house.

Karl seemed unusually attentive as he told Joey to take his shirt off so he could check to see if he had any cuts that needed to be cleaned. Other than the scrapes on his elbows that Karl cleaned with peroxide, Joey was okay and started to put his shirt back on.

"Leave your shirt off, Joey. The best thing for cuts is to let them air out."

For the first time, Joey felt a little uncomfortable. He went around without a shirt all the time, but something inside of him said he was not as safe as he first thought. His thoughts pushed back at the inner voice. *Karl is Mark's best friend. He's really cool and is treating me like a big kid. Maybe this is just how big kids think.* He had never had to use his internal warning system before and was a novice at spotting harm.

An invisible darkness moved into the room, and Karl's countenance changed from brotherly to something more distant and sinister. Joey was still wrestling with his own thoughts and didn't notice the change in atmosphere.

"My dad has some cool movies we can watch while your cuts are drying up."

"Okay."

The promise of a movie was a treat Joey rarely passed up, but his instinct was moving to a higher gear, and his internal struggle stifled his enthusiasm.

"What's wrong, Joey? We can watch something else if you want. It's your choice."

Joey felt the pressure to be a good boy and watch whatever Karl wanted to watch because it was his house. And after all, Karl had helped him when he fell off his bike. He really wanted to watch Scooby-Doo but felt too childish and selfish to ask.

"It's okay, Karl. We can watch your dad's movie if you think it's good."

Karl popped the movie into the DVD player and grabbed the remote. But instead of sitting back down on the armchair, Karl sat right next to his guest. Joey was used to sitting close to his brothers, and they would often sit right on top of one another to annoy one another, but this was different. He could feel the hair on Karl's arms touch his skin, and he was aware of his breathing. He didn't like the feeling, but again, he pushed his fears to the back of his mind and rationalized his circumstances.

The movie wasn't what he had expected, and he didn't understand what was going on. There were no kids in the movie, and the grown-ups seemed really intense. After a few minutes, they started to take off all their clothes and do things to each other that shocked Joey. Karl sensed the shift in his companion. "Don't worry, Joey. This kind of thing happens in grown-up movies all the time. It's part of being a big kid. You do want to be a big kid, right?"

The darkness had intensified, and for the first time, Joey noticed a change in the demeanor of his host. The quiet, internal warning had escalated to alarm bells. He wanted to run, but he was paralyzed with fear. He wanted to yell, but his tongue wouldn't respond. All he could do was hope that his fears were irrational and that maybe the movie wouldn't have naked people in it the whole time. The safety he had felt just moments ago in the care of his big brother's friend had completely dissipated, and in its place was the most fearful moment Joey had faced in his young life.

"It's all right, Joey. Look, touching each other is part of growing up. Let me show you."

Joey couldn't believe what was happening. The room might as well have been spinning, as he was rooted to his seat in fear. He couldn't muster any courage since nothing about these circumstances made any sense. He had no experience in how to protect himself. Nobody had told him that you don't allow other people to touch your privates. It was not something that was ever mentioned in his home. He knew about stranger danger, but Karl was not a stranger. Maybe this is really just part of being a big boy, and nobody had told him. He clung to this thought as his only source of comfort while Karl proceeded to duplicate the things they were watching on his dad's movie.

"Put your clothes back on" were the only words spoken after what seemed to Joey to be an eternity of abuse. He felt so wrong. So ashamed. So dirty. "Don't you dare tell anyone. I went out of my way today to help you be a big boy. If you tell anyone, I mean anyone, I will tell them what you did. You were the one who started this. I didn't want to make you a big boy. You chose to watch the movie. I gave you the option, and you picked it. You were the one who needed help understanding the movie, not me." None of this made sense to Joey, but it all was true—wasn't it?

Maybe this is my fault. This was all too much for a seven-year-old brain to process. God never intended for a child to have to sort through these thoughts, but Joey didn't know that, and a deep shame like a small black cloud entered his innocent heart that day. He told himself he would just forget it ever happened and never go back to Karl's house. But Karl continued to use the same scare tactics to lure his innocent victim back into harm's way, and the abuse escalated. It took far too long before the cycle was broken, and by that time, darkness had infiltrated every area of Joey's self-worth.

Chapter 13

Officer Smith

Months of torturous physical therapy and a boss who wanted to reward the sacrifice he had made left young Officer Smith at a crossroads. His bout with testicular cancer meant he could never have kids, and his injuries meant he would not be much use as a beat cop. His temperament wasn't suitable to a desk job, and his ambition wasn't suitable for most of the remaining options. His boss, Captain Halliday, proposed a position with a very specific task. It would involve a promotion and a chance to become a detective well ahead of the normal schedule.

"Look, Smithy, it's a promotion that puts you at least two years ahead of any of the other guys who graduated in your class. It's not overly demanding physically, and you get to put some really bad guys away. Most of our guys have kids and can't handle the issues associated with being a child abuse investigator, but you can't have kids, and this way you get to protect a bunch of them from these sick bastards. You should be jumping on this. 'Yes, Captain. Thank you so much, Captain' is what I expect you to say."

There was no way the captain could have known the anguish this tortured soul was facing because of this opportunity. Memory after memory of his abuser came crashing to the forefront of his conscience. Images he had repressed, some on purpose and some without knowing, were tormenting him. Deep in the basement of his emotions, a beast called out to be released. *Let me kill him. I am a cop. I can work out some way to do it and get away with it. He deserves to die. Who knows how many other kids he took advantage of? Yes, let me kill him, and the world will be a better place.*

Something interrupted his internal dialogue. It was a memory of a thought, a faint lingering of a resilient Bible verse making itself known in the first person. *Cast all your cares on Me, for I care for you.*

His captain was staring at him, waiting for an affirmative answer to his perceived generous offer, when another voice, subtler and more appealing, shared a new perspective.

This job will give you the chance to get revenge. You can take out your anger on the scum that hurt the most vulnerable among us. You said you were done with God and His perverse, painful love. You said you were done with Him and His sick sense of humor. There is another way. There is revenge. You deserve revenge. You just have to want it enough. You just have to want it more than anything else. You just have to not care what the cost is or whether you live or die. Revenge is worth everything you will pay to get it. For once you get revenge, you can rest in peace knowing a wrong was made right and God didn't get His way."

The voice made a compelling argument, and the heart of this 20-year-old found a new form of comfort. A new form of empowerment. A new god to put his faith in. A new outlet for his painful emotions. A new category of scumbags on whom to bring retribution.

"Sorry, Captain. You better believe I want this promotion. I will give it everything I've got. I will be the most successful child abuse investigator this state has ever seen."

"Now that is the Smithy I know. You start training next week, and you'll be putting away bad guys before you know it. You'll be glad you did this, son."

The fatherly expression was lost on the young officer. At another time, he would have reveled in the attention of a mentor he respected. Instead, his countenance was changing. His eyes were more sullen, and his gaze turned into a glare. The muscles in his face tensed, and he adopted a scowl that fought to become his permanent disposition. The pain and discomfort from his injuries began to fuel his focus. Adrenaline coursed through his veins as he meditated on getting revenge.

As the soon-to-be Detective Smith made his way home that evening, he did something he had not done for a very long time. He pulled into the Waffle House parking lot, which was almost empty except for the two cars

43

of the employees inside who were staring at each other, wondering why they bothered to come to work that day. Smith got out of his patrol car and walked around the back of the building and into the field right behind the diner. He and his brothers used to play on their bikes back there. The hills were perfect for doing tricks, and some of his best memories were the times he overcame his fears and made a new record jump. As he meditated on those memories, the voice that had shadowed him since that fateful day in the hospital moved right into the young officer's head. The voice that had guided his recent decision-making re-engaged.

This is the life that was stolen from you. This is the life that you will protect for other boys and girls. I am the god you want to serve. I am the god of anger and vengeance, of retribution and destruction. Your life for theirs. Your life is already wasted. Give it to me, and I will make something meaningful out of it. It is your choice. The voice went silent, but the message rang clearly, and it was the only thing that made any kind of sense to this wounded soul.

"It is yours. Take it," Smith said out loud. "Make something worthwhile of it. All I have is anger and hate, so use it whatever way you can. I don't know who you are, but I will make an agreement with you. If you will open the doors for me, I will walk through them. If you give me opportunity, I will take it. If you will make my life into something, I will dedicate it to you."

The figure in the shadows was smiling with the same look of glee that gave the Cheshire Cat its name. It was a look of wicked pleasure over a life being destroyed, a nod of another notch in his belt, another scalp, another trophy for the cabinet.

But there was another observer in those woods, and His stomach turned. Although He was out of sight, He had heard the dialogue between the new disciple and his master, and he had seen a different scene unfold. He saw the younger version of this man being abused. He saw innocence corrupted and weakness exploited. He saw a scared boy, afraid of living in fear the rest of his life. He saw a life manipulated and stolen. He also saw the life he had saved from the burning wreckage of a smashed vehicle being distorted. He saw the deliverance he had fought for aborted. He saw a future dismantled. He saw more than his ancient heart could bear, and he vowed to save that life no matter what the cost.

Chapter 14

Scott

The day started like any other. *Where will I get a fix today?* Scott's entire existence, his every waking moment was consumed with self-indulgence. Nothing or nobody was outside the realm of his manipulation. Old friends, old colleagues, old college buddies, old roommates, relatives, strangers, prostitutes, street evangelists, performers, garbage collectors, civil servants, homeless veterans—everyone was viewed through an insanely selfish filter of meeting a need. Scott had a mental Rolodex of all his dealers. He had them categorized according to how much he had burned them and who would, or at least might, entertain his demands for a fresh supply.

Every morning, his options looked limited, but by the end of the day, he had found a way. The odds should have been getting greater every day, but he was like an oil company squeezing the maximum production from a well. And he was always drilling for new wells in any field that looked promising. He had a knack for getting blood from stones on a regular basis. The cycle was toxic and even more so when it involved pulling others into his depravity.

He decided to try a new bar that opened before lunch. The wheels of his mind started profiling before he even saw his prey. *Any woman who is in a bar before lunch is looking to forget and is ready for something more potent.* He grinned at his plan, one that had worked on many occasions and killed two birds—two physical needs—with one stone. Bars looked different in the morning. The light of day peeking through the blinds illuminated the dirt and grime on tables where only hours before folks were eating wings and cheese fries. If he had been sober, this kind of joint would have been offensive to this former clean-freak character, but he was completely unaware of the nasty smell and ambience. He had found his source for the day.

She was at least 10 years younger than he was. She was attractive, or at least could have been if she weren't pushing enough alcohol into her system to make an elephant forget. She used the pool cue in her hand to hold herself up when she wasn't trying to hit the white ball on the table. Scott had learned long ago to find the weak one of the herd, and she definitely fit the bill. He figured she must have been mourning a breakup or some other life tragedy. It was written all over her. All he had to do was pretend to listen and empathize at a few strategic moments, and they would be headed back to her place in no time.

"You want to play?" He gestured to the other cue on the wall.

"Sure." She bent over the table and tried to strike the white ball, but she could barely focus long enough to allow the cue to hit its target.

"Your day going okay?" He realized he probably didn't even need the perfunctory small talk since she was already out of control.

"Yes." She tried to say it with conviction and then hesitated. "No. No it is not. It may actually be one of the worst days of my life." Her anger seemed to temporarily bring her inebriated mind into focus. "The asshole who I poured the last five years of my life into just told me he is dumping me for some other slut. He had the nerve to tell me that I have a drinking problem. I only drink to unwind, and he winds me up more than anyone."

She rambled on for 10 minutes before stopping to take a breath. At one point, Scott started to look for another candidate since he wasn't sure how long he was willing to listen to her woes. He decided to push the issue or cut his losses.

"I'm in the same boat. My ex told me the exact same thing. You know, we could hang around this old place all day complaining about how we were done wrong, or we could go do something about it. I know where we can get something to take the edge off your worries, and then we can go back to your place and have some fun." This was as direct as he had ever been, but he didn't want to mess around with her any longer unless he thought he could get what he needed. She looked up at him for the first time since they started talking and tried to assess his credibility, but her danger radar had long stopped working.

"You look safe enough. Sure, what did you have in mind?"

"I know a place just around the corner. Where did you park your car?"

"I left it right on the street outside." The two walked toward the door, and she handed her keys to the complete stranger she just met.

"Hey, I don't even know your name."

"Scott."

"Well, my name is Hazel, in case you wanted to know." He smiled but really didn't care to know her name.

She had a late-model Dodge Charger in pretty good condition. Cash was stuffed into the console, and Scott knew he could make her his meal ticket for a few days if he was willing to work his victim a little more gently. He decided to go to one of his less shady sources, a housewife who supplied opioids from her multiple prescriptions from a plethora of doctors she was scamming. A pill bottle with a prescription label was much less intimidating but equally addictive as a bag of heroin from a shady street dealer.

His need for a fix was much more important than his desire for sex, but Hazel was starting to look a little uncomfortable and in need of some attention. He put his hand on her leg and smiled.

"This is gonna make your day go so much better. My friend has some extra muscle relaxers she doesn't need. They're great for unwinding and forgetting your troubles."

The reassurance seemed to have its desired effect, and they were soon pulling into a nice house in an up-and-coming neighborhood near downtown.

"Crap! I meant to stop at the ATM. Do you have any cash? I'll pay you back later." Scott feigned a genuine look of self-surprise at his apparent forgetfulness, and Hazel was only too happy to help out her new friend.

"I have some cash in my purse. How much do you need?" Scott knew not to go overboard until her guard was completely down.

"Just fifty is fine. I can go to the ATM if you don't have that much."

"I have about a hundred. Take what you need." Scott took 80 and left a 20 and some ones.

They both stood on the doorstep waiting for the door to open. The housewife who answered was well-dressed and looked like she could be a member of the parent-teacher association. Hazel never thought to question what drugs the lady had given them. At Hazel's place, Scott poured them both a drink and gave her two pills. She took a swig of tequila, popped the pills in her mouth, and swallowed hard. Scott took a double dose and drank a large mouthful from the bottle. Today's wait was over. No more concerns for this day, only the sweet comfort addicts feel when they are not in charge of their own faculties.

Chapter 15

Joey

Joey stopped going on his adventures in the forest beyond his backyard. He stopped playing with the kids on the street and had become disrespectful in his daily interactions with his parents. His mom noticed the changes but didn't say anything. He had been struggling at school, and she figured he was having a hard time because of that. He was eight now, and his older brothers, who were close to puberty, had similar struggles. No mom wishes early puberty on her child, but Joey's latest regression made her hope it was something as simple as that.

"Leave me alone, Mom."

"I just said you need to get ready for your bath."

"I don't want to take a bath, and I don't want you in my room."

"Don't be silly, sweetheart. We're going to church in the morning, and you have to have a bath. I've seen you naked a thousand times."

His mom was standing in the doorway with a smile on her face, but Joey unexpectedly pushed her out of the way and slammed the door shut.

"I don't want to see you, and I hate church!"

"You do not hate church. You have always liked church, Joey. What has gotten into you?"

A mother's love is unconditional, and only moms can get away with attacking conflict head-on with their sons. A son instinctively knows his mom has no other agenda than his well-being. But this time, Joey didn't believe that.

"What do you know? You don't know what I think. I hate church, I hate you, and I hate God!"

Moms often seek to strike at the heart of the problem, and their intuition usually serves them well. Joey's mom's instinct was telling her that something was seriously wrong, but she couldn't listen to that voice right now. She had to blame it on something she could control. She didn't force her way into his room and continued the dialogue from the other side of the door.

"Is this about the trouble you're having at school? If it is, Joey, you can tell me. You know that, right?" She wanted to offer a blanket amnesty for any issue. "You can come to me about anything that's bothering you. Anything, Joey."

Kelly had heard the commotion, and his four-year-old brain wanted in on the drama.

"What's wrong, Mommy?"

"Nothing, sweetheart. I'm just talking to Joey, that's all."

"Why won't he open his door?"

She knew this was going to be a losing battle with both boys, and she wanted to give Joey time to blow off some steam and consider her offer of help. "Let's go play Legos, Kelly. I thought you were building a big tower."

Kelly bounced down the stairs, feeling victorious that he had won his mother's sole attention. She played for five minutes and then told him she had to clean the kitchen. She threatened going to bed early and offered playing quietly as a carrot that would give her a few minutes to think about how to help Joey. She went into the kitchen and stared out the window. A simple dialogue with the One she always leaned on in times of need seemed to flow subconsciously from her heart.

"Dear Lord, please help Joey. He seems so upset, and I don't know why. What should I do for him? Is it just school, or is more going on? Give his little heart peace."

The ears of the One she was addressing were always inclined to such a prayer. She knew He could see the anguish in the heart of her little boy and hated the shame and pain that had replaced his innocence. This wicked form of abuse happened millions of times all over the planet every day, and He could hear the cries and feel the pain of every tortured soul both past and present. He would help. He would not leave Joey to face this on his own, but only He could foresee the pain yet to come in the little boy's life. Only He knew the struggle for his future that would ensue.

Upstairs in his room, Joey was praying, not verbally but in the self-hatred that was taking over his young heart.

Why me, God? What did I do wrong? Why am I so bad? Why did he make me do those things? I hate everything, and I hate You.

But God took no offense. He only had compassion for a damaged soul and a desire to rescue him. There was a longing to save him from the coming pain and the knowledge that when the time came, He would make the full resources of heaven available to fix what man and the devil had broken.

Chapter 16

Officer Smith

Officer Smith's training was designed to help prepare him for the trauma of child abuse investigation. That kind of trauma impacted not just the victims and their families, but everyone who was unfortunate enough to be involved with those heartbreaking cases. Some were worse than others, but no amount of training could prepare the human soul to deal with the all-too-frequent and horrific damage inflicted on the most vulnerable and innocent among us. Some cases would mark any conscience, and some cases would haunt a man for the rest of his life.

Smith threw himself into his work and devoted himself to putting perverts behind bars. He was willing to push the limits to get confessions. Once he had a medical report of abuse and a child who identified an abuser, he could rationalize that the end justified any and all means to get a confession. Today was one of those days as he sat across a small two-by-three-foot table and looked into the face of a man he was convinced was guilty. Often, he could appeal to the offender's own sense of shame to confess, but sometimes he needed more drastic measures. Pulling out the file with images of the child and the medical report, he planned to give this offender a chance to come clean.

"Craig Drummond, you worked for Jeff Sawyers. Correct?"

"Yes."

Officer Smith knew there was power in establishing a pattern of agreement. "You built cabinets in the workshop at his house before you would install them on the job, right?"

"Yes."

"He trusted you to work on your own at times. Correct?"

"Yes." The offender started to relax slightly, as the line of questioning did not seem as aggressive as he had feared, and the officer across the table seemed quite amicable.

"Sometimes Jeff would leave to get some supplies while you continued to build cabinets in the shop. Correct?"

"Not too often, but yes."

"He trusted you to take care of things while he was gone. Right?"

"Sure, I guess."

"You worked most Saturdays. Correct?"

"Yes."

"Every other weekend, Jeff had his beautiful little girl Melanie stay with him, right?"

"Uh, I'm not sure what their arrangements were, but that seems right."

"Jeff said you were really good with Melanie."

"I love little kids. She was a cute kid."

Officer Smith had to hold in his urge to explode. "You used to be alone with Melanie when her dad left to get supplies?"

"Yes."

"Jeff would ask you to keep an eye on her if she came looking for him. Right?"

"Well, yes. He did, yes."

"How did it start?"

"What do you mean? How did what start?"

"Your relationship with her." His training had taught him that normalizing the behavior and not referring to it as abuse paved a way for the less evil of the abusers to confess.

"I just watched her for her dad when he was gone. He asked me to take a break and get a coffee while he went to the store. Melanie liked to play games. She has a creative imagination."

"Did she want to play moms and dads with you? Little girls love to play like grown-ups. Did she touch you first?"

"I never touched her. I just watched her while her dad was gone."

Officer Smith's demeanor changed. The gym had become his arena to vent his anger, and it was showing. His neck muscles bulged as he tensed up, and the veins were visible as his face went from a relaxed flesh tone to a red mass of anger.

"Look at these photos. Look at the bruises. Look at the damage to her vagina."

The accused looked away, but Officer Smith grabbed his face and made him look at the photos.

"Let me tell you what this report says. Let me tell you the damage you have done to this little girl. Her vagina was split open and torn two inches. The forceful entry caused internal hemorrhaging. The damage to her cervix is permanent. The doctors are not sure she will ever regain full functionality or even be able to have sex without pain when she grows up."

The figure in the shadows was ever present with his apprentice now. He whispered his instructions into his ear. The voice was indistinguishable from Smith's own thoughts, and Smith didn't stop to question his new master. *He did it. He is not worthy to live. He is scum. The lowest of the low. You'd better make him confess since there is no way you can let him hurt another child again. Make him confess. Make him confess!* Officer Smith grabbed the offender's face once more, but this time, he squeezed so hard the man felt like his jaw was going to break.

"I didn't do it."

Officer Smith could take no more. He smacked his suspect with his open hand, jerking his head enough to tear several muscles and make his face feel like it was on fire. The open hand ensured minimal bruising but maximum pain. As with most abusers, this suspect had never known the powerlessness of being physically abused as an adult. Abusers create a safety net for themselves that protects them from more powerful adults and exposes vulnerable children to their evil fantasies. The force with which he had been hit sent shock waves down his body and jarred him into survival mode. Officer Smith wound up for a second hit.

"Stop! Please, stop."

Smith had no intention of stopping. *Whaap! Whaap!* Two more blows with the open hand. The suspect instinctively knew his survival was on the line. Tears rushed from his eyes, and the fear he once knew as an abused child, the same fear he imposed to a much greater degree on little Melanie, came to life with a vengeance.

"Please! Please! Stop! I didn't do it. I didn't do…" *Whaap! Whaap!*

Wrong answer! Smith thought. He was starting to feel some of his own anger being soothed, but there was enough inside him to bury this suspect and 20 more. His anger flared up again as fresh fuel was poured on the fire raging inside him. *He is just the same as the pervert who raped you over and over again. He's an animal. He shouldn't be allowed to live.*

Whaap! Whaap!

The officer's hand was stinging from the force of the last two smacks, and there was blood coming from the suspect's nose and mouth. Smith didn't care as he wound up for another set of blows.

"She touched me first." The suspect braced for impact, but it didn't come. He didn't want to open his eyes since he was sure he would see the officer's hand raining down on him. A moment passed, and he quickly grabbed the opportunity to stop the torture. "She said she wanted to play a game with me. She wanted me to be the daddy and she the mommy. She gave me her daddy doll and wanted me to play. She said we should lie down together and play. She made me take my shoes off and wanted us to play under the covers in her bed. She said I had to take my pants off to get into bed. I got an erection, and she asked me what it was. She just reached over and touched it. I didn't know what to do. It just happened."

As much as the explanation sent him over the edge and as pathetic and evil as the excuses were, the young officer knew he needed to regain control of his emotions as the confession came flowing out of the offender's mouth. He needed to send this guy to jail more than he needed to kill him, even though he desperately wanted to do the latter.

For the next 45 minutes, the suspect provided an increasingly more detailed version of the events leading up to the rape of the beautiful little girl who trusted her dad's friend to safely play family. Each time Smith asked a new question, the offender rounded out the truth a little more. Then Smith handed over this abuser, the perpetrator of this horrendous crime, for processing. He pondered how good he had become at procuring confessions. He wished he didn't have so many opportunities, but the world kept offering up new monsters every day, and he feared he would never make a significant enough impact on the cycle of abuse in the human race. His guiding voice wouldn't allow him to contemplate that outcome since it could make him weak and ready to give up. Smith fixated on the next blue file on his desk.

Chapter 17

Diesel

The prison allowed inmates to visit the library only once every 12 hours. Diesel had a Bible in his cell, but he hungered for a deeper knowledge of the book that had transformed his life. The library offered what seemed like a treasure trove of options, but the holy grail of study aids was *Strong's Exhaustive Concordance of the Bible*. To get to the library, inmates had to pass through what was called Death's Alley, a narrow path bordered by several cell blocks. It provided a well-concealed place for those who carried out initiation rites or simply wanted retaliation for a grudge. Brushy Mountain Prison saw more in-house deaths than were ever perpetrated by these men on the outside. It truly was survival of the fittest.

Diesel knew Death's Alley would be an excellent opportunity for Big Red to come good on his threats. A few months earlier, as Diesel made his way to the library, an unsuspecting man in front of him and an unfortunate soul behind him were both attacked out of the shadows. It seemed to Diesel that at some point the sheer weight of the odds alone would ensure his untimely death. He would need a miracle to stay alive, so he prayed accordingly.

Lord, I am not afraid to die, but I don't fancy getting shanked on my way to the library to study. You know the only reason I come here every day is to learn about how great You are and to have something of value to offer the men in here. As the apostle Paul in the Bible told Timothy, I want to study to show myself approved to You, Lord, to be a workman who does not need to be ashamed, accurately handling Your Word. I trust you with all my heart, and I believe You have something greater in store for my life. I just want to be around to see that. Diesel winked at God to show a degree of humor but also to settle his nerves as he stepped onto Death's Alley.

Fifty feet down the path was the end of the first block and the first opportunity for attack. One of Big Red's men had a knife fashioned out of angle iron stolen from the shop. It would do the job adequately and inflict significant pain in the process. It was Cyril who had instructed the would-be assassin to be ready when Diesel went to the library and to connect with his torso on the first strike, preferably in his heart. The man held the knife in his right hand and kept his back to the wall, hidden on the left side of the path. He wouldn't even have to jump out to make his mark but just swing his blade from his hip into the body of his victim. Across the alley, his accomplice had Diesel in full view and would draw Diesel's attention away from his partner while simultaneously alerting him that their victim was approaching.

When Diesel was only 10 feet from the intersection, he could see the face of the man to his right. He knew something wasn't right, and his heart started beating faster as he braced for an attack. He had been in many fights in his lifetime, and he knew the adrenaline coursing through his veins was for his preservation and needed to be used accordingly. His instinct told him to keep his eyes on the guy to his right, but something was shouting at him to be alert for an attack from a different location.

As he was about to enter the intersection, Diesel saw the man's eyes shift from a fixed stare at him to something down the unseen portion of the alley to his left. He instantly knew there was another person waiting for him there. He braced for impact, hoping to avoid a direct hit and hoping his assailants would not want to draw too much attention with repeated strikes. He was amazed at how time seemed to slow down and how much his mind could process in the space of just a few microseconds. As his mind caught up with his feet, he saw what was waiting for him and looked directly at a man holding a makeshift knife at least eight inches long. *That will do some damage*, he thought and then shifted his body in the opposite direction of the knife holder. *Any second now that guy behind me is going to jump me and hold me while this guy rams that blade into me.*

The man who had stayed visible the whole time was staring in disbelief at his accomplice's apparent lack of willingness to strike. It was not their first rodeo, and he had seen his colleague successfully complete an attack like that on several occasions. This was not nerves. And then their target walked right through their trap without being confronted by either man.

As Diesel was putting more distance between him and his would-be attackers, he could hear the men's murmurings behind him.

"What the hell is wrong with you? Didn't you see me signal you? Why didn't you at least jump him once you saw him? I would have backed you up." His partner's look of disbelief woke him up to the strange scenario that had unfolded.

"What are you talking about? I saw you look my way, but nobody came, so I presumed you were just diverting your gaze to refocus or something."

"What do you mean 'nobody came'? Look!" He pointed down the alley at Diesel, who was a full 100 feet away by now, still hearing their elevated voices.

"Where did he come from?"

"You're kidding me, right? He walked right by you, and you didn't see him?"

"There is no way he walked right by me. No way!"

"Well, he did. As you can see, there is no way he can be walking down this alley without walking by you. Big Red is not going to be happy. There will be hell to pay, I tell you. Hell to pay!"

Unseen by either man, the One who had given Diesel the strength to stand for his Lord was chuckling at the scene. With one hand, He had prevented the man with the knife from seeing Diesel as he walked by, and with the other, He had held the watchman accomplice at bay. The dark forces behind the assassination attempt had failed, and the planned homicide became a non-event as the men scampered back to be chastised by their boss. Diesel, on the other hand, made it safely to the library and praised God for the miraculous protection he had just witnessed.

"Thank you, Lord! Your Word says You will send Your angels to watch over me and protect me, and You have certainly done that tonight." His celebration was quickly tempered with the knowledge that Big Red wouldn't stop trying just because a couple of his goons had failed. "Lord, I know they will try again, but Your Word says I should not fear those who can kill the body, but instead I should have a reverence for You. Lord, I need You to continue to protect me and provide safe passage." He paused to meditate on his request and search his heart for a response. It came in the form of a scripture from Deuteronomy 31:6.

> *Be strong and of good courage, do not fear nor be afraid of them; for the* LORD *your God, He is the One who goes with you. He will not leave you nor forsake you.*

Diesel smiled and breathed more easily as the truth of God's love and protection was more real now than ever before. He couldn't help but think he may have a fresh swagger as he shared the gospel with whomever he could get to listen the following day. With that thought inspiring him, he settled down with the concordance to glean some more truths from the passages of the Bible he had been studying.

Chapter 18

Scott

Scott tossed and turned in bed. His newest companion lay passed out next to him. He was caught between two worlds, and his dreams were being ravaged by his subconscious. A scene was unfolding before him. It was a scene he had watched a thousand times before—a vulnerable young boy being abused by a predator. The young boy was helpless to defend himself as his future was being scarred forever by this evil act. He wrestled with the image and watched how the abuse unfolded until even his subconscious could no longer handle it. He jolted upright in the bed.

Tears of anger streamed down his face. If only he could go back in time to protect that boy. He was big now, bigger than most others, and certainly vicious enough to take on any of the bigger opponents. He was smarter now also, too smart to be taken advantage of by anyone ever again. If he could get his hands on that monster, he would rip him to shreds. It had been a very long time since he had addressed his Creator, but a rare prayer left his lips—a prayer of anger but a prayer nonetheless. "Why didn't You help me? Why didn't You do something? Why did You let that bastard lure me away? Why? Why? Why? I don't even know why I am talking to You. I don't even believe in You." Despite his atheistic claims, he continued his prayer. "You could have just stopped it from happening, but You just closed Your eyes and let it happen. It ruined my life. It ruined everything. I haven't been able to have a relationship that doesn't end in disaster. I can't even get a night's sleep."

As soon as the rant came to an end, he immediately went into self-medication mode. It may have been the middle of the night, but he was awake now, and it was a new day for him. His mission for that day, for every day, kicked into gear. Get high.

Scott climbed out of the bed, not even taking a moment to check on his companion, who thought she had found a like-minded person who could console her in her pain. She had offered her home and body to the silver-tongued predator who was now roaming her house as she slept. He riffled through all the usual spots to find any medications that might tie him over until the morning or any cash to go get a fix. He found cash in a drawer in the bedroom and then put on his clothes.

The tormentors who had been attacking his dreams for so long watched his movements and enjoyed his predicament as they laughed at their handiwork. The abused had become the abuser, and his life was firmly in their grasp. He was now just a tool to destroy as many lives as possible before he completely self-destructed. The circle of abuse brought them delight as they followed his movements into the kitchen. He grabbed Hazel's car keys and headed for the door.

He figured she wouldn't wake up while he was gone, but he didn't care. He had $160 in his pocket and a borrowed car. That translated in his mind to nothing more than getting a good buzz. It was a way to get that horrible dream to stop haunting him and put the shambles of an existence he called life back on life support.

He wasn't fit to drive, but that was never an issue when he wanted to get high. Everything was a risk, and life became a process of managing and prioritizing risks. At the top of his risk list every day was the risk of not getting a fix. It superseded all other risks at all other times. Addicts don't like the bondage they find themselves in, and Scott was no different. As he drove down the street, he pondered what he would do if he ever had to choose between the safety of a loved one and avoiding the pain of withdrawal.

Get a fix.

He decided to play devil's advocate against himself.

You don't even have a loved one anyway.

I have Mom.

You would sell her out for $50—you've done it before.

I would never hurt her, though. I would never make a choice to harm her just to get my dope.

He thought about that for about 10 seconds, and the honesty of his own answer scared him. *You have already hurt her time and time again. You know if it came down to it, you would see her in her grave if it meant getting your last high.*

Scott wanted his brain to stop working, but that wouldn't happen until he could get to the supplier. He was in the zone where the drugs had not fully worn off. His body didn't feel like he was coming down with the plague yet, but he was lucid enough to articulate and analyze his own thoughts. It was the time when he felt most normal and, thus, the time when he hated himself the most. His self-loathing propelled him just as fast, if not faster, to the next buzz.

How did you let yourself get into this state? Since when did you become the guy who picks up girls in bars just to rip them off? What happened to you? When did you become such a scumbag? You used to be a normal guy. You had a job, a career with a future, a pension, and benefits. You had a wife and adopted her son. Who the heck in their right mind just gives all that up for some dope?

The word *dope* resonated with him. He had googled it once and found that the word had a history going back almost 200 years. For more than 100 years, it had referred specifically to a drug mixture. Its original meaning was slang for a stupid person, an idiot. *How fitting*, he thought. *Only a dope, an idiot, would make the choices I've made.* In his weaker moments, he longed to go back and make things right, but three attempted rehabs convinced him he would never be able to kick his addiction. His only viable option was to not allow himself to live in deep regret since he felt suicidal when he did. Instead, he went headlong into the identity of an addict and accepted it as his fate. *If I am going to hell, I might as well do it in style. Redemption is reserved only for folks who have something redeemable.*

His car pulled into a seedy neighborhood. All the streetlights were broken, but he could have found his way to the driveway with his eyes closed. Shelley had the best drugs in the city, but there was no messing around with her. You didn't show up at Shelley's without money in hand. The cops in the area were on the take, and all she had to do was make a call to get you hauled off to jail. Her cops were known to pick up bodies and then pin the crime on local gangs. She didn't put up with fools either, and had a muscle on hand to crack a skull or two if someone tried to pull a fast one. There were many poor souls who thought they could take advantage of this senior citizen only to wind up in the hospital or the morgue. Scott reserved his visits to her place for times when he could buy whatever he wanted.

An oversized goon was hanging around Shelley's front door.

"Shelley inside?" Scott didn't feel comfortable trying to walk by this guy since he was not one of her regular security people.

"Who's asking?" He stood to attention, towering even more than his large stature suggested when he was sitting down.

"Scott. She knows me." He just wanted his fix. He wasn't daunted by the guy's size and was never one to back down, especially when someone tried to intimidate him. But his pride was only a secondary priority right now.

"Let him in," came a voice over the wire in the tall guy's ear.

"She's in the back room."

Scott didn't bother with formalities. The outside steps to the front door were wide enough for two or even three normal-sized adults to walk side by side, but Scott and the goon were not normal-sized, and the big guy wasn't budging. Scott pushed his way past the goon and noted that he felt as thick as he looked.

He walked through the house to the back as he had done dozens of times before. Even though there were lights on, the place felt dark. He was still under the influence of the drugs he had taken earlier, but a dark feeling seemed to seep inside him. It wasn't just the lack of lighting; he could feel the darkness. It was almost like he could taste the evil there. Shelley was sitting on the couch knitting a blanket.

"It's for my new grandson. He'll be number 10, and I have made a blanket for all of them. I could buy one, but nothing is handmade anymore. The cheap crap from China is everywhere, and the best of America is made by a machine. No artistry, no craft."

Shelley was unusually talkative. Scott didn't care to hear the ranting of this old, eccentric woman, but he knew she never hesitated to kick people out on a whim if they annoyed her.

"Do you have kids, Scott?" Now he would have to answer.

"No, Shelley, no kids." It was technically a lie, but he never acted like a dad and didn't feel like he could really claim his adopted child as a son.

"Do you ever wish you had kids?" Scott didn't like this line of conversation.

"I didn't have a good childhood and don't want to create another life that would be just as miserable as mine." He surprised himself with his vulnerability and practical honesty.

"I don't know what I would have done if I didn't have my kids. They mean the world to me. I would give up anything for them. And then there are grandkids. They are the game changers, Scott. I have fully funded college for each of them. I have trust funds in place to fund their futures and the futures of their children. I studied how the Rockefellers preserved their wealth, and then I made my own version. Sometimes it's a chore having to clean the money, but when you get to my age, you need a motivator to keep going, and I don't want my progeny to live the life I've lived. I want them to have legitimate wealth."

Scott's annoyance at the old woman's ramblings turned to melancholy as he realized that even this woman, who had lived in the drug world for decades, had a perspective on life that was at least semi-normal. His thoughts were drifting as she asked him a question that pierced his conscience.

"Why do you live like you do, Scott?"

"Because I am an addict."

"I don't mean that. Why do you choose to be the type of addict you are, Scott? You have a reputation. I know you shop elsewhere when you don't have money, and you have several skeletons in your closet, leaving normal folks marooned in your wake. You are one of the most destructive addicts I know." There was an awkward pause before she started again. "When you came to me in the early days, you seemed like a decent guy. I thought you would turn things around and maybe even quit. I liked you and felt like you were the kind of client who would make my business better. I like doing business with good guys. I like feeling like I make people's lives more enjoyable." She paused and looked Scott right in the eye. It seemed like her eyes got darker, almost black. Scott thought his half-drugged eyes were playing tricks on him. "You are a miserable piece of crap, Scott. I don't like how you make me feel when you come to my house. You have darkness in you—the sort that has no goodness, no redemption. I bet you would kill your own mother to get a fix."

Scott lurched backward. He tried to process as quickly as he could what was happening. The new guy at the front. The dark feeling in the house. The weird conversation. The accusations. The clairvoyant knowledge of his thoughts. He had experienced some trippy things on hallucinogens, but this freaked him out. He knew he was in danger. He formulated a response in his mind that he threw out like a Hail Mary hoping it would de-escalate whatever was going on.

"Life has been hard on me, Shelley, but I have people I care about. People I would protect no matter what." That was a lie, and both of them knew it.

The room was full of unseen observers. Each had played a role in this moment. They had colluded in the plan to end Scott's miserable life and strengthen their control on the drug business and law enforcement that was empowering it. They may not have been the hands doing the dirty work, but they were undoubtedly the cause that created the effect unfolding before them. Their faces lit up with anticipation of the pending crescendo.

Scott saw murder in his supplier's eyes. He had never known Shelley to get her hands dirty, so he figured he may have a moment before one of her men came crashing through the door with guns blazing. His adrenaline was firing up, and it shook the remaining drug fog from his brain. His instinct was always to survey his surroundings, and today had been no different. He knew one side of the house had no fence. Her guys usually guarded only the front and back. He could not run fast enough to get away, so he would need the car. The car door was open, and he could only hope the goon had not decided to disable the motor. If he went too soon, he would be picked off at the front as he made his escape. He had to gamble on waiting for his assassin to open the living room door before he would crash into the glass of a side window and hope his mass was strong enough to break through the reinforced wooden frame. He could catch some serious wounds from the glass, but the bleeding probably wouldn't be enough to slow him down right away. He could see Shelley pushing a button to summon the perpetrator for her dirty work.

"Look, Shelley. I just want to pay you for some drugs and get out of here. I won't come back again. I promise." The more desperate he sounded, the less she would expect him to jump out her window.

"You're not getting any drugs today or any day ever again." Her face seemed to screw up with unnatural facial contortions, her aged skin looking hideous around her black eyes. He heard the front door handle turn, and he jumped into action. As he leaped for the window, the awful thought hit him that the glass may be bulletproof or shatterproof. But it was too late to change his plan, and he was grateful when the glass shattered from his weight and he tumbled to the ground outside.

No time to check yourself for injuries. Just run! His thoughts were racing, and time seemed to slow down as he picked himself up and bolted for the car. As he rounded the front corner of the house, he heard shots from behind and felt one buzz right by his head and hit the siding of the house. *Get to the car! Get to the car!* He coached himself through the next steps as he pulled the keys out of his pocket. Every instinct in him wanted to ram the keys into the ignition and speed out of there, but he knew he had to slow down just for a second so he didn't miss the ignition or drop the keys. That could be the difference between life and death. *Put the key in the ignition, Scott.* The key went in the first time. He knew the Dodge had some get-up-and-go, so he floored the gas pedal and allowed the engine to roar into action. He caught sight of the gunman coming through the front door, and bullets ripped into the back end of his car as he sped off, out of sight and out of range of his would-be murderer.

When he was safely out of the neighborhood and his heart rate slowed down slightly, he examined the injuries he was starting to feel. There was blood everywhere. He had several shards of glass sticking out of his legs and arms, and he was bleeding from many other places. His shirt was shredded. He needed to get to a hospital.

What the heck have you done, Scott? How bad do you have to be for someone like Shelley to want you dead? I may be going to hell, but this is not how I planned on getting there. I need to get out of town after I get patched up. Hope for change almost sparked into existence, but it was quickly crushed by his constant companions who had orchestrated the night's events and were angered by the failed execution. They whispered in his mind, as they had done so many times before. *You are a waste of space, Scott. You are not worth the dirt on your feet. You are the scum of the earth, and it would have been better for everyone if you had died tonight.* Scott hung his head in shame as he sped to the hospital.

Chapter 19

Joey

Joey wandered down the path from his backyard into the woods as he had done so many times before. His mother had seen his sullen face as he left the house but cheered herself up as he headed up the old familiar path. Maybe going on an adventure will make him feel better. Things had continued to be rough at school, and he had grown detached from all his friends. His mother had hoped he would grow out of this. He was nine now and should be playing ball and getting into mischief, but instead, he stayed in his room and fought against the status quo anytime he could. She gave him over once more in prayer to his Maker.

Joey wanted to feel the same joy for the woods that he had before his encounters with Karl. Everything was better before him. Everything felt dark and gray after him. The sounds of the woods used to simultaneously excite and scare him, especially near dusk. Now they barely even registered. The climb up to the vantage point where he had spent so much time over the years held no pleasure. It was now just a chore that meant nothing. As he sat down and stared at the world below him, he wondered how he could fix things. Some boys are doers, and some are thinkers. He had always been a thinker. But doing should flow out of clear thinking, which should be engaged first if there is a problem to solve or a question to answer, or if you want to discover a new insight or explore a new path. His processing was unusually advanced for such a young boy. Details and thoughts stuck in his mind—details of a behavior that seemed to emanate from action that had no logical beginning. So the self-dialogue would begin once more in a circle of unsatisfactory conclusions.

Why did I go into the house with him in the first place? I didn't care about the blood. I could have gone home just as easy. I must have given him the wrong idea somehow. He paused in a genuine effort to remember his emotions and thoughts at the time he went into the house, but as in every instance, he couldn't pinpoint his dominant thought.

Why did I watch the movie with him? I didn't understand it, and I didn't like it. Again, he paused in hope of a new revelation, but none came.

Why did I let him touch me? I was scared of him. I could have left. He didn't pause as he launched into his next line of self-interrogation.

Why did I do the things he told me to do? He could have rationalized all these events except for the next question.

Why did I go back? That was the kicker. That was the one that lay so much of the blame at his own feet. He never started a day planning to go to Karl's house, but somehow he found himself back in the same place doing the same things and worse. It was a sick *Groundhog Day* feeling. It was the stuff of self-inflicted nightmares, of irreconcilable failures that ultimately pointed most, if not all, of the blame firmly at his feet.

As he stared at the beautiful scene before him, the gray feeling on the inside started to dominate what he saw on the outside. All the beauty disappeared, and he saw only function. One thing led to another. The birds, the animals, the trees, the sky—everything was just function. They all came and went, and nothing changed. None of them mattered. None of them could change the wrong he had done. None of them could ever bring color back to his heart.

"I wish I was dead." The words came out of his mouth unexpectedly. For a moment, he was not sure if he had actually verbalized them or just thought them. He could still feel the sensation of his lips and jaw moving, so he assumed he must have said them. He contemplated the words for a few minutes. They offered a solution he had never thought of before. It was a solution that seemed to inflict the right amount of punishment on him and—dare he say it?—God. In this quiet place, he let his feelings flow unrestricted as words poured out like water from a faucet.

"If You had not let me get hurt. If You had made me go home instead. If You had made the movie not work. If You had stopped him from doing anything. If You had made Mark stay instead of go home. If You had done something." He paused and looked at his dirty hands. They were dirty from the climb up the mountain and dirty from the bad things he had done with Karl. They were dirty like his soul before God. Dirty. So dirty. "If You had done something."

The repetition didn't help the shame that was flowing to the surface. *How can I blame God for what I did?* His rational thinking was advanced for his age, but he could not have known how flawed it was. He could not have known how the God he was accusing longed to tell him that He loved him, and that He had already paid the price through Jesus to have the gray removed and replaced with color and wonder once more. He longed to tell him that it was not his fault. He did not hold him responsible for his actions because he was just a confused little boy who had his innocence ripped away. He did not have the faculties to process any of the decisions he was forced to make that day or any day since.

On one side of Joey sat a dark presence who was inspiring this misguided dialogue. It was this dark presence that had inserted himself into the boy's life that fateful day. It was this dark presence that had orchestrated events so many times to put him back in the position to be abused over and over again. It was this dark presence that had been responsible for the gray and the absence of wonder. It was this dark presence that suggested that death was a good solution. But his voice was being minimized, mitigated, and diminished by another presence full of light sitting on Joey's other side.

If it were not for the rules, that light-filled presence would have rid his charge of this dark blight long ago. If it were not for the rules, the boy would not be in this predicament. Joey had debated in his own mind the merit of free will. He knew there could be no legitimate love relationship with God without it, but he still found himself wishing the rules could be changed or at least suspended long enough so he could exact some punishment on the enemy he faced every day. He knew there was not much he could do—at least not yet— but he consoled himself with the hope of a day when all that might change.

The light-filled presence reached out and put His hand on the boy's shoulder. Although He could not fix his wrong thinking or penetrate the gray with much color, He still could bring peace with His touch. He could still provide some light to the dark vein of thought inspired by the one tormenting him.

You are loved by many. The impression in his mind seemed just like his own thoughts, but he noticed the third-person wording and thought it odd that he would think like that. He thus gave it a little more attention and scrutiny than he might have otherwise. He tried to put the thought in submission to the self-hatred he wanted to stay attached to, but it would not submit. And then another thought arose: *They would all be sad if you were gone.* It was the same third-person wording and the same resistance to his previous train of thought. This time, however, he had a fleeting emotion of hope that he could feel loved again one day. It did not linger long, but it did remove the fog of self-annihilation, and it did sow a seed for another day.

Chapter 20

Officer Smith

In Officer Smith's hand was a case file that would alter the course of his life forever. Never before had he contemplated the horrors he would discover in this case. It was an atrocity so despicable that he would be pulled into a permanent hatred of the dark side of man and, therefore, a hatred for self and ultimately the God who had created such evil.

As he pulled open the file, he saw the mug shot of a man accused of the murder of his own son. The man had denied the charge, and because there was no body, they had to release him. After reading the rap sheet of the suspect and the testimony of the distraught mom, Officer Smith intuitively felt the guy was guilty. The report told the mother's story:

Ms. Everitt: Aiden, the baby, had been crying almost nonstop for two days because he was colicky. Larry, the baby's daddy, was so mad at Aiden because he was crying. Larry had been using drugs.

Officer Harley: What kind of drugs?

Ms. Everitt: I'm not sure. He did lots of different drugs. Mostly meth.

Officer Harley: Methamphetamines?

Ms. Everitt: Yes, and other drugs, too, but mostly meth.

Officer Harley: Then what happened?

Ms. Everitt: He was acting all sort of crazy and yelling at Aiden to stop crying. He grabbed him out of his crib and started shaking him.

(Note: Mother broke down crying for several minutes.)

Officer Harley: Please continue, Ms. Everitt.

Ms. Everitt: I took Aiden from him and put him back in his crib. He stopped crying after a little while, and Larry seemed to chill out. I didn't think he would do anything.

Officer Harley: What did he do, Ms. Everitt?

Ms. Everitt: He killed him. He killed my baby. He killed my Aiden.

Officer Harley: Did you see him hurt Aiden?

Ms. Everitt: No. I left to go to the grocery store, and I told him to call me if the baby started crying again. I came home about an hour and a half later, and they both were gone. I called him over and over again, but I knew in my gut that something was wrong. I knew he had done something terrible.

Officer Harley: What happened next?

Ms. Everitt: I called his mom and his brother to see if he had brought Aiden to their house, but they hadn't seen him. I called my mom to ask her to come over and help me find them. After about four hours, Larry came home without the baby. I asked him where Aiden was, and he said he didn't know. He said he had just gone out to get some air and assumed the baby was sleeping and would be fine.

Officer Harley: How did he act when you told him Aiden was missing?

Ms. Everitt: It was horrible. He said nothing. He didn't even act surprised. That's why I know he killed my baby. Who does that? Who kills their own baby and then hides his body? How can he have no feelings? He is the devil. He is the devil.

Officer Smith had read enough to discern that this was not a typical abuse homicide. It did not fit the bill of a usual abuser. He flipped over to the transcript of the suspect.

Officer Harley: Tell me what happened when Aiden went missing.

Mr. Walsh: I told you. I went out to get some fresh air. The baby was sleeping, and I thought he would be fine.

Officer Harley: You were gone for at least four hours. What did you think would happen to the baby if he woke up?

Mr. Walsh: He never wakes up. He always sleeps.

Officer Harley: Aiden's mom says he had been colicky and was not sleeping like normal. Was his crying getting to you?

Mr. Walsh: I don't think so.

Officer Harley: What do you mean you "don't think so"? Either it was getting to you, or it wasn't. Which is it?

Mr. Walsh: I don't remember, okay?

Officer Harley: Why don't you remember?

Mr. Walsh: I had been using.

Officer Harley: What where you using?

Mr. Walsh: I was smoking pot, man.

Officer Harley: Just pot?

Mr. Walsh: I think so.

Officer Harley: I have your tox screen here, and it says you had high levels of methamphetamines as well as marijuana.

Mr. Walsh: I guess I did some meth, too.

Officer Harley: How old is Aiden?

Mr. Walsh: He was six months old.

(Note: Suspect referred to the missing child as deceased.)

Officer Harley: What do you think happened to Aiden?

Mr. Walsh: I don't know.

Officer Harley: You don't seem to care.

Officer Smith had to stop. He couldn't bear the suspect's complete disregard for the life of his child. Smith was unable to have children and unable to go home to a family and wash away the horrible abuse and twisted acts of sick and perverted men. He couldn't filter it like other cops. He would never feel the hand of his own child resting in his hand or the kiss of his little girl putting her trust in him. What difference was he making if it kept happening? He was not saving any of these children, only punishing who had hurt them.

He finished reviewing the file and realized the only charges they could make stick were drug use and neglect. His gaze focused on the file, and his heart became determined to find out what had happened to the child, to six-month-old Aiden. He grabbed his gun from his desk and headed to the trailer home located on 20 acres just east of town. It was being treated as a crime scene, so he knew any evidence would be preserved and he would have complete access to the circumstances leading up to Aiden's disappearance—to his death.

The place was a complete mess, and it stunk. It was just what he expected from a couple of junkies. There were at least the basics of what was needed to take care of a baby, so there was no immediate reason to expect a long-term abuse or neglect situation. Officer Smith was blessed with an incredible mind for details. His superior wasn't aware of this gift when he promoted him, but it had shot him to fame in his region as a talented investigator and exceptional interrogator.

He spent several hours inspecting the scene. Room by room, he visualized what kind of activities may have taken place close to Aiden's disappearance. But it was not until he sat down at the kitchen table that he noticed the dent in the wall. There were several dents and marks on the wall, but what made this one stand out was its unusual shape. He walked over to the spot and measured it with the size of his fist. It was a little bit larger. The suspect was bigger than he was, so it could be a mark made by him punching the wall, but there was something about the dent that bothered him. He pondered the scenario.

"What caused you? You don't look like a typical fist dent in Sheetrock. How did you come about?"

If someone had been in the room with Smith, they may have expected the wall to respond to those questions, given how intensely he was staring at it. He moved to within a couple of inches of the spot and stared.

"You are too round. A fist has an oval shape, and the impression in the wall should match the force of the individual fingers. One side of the dent would be a quarter to a half inch deeper than the other side where the leading fingers connect first. But here, you have an even, round impact like, like—" He stopped talking as it dawned on him what made the dent. He pieced together the scene in his head.

The baby wouldn't stop crying. Dad was coming down off his meth and didn't have enough to get high again. Aiden's crying was driving him crazy. He picked him up and shook him to make him stop. Aiden kept crying. Dad's temper rose, and he shouted at the boy for crying as he paced around the room holding him at arm's length. He lashed out in anger at whatever was in his way, probably hurting himself and making his frustration worse. And when he got close to the wall... Smith paused in his mind to allow an alternative scenario to present itself. But as he stared at the dent in the wall, he noticed a smaller, much fainter dent a few inches below and to the right.

"You slammed Aiden into the wall, causing his head to suffer a fatal blow after the violent shaking had started internal bleeding. You are right-handed, and naturally you would have led with your right hand, gripping Aiden's upper body and making a second dent on the wall."

He felt sick as he realized he had most likely uncovered the events of the murder. As he replayed the scene over and over again searching for flaws, the same scenario kept presenting itself. He became convinced that he had run the scene out just as it happened, give or take a few minor details.

"What did you do next, you scumbag? What did you do next?" He walked away from the wall and paused, just as he thought the suspect would have since the baby would have stopped crying. "You realized you had hurt Aiden pretty badly. Within a couple of minutes, you would have realized you killed him. So what did you do next?"

Officer Smith instinctively walked out the front door and surveyed the scene with a new set of eyes. It was the middle of the day, and he had perfect visibility, just like the suspect at the time of Aiden's death. He looked around to see what he might do to get rid of a baby he had just killed. Sometimes, when everything is a mess, the only thing that stands out is something that looks taken care of. Smith noticed a spot of dirt next to an overgrown vegetable garden that had obviously not yielded a crop for some time. The dirt was disturbed just like many other parts of the yard that had been dug up by the dogs and chickens walking around, but this patch of dirt was level, like someone had run their foot over it to make it less obvious. It was a subtle difference from the rest of the yard, but it was enough for him to notice. In the few seconds it took for him to walk the 30 feet to the vegetable garden, he had convinced himself that he would find Aiden or at least some evidence buried in the dirt.

As he shoveled away the dirt with his penknife, being careful not to disturb any potential evidence, he saw Aiden's hand. He gently scooped dirt away from the area where he expected to see the rest of his body. As he got to the end of his arm, he realized that the limb was no longer attached to the body. His mind was reeling at this point. *No, no, no! You did not do this to your little boy. It's bad enough that you would smack him into a wall and then think to bury his body, but tell me you didn't do this.* He couldn't even say the words.

He called in the report to the crime scene investigators, and a team met him at the house. They spent the next four hours digging up 18 parts of little Aiden's body. They assembled it piece by piece on site to make sure all his remains had been accounted for. Every time Smith found another piece of this little boy, he brought it to the five-foot folding table set up in the front yard. He saw the body of this precious little boy being reassembled like a dirty Lego set. His heart could take no more. He compartmentalized his emotions as long as he could, but when he got home that night, he cried, and he cried. He cried for the pain he felt for Aiden and for the rest of his family that loved him. They would have to live with the knowledge that he had been carved up like a turkey at Christmas. He cried at the reawakening of the awareness of the depravity of an abuser. He cried at the wickedness from which he would never be free. He cried at the absence of a family of his own to restore his sanity. He cried at the wickedness of a God who would stand by and allow such atrocities to occur. And he drank like he had never drunk before.

The alcohol didn't wipe away the pain that evoked more tears than he had cried in the past decade. As he took another swig, he heard a suggestion inside is head. *You have some Xanax the doc prescribed last year when things were rough on the job. It will take the edge off. It will help you sleep.* He didn't question the source of the suggestion. He only welcomed the potential relief. Little did he know that he had just opened a door that he would never again be able to shut.

Chapter 21

Scott

Dr. Johnson was the attending physician in the ER when Scott rolled in, covered in blood. The doctor immediately judged, correctly, that the wounds on his body were a direct cause of some self-centered pursuit. He may not have inflicted the wounds, but his narcissistic worldview was definitely to blame.

"I can't believe he is still alive," he said to the orderly nearby who had no idea the doctor was addressing him. "How does someone like him manage to live past 30, let alone 40?" His observation had a degree of genuine wonder without any real malice. He intently disliked Scott and all men and women who pursued self-destruction with such vigor. He watched as so many good living people, young and old, were unsuccessful in their attempts to cling to life, finding themselves in life-threatening predicaments through no fault of their own. He had witnessed parents, children, spouses, and friends station vigils by their bedsides, only to watch as the ones they prayed so desperately to save slipped out of this world, leaving behind only memories and sorrow.

"It's as close to a negative miracle as I will ever encounter."

The orderly started to suspect he was the target of the doctor's ramblings. "Are you talking to me?"

"He has been in here at least six times since I've been working here. Every time he has nearly fatal wounds, or he narrowly misses some artery, or he manages some other miraculous escape from some ridiculous situation he orchestrates through his recklessness."

"I'm not sure who you're talking about, Doc."

"Over there. What's his name? What's his name again? Uh, Scott. Yes, I even remember that numbskull's name—Scott. How often do you need to be in the ER for the doctors to know you by name?"

"Would you like me to attend to him, Dr. Johnson?" The orderly was very confused about why the physician was choosing this moment to talk to him for the first time and even more confused about what he wanted to happen as a result of the conversation.

"No, no, not at all. I am off in two hours, so hopefully we can stall him in triage long enough so I don't have to see him."

"He looks like he's lost a lot of blood and may need immediate attention." As soon as the words left his mouth, the orderly knew he had overstepped his boundaries and regretted getting sucked into the doctor's meanderings.

"So, you are a doctor now? Would you like to treat him?" His sarcastic tone and words were matched by the sarcastic look he threw in the direction of his unwilling and unwitting debater.

"I'm going back to work now, Doctor," and he retreated out of the sight of his predatorial conversationalist who had unfairly trapped him in this argument.

Scott was attended to right away and rushed to the ER examination area. As the nurses cut his clothes off, they noticed he still had several shards of glass lodged in critical areas of his body. The most disconcerting one was a particularly thick shard in his groin, which was bleeding at a steady rate. Jennifer was new to the hospital and had never seen Scott before. She had dealt with many drug addicts and was not easily suckered into a sob story, but something about Scott caused her to have compassion for him.

"Get Dr. Johnson as soon as you can." Her tone of voice enlisted the appropriate response from the assisting nurse. She turned her attention to Scott to try to uncover the reason he was in this predicament and, more importantly, why she was drawn to him.

"So, Scott, can you tell me a little bit about what happened?"

"I jumped through a window." His forthrightness had much more to do with his impatience than any genuine willingness to help her with her job.

"Was it a first-floor or second-story window?" She didn't even bat an eye as she rebutted his brashness with her own apparent indifference.

"Does that matter?" Scott was duped by her diversion and found himself being sucked into this redhead's mind games.

"Not really." There was a full grin on her face, and for a minute, Scott forgot his overwhelming urge to get as many drugs as possible.

"Let's get you cleaned up as much as we can and get these smaller shards removed and treated while we're waiting." He knew he would be fine without getting some kind of fix, at least for a short while, so he allowed himself to enjoy her presence.

"Sure." He found himself being glad he had landed the new nurse. She and her assistant removed about 12 pieces of glass, each one about two inches long.

"We'll leave the big shard for the doctor."

"Thanks, Jennifer." He had never cared to look at someone's name badge before tonight, but he wanted to keep this personal connection alive as a distraction, at least for now. It had been a very long time since he had known and experienced the company of a woman who meant something more to him than a means to an end. That thought had barely left his mind when he remembered his original and constant primary objective: to get high. A potential relationship, however appealing in the moment, was not even on the radar.

Dr. Johnson approached Scott's bed with the same disgust as when he had arrived, and he didn't care to mask his distaste for his repeat patient. "We need to take this shard of glass out of your groin, Scott. I will need to work on it in the OR within the next hour since it is dangerously lodged against your main artery. We'll just need a local anesthetic to deaden the area while we stitch the wound closed."

"What can you give me for the pain, Doctor?" Scott was in pain, but he was entering the beginning stage of withdrawal, which in many ways created more fear and torment than detox itself.

"It looked to me like you were flirting with Nurse Womack, so I can't imagine you need anything more than what you have been given already. The local anesthetic will be ready in about 30 minutes."

Scott's anger flared up, and he tried to protest, but he knew it was futile. He was not in the mood to pick a fight with the determined doctor who already had his number. He backed off and turned his attention back to the pretty nurse, hoping to reignite whatever had started kindling between them. As he did, he realized he needed a distraction more than he originally thought. Thirty minutes felt like an eternity at that moment.

Chapter 22

Joey

The principal stared at Joey's parents across his large cherrywood desk. He paused from making his dissatisfaction with their son known before launching back into his articulation of the many rules he had broken.

"After he blatantly ignored his teacher's request to be quiet, he threw his pencil at the student he had accused of stealing it from another student. The teacher, in an attempt to establish order, told him to report to my office, but instead, he ran to the other boy and started hitting him. As parents of four boys, you must understand that anarchy of this nature is simply unacceptable in any environment."

If they were to read the principal's body language, they would have felt like their son had committed an unpardonable sin. The principal embellished the importance of this issue, and the parents couldn't deny that this kind of behavior was not only unacceptable but also deeply concerning since Joey had never gotten into a fight before. Dick looked at his wife, who seemed at a loss to explain how her once sweet little boy was now a scrapper and self-declared vigilante of sorts. He then looked at Joey, who had been staring at the ground the whole time.

"Joey, is this true?" His father thought carefully about the next words he would say. He could see the sullenness of his son's countenance, and although he did not know why, he could also see the brokenness of his heart. "If there are any circumstances or any other information surrounding this situation that you think would help us understand why you picked a fight with this other student, then please tell me, and we can address them right now with your principal."

The principal seemed horrified that Dick was not towing the line in his attempt to reprimand their son. "This is not a tribunal. Joey has broken school rules and will be punished accordingly." If the principal had not already made up his mind, Dick's actions now galvanized his convictions as he pronounced the punishment. "Joey will be suspended for three days and will have to make up all his work at home."

Dick looked at the principal in a manner that would not be considered fitting for a pastor, but he held his tongue, at least for the first round of thoughts that came to his mind.

"Principal Lark, you are entitled to administer whatever punishment you see fit for my son, but you are not entitled to tell me how and when I can discuss my son's actions with him. I have been a pastor for more than a decade and a youth pastor before that. If there is one thing I have learned, it's that there are always two sides to a story, and it is not my intention to throw my son under the bus until he has had a fair chance to explain what the circumstances were surrounding this incident. There is always more than meets the eye, and you would do well to consider that instead of taking a draconian approach to your discipline." As soon as that last phrase left his lips, Dick knew he had gone too far, but there was no turning back. "So I will take *my* son home with me, and he will serve his suspension in *our* home, and in the meantime, you might want to check into the allegations of stealing that made my son feel like he needed to take action. If he did, indeed, fight to defend another child, then he was following the principles of our home, even if he was misguided in how he did it."

Joey stared at his dad almost in disbelief. He had always known him to be strict and fully expected him to line up with the principal's opinion of his disobedience. His dad's impassioned defense made something inside him respond. It was hope—yes, hope. It had been so long since he had felt hope that he had forgotten the warmth it brought to his heart. Winter had set in long ago, and spring had failed to appear so often that he was sure it would never arrive. But as quickly as hope had darted out from its hiding place, the voice of winter attempted to assert itself as it had done so many times before. *Your dad won't understand. How could anyone understand? You are broken. God is disgusted by you. You will never amount to anything. When you get home, your dad will tell you what he really thinks, and you will wish your principal was the only one you had to answer to.*

Dick watched it all play out in front of him. He couldn't hear the internal dialogue, but the hope that spread across Joey's face after he jumped to his defense had given hope to his own heart. He had not been able to connect with his son for so long that he had forgotten what an affirming facial expression looked like. He always erred on the side of discipline and took literally the Scripture that guided his own parents to spare the rod and spoil the child. He sometimes felt he was overly strict, but having four boys made it almost impossible to show individual leniency, let alone change his parenting style to match each kid despite the assertions of the latest psychology books. But his hope of building a new relational bridge to his son was quickly being extinguished as he saw Joey's expression retreat to his more familiar withdrawn demeanor. The voice of winter had affected both souls.

Dick knew he was at a critical point. It felt as if his son were being sucked away from him in a vortex of misunderstanding and circumstantial half-truths. *What is going on in your head, son?* His thoughts strived to solve the problem. *How did I lose you? When did I lose you? What happened to you?* He knew Joey would not answer him, even if he could hear the questions. Somewhere deep inside, Dick felt an urge to fight for his son and their future. It was like he was holding a fishing line that was being pulled through his hands by a fish seeking to evade its captor. If he did not pay attention, it could slip right through his hand. If he was not deliberate enough at this moment, he might unwillingly let the circumstances unfold whatever way Joey was letting them go. In that moment, it felt easier to believe it was a phase, but his intuition told him to fight and not leave his son's future in the hands of destiny and whatever that might mean.

His heart drew his mind to his favorite parable in the Bible about the lost sheep. It was critical to how he understood the love of God and how he had turned away from a wayward path as a young man. In the parable, the Good Shepherd had 100 sheep. One of them went astray, and out of his great love for his sheep, he left the 99 who were safe and sought out the one lost sheep. The shepherd carried the sheep on his shoulders and built a foundation of familiarity and safety in the process. *I need to pursue my lost boy. I need to draw him close, and if he won't let me in, I need to get someone else to help him. I will not let him face whatever he has going on by himself, not if I can help it.* Hope may not have been rekindled to the same degree as a moment ago, but the sound of the coming of spring definitely echoed more loudly in his heart.

He looked at his son once more and put his arm around his shoulder. "Come on, son. Let's go home and work this out." Principal Lark's expression left no doubt that he disapproved of Dick's parenting tactics, but Dick didn't care. All that mattered was his son's well-being. He looked at his wife, who had been just a bystander in the events of the last few moments. He was not sure what to expect, and her neutral expression gave nothing away, but as they turned to walk to the door, she grabbed his hand and squeezed it. They would be together in this, and that made it all the more possible to press on. Dick now knew what he had to do. There was someone he knew from his days as a youth pastor who might be able to reach Joey with the right measure of compassion and discipline. He just needed to make the call.

Chapter 23

Officer Smith

A dozen cases had come and gone, each one with an offender now behind bars, but Officer Smith could not get the image of the pieces of that baby on the table out of his head. It haunted his thoughts. *That was a real child. His mother is traumatized. His grandparents' hearts are broken. He was a real person. Aiden. Aiden. What kind of monster does that? It would seem incredibly inhumane to do that to an animal, but a baby?* He simply could not wrap his brain around the depravity, no matter what the circumstances, that would lead a man to do that to his own flesh and blood. *Even if he had killed him accidentally, how do you do that to such an innocent life?*

He had a bottle of vodka in his hand, and a bottle of sleeping pills were on the table. His work colleagues had made comments about his drinking a little too often. Vodka was virtually undetectable as long as he could keep his act together. He would not be back on his shift for another nine hours. *I can drink for a few more hours and sleep it off. I just need enough to stop these images from tormenting me.* He did his best to hit that goal, but when he eventually acknowledged his failure, he took the pills.

The alarm never went off, and he fell out of bed four hours after he was supposed to be at work. His phone had several messages, but he decided he'd better shower before he listened to them. He would probably have to jump into action once he knew what they were about. The pressure of being late for work dominated his thoughts, and he was glad to have something else on his mind, even if it was just for a few minutes.

"You're needed at a crime scene on West Brown Street. They're waiting for you to get there before they do a full crime scene investigation. They want you to see the physical evidence. I'm sorry, Smithy, but this sounds like a bad scene."

It was not often he got dispatched by his captain. Halliday was a good man, a family man. His kids were grown, and the youngest was off at college, but he often remarked how he hated being responsible for child abuse investigations. He said he had often gone home at night after investigating a case, crawled in bed beside his kids, and just held them while they slept. *How bad could it be?* Smith thought as his mind immediately re-created the scenes from Aiden's murder a few months ago. *How bad could it be?*

He pulled his cruiser over to the side of the road behind the six other department vehicles. The scene was taped off, but there was not the usual hustle and bustle he was used to. There was a somber mood in the air, and people weren't making eye contact. They all seemed buried in their own thoughts. Officer Bennet was standing in the driveway, staring at the ground.

"Hey, Bennet. What's with everybody? It is like a funeral around here."

"It's best if you go look for yourself, Smithy. I don't know what to say."

He didn't want to ask any more questions, and for the first time, he really didn't want to go into the house and see what had happened. With one foot in front of the other, he compelled his resistant body through the door. The first thing he saw was vomit that had been partially cleaned up and put into a sanitized bag. *Must be one of the first responders or they wouldn't have bagged it yet.* He was used to vomit at crime scenes, but it must have been something pretty gruesome to cause a first responder to react that way. He wished he had not spent the previous night drinking, putting his stomach on notice that he'd better not throw anything at it that it couldn't handle. Just outside the kitchen, he saw another familiar face. His head was down.

"John, what happened?" As his friend looked up to respond to his question, Smith saw tear stains on his face.

"The body is in the kitchen." No warmth was present in his response. He gave no clue that would prepare him.

Smith stepped into the kitchen, expecting to see a bloody massacre, but there was nothing except a very large soup pot on the stove.

He searched the room for another possible place for a body to present itself. He didn't want to look inside the pot, but he forced himself to step toward it. When he was a few feet away, he could see part of the inside rim. Again, he was expecting a bloodbath, but it was clean. As he took his next step, he saw a reddish limb. He stopped in his tracks and turned his head to process what he had just seen. Inside the pot were the remains of a bloated, burnt-red, blister-covered three-month-old baby. He wanted to bolt out of the door and scream, but he knew his place and knew his responsibility. He was a child abuse and murder investigator, and this was his crime scene.

He couldn't control the tears streaming down his face. He re-created the events that may have taken place as this defenseless, innocent child was forced alive into boiling water, screaming in response to the unimaginable pain of his skin and organs cooking. Smith could tell by the baby's contorted features and the way the burns had formed that he was alive when someone put him into the pot. It was highly unlikely that he would have drowned quickly enough to avoid the majority of the pain. Smith's stomach let him know that it had never signed up for this kind of evil, and he looked away to steady himself once more. Then a familiar inner voice added its opinion to his mental processes. *What are you going to do about this? Whoever did this deserves to die, not by lethal injection since that would be too merciful, but by torture, just like this baby experienced. This atrocity can't go unpunished. The system will be too lenient.*

The words were followed by an image of Smith torturing the person who did this. He could see himself skinning the person alive and using a blow torch on the body. Then he saw himself taking time to treat the wounds and administer intravenous fluids so he wouldn't die, only to start all over again and again until the person was begging for death. The image startled him. He had never even considered hurting someone like that. However, once the initial shock wore off, he couldn't help but think how fitting such a death would be for the animal who had killed this baby.

The self-proclaimed god who accompanied Officer Smith smiled at his own handiwork. He delighted himself with his wicked imagination and how easily he could insert his hellish plans into his defenseless puppet's consciousness. He got a reprieve from the unperceived tormentor and sought out another person to flush out the murderous thoughts that had gripped his heart and mind so easily. It would be a lot harder than he could have imagined, as murder had been planted in the fertile soil of a hateful, angry heart, where it would grow like a cancerous mass.

Chapter 24

Scott

Jennifer was the first to come to his room while he was in recovery. The drugs in his system were still potent, and he knew he would be sufficiently medicated for the next 48 hours. It had been a long time since he had relaxed like this. The times when he went on benders without worrying about his next fix seemed like a lifetime ago. He had been hustling from fix to fix for as long as he could remember. This was a rare break to know he didn't have to dig into his resourcefulness to take care of his addiction.

Addiction. The word reverberated in his mind as he looked at the pretty nurse who was paying him more attention than he deserved. *Addiction.* Such a simple word that carries the threat of hell and death in its undercarriage. How could nine letters adequately describe the millions of lives killed and the countless millions more destroyed by its effects?

"Scott! Scott!" Jennifer was smiling at him as she gently shook him and tried to get his attention. "How are you feeling?"

The simple question seemed to offer no real context for an answer. *Awful, terrible, ready to quit, ready to die, in love.* His thoughts pulled his emotions into action again, but where did that last one come from—*in love*? He tried it again to see if it was a cosmic joke. He could never love again. He had proved he was incapable of love before he had gone headlong into his life of addiction. Jennifer was still shaking him and had no intention of stopping until her patient showed signs of coherence.

"Uh, okay, I guess."

"Let's take a look at those wounds again." As she examined the main wound, she talked through the procedure, mainly to herself, to make sure she checked everything. As she moved to the cuts on his torso, she noticed a fairly prominent scar near his diaphragm. Although his body had scars all over, this one looked particularly nasty.

"What happened here?" The image of his ex-wife flashed through his mind. She was beautiful and crazy all in one. They were two lives that had come together in pursuit of getting the most out of a relationship with the minimal amount of effort. Both had an inflated sense of the value they brought to their relationship, but the moment she crossed the line was still a very painful memory. They had been physically abusive with each other in the past, but Scott had never hit her. She, on the other hand, knew very little restraint when it came to expressing her dissatisfaction with their marriage. It was in shambles, and he was a big enough boy to take whatever beatings she would muster up. The truth was, he was happy to take a few hits since she would always use sex as a way to alleviate her guilt, and sex was why he was with her in the first place. However, you can only push a girl so far before she breaks, and he had the scars to prove it.

"Long story and not very pleasant?" Jennifer looked a little disappointed that he wouldn't share the story with her, which took both of them by surprise.

"Um, I didn't mean I wouldn't tell you. It just isn't a nice story, and it definitely will need some context or you'll think I'm a freak."

"I already think you're a freak."

He was starting to get used to her sense of humor and was also starting to enjoy it. "Well, let's just say it was inflicted by someone who said they loved me." He looked at her in anticipation of a shocked response, but it didn't come. "Go ahead and say it."

"Say what?"

"That you would hate to meet my enemies. You know you were thinking it."

"I was actually thinking what a loving act it was to try to put you out of your misery."

He couldn't hide the fact that he was an addict. The tracks on his arms were unmistakable, but so was the warm tone in her voice that was a good companion for the tone of humor. She was not put off by his poor life choices.

"Well, it would have been, except I still woke up the next morning."

"It looks like it never got any proper medical attention."

"No, I sat around for a week hoping not to die because I didn't want her to get in trouble for what she had done."

"Didn't want to get yourself in trouble is more like it." She was closer to the truth than she could have guessed, but he wasn't about to reveal the whole story.

Jennifer checked in on Scott more than any other patient in her care during her 12-hour shift, and she felt her heart being drawn to what appeared to be an oversized teddy bear wrapped in the cover of a drug addict with a death wish. *Stay away, girl. He's not the type of man you want to develop a liking for.* But she knew it would take stronger self-talk than that to prevent a growing fondness for him. *You always try to rescue the ones that are too far gone. Maybe, though, he will be different. Maybe there is something in him worth rescuing, despite what Dr. Johnson thinks.*

As the hours rolled by, Scott's thoughts started to mirror hers. *Maybe there's a chance I could have a real relationship with a woman again. Maybe I can be rescued. Maybe I've something to offer.* As her night shift came to an end, the redheaded nurse in her mid-30s came in to check on him one last time and say good morning, as the sun was already high in the sky.

As she departed and he watched her walk away, his gears subconsciously made plans for the coming days, and he began mapping out how he might get his next fix with no thought of the cost. *You are only kidding yourself, Scott. You don't have any room in your life to care about a woman, no matter how attractive or how interested she is in you.* He looked at the current predicament and tried to use his damaged imagination to picture a world where he could be with someone and build a future, but it failed him. Once more, the cost of pulling himself out of this slow death march would be more than he could bear, and he would have to move on.

Before Jennifer returned for her shift the next evening, Scott had already discharged himself from the hospital. Shelley had no doubt doubled the price on his head, and he needed to make a plan. He had already worn out his welcome in the houses of everyone he once called *friend*. He knew he had only one course of action left. It was the one thing he had been dreading. Nonetheless, it was now a matter of imminent death, and he had to go back home for the first time since his mother kicked him out. He hated his hometown. The memories of a once-promising life now wasted were around every corner.

As he left the hospital, he took one more look at the building and what he knew would have been his last chance at love. He knew his life was over—maybe not today, maybe not at the hand of a drug dealer, but he knew there was nothing strong enough, no hope powerful enough, or no love deep enough to rescue him anymore from this pit. As he walked out, he knew he was only delaying the inevitable by going home.

Chapter 25

Officer Smith

The call from the minister took Officer Smith by surprise. He instantly remembered the voice of the man who had been his youth pastor, the man he had been forced to listen to in their little Missionary Baptist Church. For quite some time, he had distanced himself from anything church-related and was caught off guard when the call came in. He reluctantly agreed to meet with the man's 10-year-old son, who was having problems at home and at school.

What the heck am I doing here? he murmured to himself as he waited at the corner table of the local diner where he and the boy were to have lunch. *Maybe he won't show and I'll be off the hook.* He felt badly that he didn't want to help, but not bad enough to hang around past the agreed upon time. *Another five minutes, and I'm out of here.* The words had barely left his lips when he saw his former youth pastor walk through the doorway. His son was about eight feet behind him and obviously felt as uncomfortable about this meeting as he did.

"Thank you, Officer Smith, for meeting us today."

"Don't mention it, Pastor."

"Just call me Dick."

"Sure." He didn't argue with him, but he knew his subconscious wouldn't let him say anything other than *pastor*.

"Joey here is having a tough time at school and has not been himself for quite some time. He got into a fight with another kid who stole some money from his friend and has even been suspended for a few days. When we try to talk to him, he shuts down." It was obvious that Dick was understating the problem so he wouldn't alienate his son. Dick was a preacher, and Joey was a preacher's kid, just like Officer Smith, who had a modicum of sympathy for Joey, but it did not extend too far. He knew firsthand there were a lot of things worse in life than being a preacher's kid.

Dick had mentioned in their call that he didn't know what to do with his Joey and that he felt he was at a vulnerable point in his development. "I have been hard on Joey in the past, and I don't want to push him away, but I feel like he needs somebody to play bad cop while I try to be good cop for a while." He remembered those words in the hours after the call and replayed the irony of being called bad cop. "I guess it won't hurt to put a little fear of the law in Joey since the fear of God was always too far in the future for me to create enough pressure to bring about change in the present."

The request did not sit well with him, but his thoughts left him no room to say no. *What do you say to your old pastor, especially when he calls you out of the blue?*

"Leave him with me, and we'll have a chat, Pastor, uh, Dick, I mean."

"Thanks, Officer Smith. Make sure to share your experiences of people who struggle to follow the rules." He winked in an awkward kind of way, and both men felt a little uncomfortable with the request.

"Ten-four." He didn't want to affirm his acquiescence to the last request. His response was deliberately broad enough to give him leeway to take the conversation in whatever direction was needed to bring this awkward meeting to its earliest possible close. He watched as his former pastor turned and walked out the door. He continued to stare as he drove off before he ever turned his attention to the young boy in front of him.

"Hi, Joey." There was a short silence, almost enough for Officer Smith to say something else, but the boy eventually answered.

"Hey."

"Do you know why you are here?" Ever the cop, he felt like he was talking to a guy he had pulled over for a broken taillight.

"I guess."

"Well, what is your side of the story?"

"There is no story." The boy looked down and to his left. He shifted his feet and then looked toward the door. Officer Smith was all too familiar with subconscious human behavior, and he had seen this kind of reaction in the victims and perpetrators he interviewed. There was something the boy did not want him to know, something more than trouble at school. He suddenly forgot his discomfort in talking with his pastor's kid and went into investigator mode.

"I know you don't know me, but I work with kids all the time." He waited until Joey made eye contact before continuing. "What is your favorite sport?"

"Football."

"Do you play?"

"Just in the neighborhood."

His brain started to interpret Joey's body language and add up the percentages of the likelihood that this kid might open up to him. *Two affirmative responses. Give him another couple of soft questions to build some rapport.*

"What's your favorite team?"

"University of Tennessee."

"You like college ball, then?"

"Yes, sir." The boy's eyes brightened a little. He felt his chances of getting out of this meeting unscathed were increasing.

"You look like a strong kid. Maybe you will play for them one day."

There was no response, but a wry smile was enough for Officer Smith to feel confident that he had a chance of connecting with the kid. For the next hour and a half, he mixed small talk and yes-and-no questions with some strategically placed hunch questions. He could see himself in this young boy sitting across from him. He was cold but warm, disinterested but responsive. He was hiding but reaching out. They even had similar hobbies and really enjoyed the outdoors, especially trekking up the Tennessee mountains. Smith did not like his suspicions that were developing. By the way Joey shut down at certain points, it seemed like he may have suffered some sort of abuse. As their time came to a close, Joey let something slip that made the officer's heart sink, and he realized he had most likely found another victim of sexual abuse.

"Do you like watching movies with your friends, Joey?"

"Yes. No. No, I don't. I don't watch movies with other kids. I have at birthday parties, but no other times." The intensity of the response was in sharp contrast to the lighter mood he had established in the previous round of questions.

"What kind of movies do you watch when you go to parties?"

"Just whatever. I don't remember. I don't really like movies."

"I understand. I am not a fan of some movies either." He hated that his hands were always tied unless the victim would admit to the abuse. Despite being convinced that Joey was most likely a victim of some form of abuse, he had nothing to offer either Joey or his dad. He had to push it and see what reaction he would get.

"Joey, I know this may sound a little bit weird or out of left field, but I had a really hard childhood, and I struggled a lot when an older kid did some things to me that he should not have done. You can tell me if there is anything you are dealing with, anything at all."

For a second, it seemed like Smith might have gotten through to Joey, who was processing his thoughts and searching his brain to utilize the safest words possible to answer such a loaded question. But Joey stopped himself and looked downward again. Shuffling his feet, he said, "No. No, Officer Smith. Nothing like that."

The inability to help a child was harder than facing his or her offender and extracting a confession, however coerced it might be and whatever toll it took on his conscience. But it was painful knowing he could help and maybe even prevent further abuse but was unable to intervene because Joey wouldn't talk. That was causing him to unravel. Joey's dad walked in the door just as Joey was beginning to avoid Officer Smith's gaze. Dick looked in Smith's direction, looking for the nod to come back to the table. In the last minute, Smith had established beyond his reasonable doubt that Joey had been physically or sexually abused and that he would probably never have an opportunity to help the boy. His nod back to Dick was one of defeat—a come-get-your-broken-kid kind of nod.

"Thank you, Officer Smith. Were you able to talk a little sense into my boy?"

Officer Smith did not want to reinforce the negative self-image that was growing in Joey and ignored the question by making a positive comment. "You have a fine boy on your hands, Pastor, or I mean, Dick. Sorry!"

"Well, his mom and I like him anyway."

"We had a good time together. I would recommend that you give him a little latitude as long as he shows some progress at school." He managed a weak wink in the direction of Joey who seemed to appreciate the effort to make his life easier.

As the boy and his dad left the diner, Smith couldn't help but try to visualize the offender. The face of the one who victimized Joey was unknown to him, but he could insert his own abuser's face. In doing so, he unexpectedly resurrected the thoughts of the murderous act he had dreamed of committing and, as a result, had so vividly been engraved on his imagination several months before. He let himself play out the scenario longer this time than before. His soul was in torment, and all he could think about was getting to a bar as quickly as possible.

Chapter 26

Diesel

Diesel approached a new inmate who recently transferred to Brushy Mountain.

"Hey, dude. What's your name, man?"

"Sammy." He made a face as if he wished he had used a more impressive alias as an introduction to his new home.

"Well, Sammy, welcome to Brushy Mountain State Penitentiary."

"Thanks, I guess."

"Listen, Sammy, before you get accosted or enlisted by one of the gangs here, I would like to give you some advice."

"Okay."

"There are more people who leave here in body bags than I care to count. It seems like almost every day someone is hauled away unceremoniously because they were the victim of a gang initiation or because they got on someone's bad side. You look like a decent guy, so I thought I would tell you how I survive here." His newfound friend was not sure if he was the target of a new-guy prank or if he was getting a pitch for prison's version of a multilevel marketing scheme for protection.

"Okay."

"Let me ask you a question. If you were to die tonight, where would you go?"

"To the morgue, I guess."

"Not your body, dude, your soul. Where would your soul go?"

"To heaven, I hope."

"Why do you think you would go to heaven?" That was the first time Diesel had heard that response from a fellow inmate.

"Because I'm a good guy, or at least I'm better than most." Diesel had to keep himself from chuckling. He decided this guy was either a little detached from reality or he was playing with him. The fear he saw in his body language made the latter seem improbable.

"So I guess you're going to tell me you're innocent?"

"No. I killed someone in an accident while I was drunk."

"Have you ever heard of the Ten Commandments?" It was hard for Diesel to avoid sounding sarcastic since he was genuinely having difficulty understanding why Sammy thought he was going to heaven.

"Of course."

"Well, one of those commandments is 'Thou shall not kill,' and by your own admission, you killed someone."

"But that doesn't make me a bad guy."

"Actually, it does. We are the sum of our actions, not our intentions." Diesel wasn't sure if that statement was accurate, but this was not the time to second-guess himself.

"Well, I'm a Catholic and have had the sacraments." He looked as if he had just offered a watertight argument for his hope of salvation.

"Hmm, if I am not mistaken, Catholics have things called mortal sins, and murder is one of them. You can be forgiven for venial sins, but not mortal." Diesel felt like this conversation had gotten him in way over his head since he was now just repeating things he had heard the Catholic chaplain say to one of the other inmates. He wanted to get the conversation back on track and didn't want Sammy to throw him another curveball.

"Look, Sammy. The Bible is very clear that our sins, small and large, separate us from God and that the penalty or sentence for our guilt is hell. Jesus, the Son of God, came to earth and lived a sinless life so He would be a perfect sacrifice to take on the guilt and sentence of hell for all who believe in Him. You can have your sins forgiven and be given new life in Christ today. You can have hope that if anything happens to you, in here or otherwise, God will receive you with open arms." Diesel paused as much for dramatic effect as to see the reaction of his would-be convert.

Clap. Clap. Clap. Clap. The sound was coming from behind him. Diesel swung around, perturbed to see he had been the subject of an undesired and unwelcome conscientious objector. "Great performance, Diesel. Did you tell your proselyte that all the contradictions in the Bible are easily explainable and that the same God who killed innocent women and children and even babies is the loving God who can be trusted to *freely* forgive us our sins?"

Diesel was angry, and Sammy was confused. Diesel wanted to salvage this meeting, but he was fighting an uphill battle.

"This is none of your business, Big Joe." Big Joe was not big in the way Big Red was big. There was nothing intimidating at all about Big Joe. He got his name from the rumor that he had to get extra-large custom denims made. The only thing that made Big Joe intimidating or, more accurately, annoying was his intellect and his extremely sarcastic sense of humor. Several of the gangs had grown fond of his jokes and leaned on his knowledge to help them with whatever scheme was brewing at the time. Unfortunately for Diesel, Big Red was a fan of Big Joe and had commissioned him to help shut up Diesel in return for a new round of protection.

"But it is my business, Diesel. You are misleading young, impressionable souls like Sammy here and offering them an empty hope based on an ancient book that is riddled with contradictions."

Diesel knew he was not yet in a position to effectively debate Big Joe. Previous encounters with him had uncovered his history. He had been raised in a strict Christian home that required him to memorize whole chunks of the Bible. Then he had become a successful real estate broker and gotten mixed up in white-collar crime.

"Big Joe, are you willing to take responsibility for Sammy's soul going to hell?"

"I am, but let me ask you a question. Are you willing to take responsibility for Sammy putting his hope in a God that does not exist?"

"You better believe I am." As soon as the words came out of his mouth, Diesel knew he should have made a qualifying statement first.

"So you agree that God doesn't exist?"

"That's not what I meant, and you know it."

"It seems to me that you do *not* know what you are saying or what you believe." Diesel said a quiet prayer in his heart and asked his Savior to help him navigate this encounter. A thought came to him that was better than any other option he had, so he took a step of faith.

"Listen, Big Joe, one day you are going to have something happen to you or someone you care about. In that moment, you are going to hope beyond hope that there truly is a God and that if He does exist, which He does, that He is indeed a merciful God. When all your smarts and humor are useless to connect you to the help you so desperately need, you will look to someone who can reach the God you hope exists. On that day, you won't look to your yard protection, you won't look to the philosophy books you are so fond of, and you won't look to the New Age gurus you follow. No, on that day, you will come to me, because you know I do not doubt what I say. You will come to me because I met the risen Savior in my prison cell and saw Him take my broken, hopeless, desperate life and turn it into something that can be used for good." He took a step closer to his verbal sparring partner who unexpectedly was listening intently to his monologue. "On that day, Big Joe, I want you to know that I will be here and will listen to you and pray for you and your loved ones, because that is what Jesus would do, and that is the heart of God toward mankind."

He stopped as his thoughts of what to say next dried up. It was not an argument he would have thought to offer, and he could see how it visibly rattled his detractor. Diesel had lost several arguments to Big Joe and knew not to let his own thoughts get in the way when he perceived that God was doing the work.

"I hope that day never comes." That was the only response Big Joe offered as he walked away, leaving Diesel with the upper hand in the conversation and an unexpected platform to continue his conversation with Sammy.

Diesel searched his heart again to find the words to re-engage the lost soul who had just witnessed him overcome an obviously smarter and more educated man. A thought came to him that he had heard Spencer tell him when they shared a cell. *God planted a longing for eternity in the hearts of men, and even though they may act like they do not want to know God, every man still has that longing deep inside.*

"Sammy, I know you're new here and it's hard to find your way. I want to help you in the process if you need it, but I am honestly much more concerned about your eternal well-being than how you settle in while you are in this place. Jesus is the way, the truth, and the life, and He came to give eternal life to those who repent of their sins and give their lives to Him for the expansion of His Kingdom here on earth. If you want to know more about the true God, the God of the Bible, I am here." With that, Diesel did something he had never done since he had become the so-called self-designated yard preacher. He walked away first from a conversation about God, and he started to realize that what Jesus had to offer was far too valuable to indiscriminately give it to those who did not want it.

Chapter 27

Scott

Scott walked down Main Street toward the highway. He had no bag or possessions to speak of, just the clothes on his back. He was accustomed to minimalist living and knew how to work the local charities to get food and clothing. His picked up some pants from a clothing ministry near the hospital, but his shirt was still bloodstained and ripped from the glass shards. His normally shaved head had four-day-old stubble, and with his six-foot frame and larger-than-life build, he looked like a washed-out wrestler coming out of a bar fight. *Who the heck is going to stop to give you a lift?* The thought was reasonable given his appearance, but he had no other options. The need to get a fix was driving him out of this town as quickly as possible. Shelley would have spread the word that nobody was to sell to him, and she controlled 90 percent of the flow of drugs on his side of town. If he didn't get a ride soon, he could add the ugly symptoms of detox to the list of reasons nobody would stop to pick him up.

There was a Flying J a little less than a mile away. As he had done so many times before, he assessed the folks in the store to find the one who would most likely be moved by a sob story and a tale that would explain his appearance. He needed to find someone going the right direction, but he couldn't start asking everyone in the store. He was sure the customers would just blow him off. He needed to be selective. He had worked in security before and was confident in his ability to profile people. He spotted a large guy sipping coffee. He was wearing a T-shirt with a large picture of a group of people and the name of a church. Scott recognized the church from his hometown. *He won't be intimidated by my size. I'll have to listen to a sermon, but he might give me a few dollars if I work the details on how hard my life has been.* He mentally prepped himself for the presentation as he approached him by the chips. *Don't go for the prize until you have disarmed his reflex action to resist.* He had his pitch ready.

"Hey, man, my name is Scott. Can I talk to you for a minute?"

"Sure, buddy. What can I do for you?" His facial expression was friendlier than he expected.

"Well, to be honest, I need help getting home. I was working security at a concert last night and had a couple of guys try to force their way into the bar. They smashed a bottle and cut me a few times before I could get the situation under control. I had to go to the hospital to get stitched up. While I was there, I got a call that my mom is in the hospital back home and in a bad way. I discharged myself from the hospital, but my car is across town and my buddies are not answering their phones. They usually sleep during the day when we work nights. I see you are wearing a shirt from Lafollette and was hoping I could catch a ride with you if you're headed that way.

"I sure am and would be happy to give you a ride. I'll be going right by the hospital and can drop you off there."

"That's great. Thanks so much for helping me out."

"You're more than welcome, Scott. I just hope you like listening to Christian music while we drive."

"Your ride, your music. I'm just grateful to get a ride."

"My name is Chris, Chris Wallis." The big man stuck out his hand and Scott grabbed it. He always made a point of having the stronger grip in a handshake, but this guy matched his and then some.

"Pleasure to meet you, Chris, and I really do appreciate the ride."

Chris took one more swig of his coffee. "Well, let's get on the road so you can see your mom as soon as possible."

They chatted as they crossed the parking lot, and Scott could tell his new chauffeur was a genuinely caring man. Chris drove a big rig and kept it impeccably clean with three-by-five laminated cards strategically positioned to catch his attention without distracting his eyes from the road. Each card had a Scripture verse with a promise of God highlighted. His candor was peaceful and his tone respectful. He wasn't the self-righteous bigot Scott had expected. For the next couple of hours, both men chatted like old friends. Chris shared funny stories about his kids and some of the challenges he faced by being on the road. Scott gave vague but truthful details about his past, his failed marriages, and his regrets for never having kids. Scott felt as close to a normal person during that ride as he had for as long as he could remember.

The sign on the highway said the exit for the hospital was two miles ahead. "Okay, Scott. We're coming up on the hospital. I'm going to ask you to be honest with me. You're not going to the hospital, are you?" Scott opened his mouth and raised his hand all at the same time. He planned to mount an objection and a defense of his story, but no words came out. His own muteness took him by surprise and gave him a minute to formulate the response that this man who had shown him such dignity deserved.

"No."

"There's nothing wrong with your mom, is there?"

"No. I'm sorry, Chris."

"It's all right. I knew from the time you came up to me in the store that you weren't telling the truth, but the Lord told me to do whatever you needed without asking questions."

"He did what? I mean, who did what?" Scott had heard the statement, but he couldn't accept that someone could hear God while drinking coffee in a Flying J or that God would instruct someone to help him.

"You heard me correctly, and yes, I do talk with God. In fact, I believe God wants to talk to you right now."

"No way!" It was not so much a rebuttal of his new friend's statement as it was a disbelief in the possibility of such a proposal.

"Yes way, Scott. Jesus is the way. The only way. The Holy Spirit told me that you were a drug addict and that you are fleeing danger. Is that correct?" Scott was speechless. How could this country bumpkin whom he thought he was scamming read him like that? "You see, Scott, I get what the Bible calls words of knowledge. The Holy Spirit shares some information with me about other people to get their attention so He can deliver a message to them without their unbelief blocking their thinking. Do you want to know what He wants to share with you?"

"I'm not sure. You are probably going to tell me that I deserve to go to hell, and you would be right."

"Ah! Ha ha!" The big man let out a hearty laugh. "We all deserve to go to hell, my friend. We have all earned that destination by the sins we have committed." Scott was almost annoyed that the man was not taking his immoral life choices seriously enough.

"I'm serious," Scott explained. "I have not lived well. Not at all."

"I don't doubt that, Scott, but your expectation couldn't be further from what the Holy Spirit wants to share with you. However, I respect you enough not to force this on you, so I will ask you again. Would you like me to share what the Holy Spirit showed me?" Scott took a minute to think about the ramifications of hearing or, even more fundamentally, actually believing there is a God. His curiosity and hunger for more of the warmth and peace he had experienced on their trip overruled the fear in his heart.

"Yea, Chris, I kinda do want to hear it." Chris had already exited the highway and pulled his rig into an empty parking lot at an abandoned warehouse. He looked at Scott with nothing but love and compassion in his eyes.

"God wants you to know that He has watched you from the time you were young. He saw all the pain you suffered and how you were abused. He saw the heartache and hurt of rejection from your marriages. He saw how your career offered you so much and ultimately rejected you."

Chris sighed as if processing the words from the Holy Spirit in real time.

"He knows you blame Him for it all, but His message to you today is that He loves you, that He has always loved you. You think you are too far gone, but God says that you can turn your life around right here in my rig. He can heal you of your wounds and deliver you from your addiction if you will surrender your life to Him. If you have never heard it before, Scott, Jesus died on a cross 2,000 years ago so you could have life today. He paid the price for all the wrong things you have done so you don't have to."

Chris took a moment and looked his passenger right in the eyes.

"If you will believe in Jesus, who is reaching out to you today through me, and ask Him for forgiveness, He will give you new life. Scott, I have one caveat. He gave His life for you, and He asks that you give your life for Him."

The words hit Scott like a ton of bricks. "You mean I have to die?" If the moment had not been so somber, his tutor would have laughed.

"No, Scott, but Jesus asks you to follow Him with your whole heart and allow Him to change you from the inside out."

The message was unlike anything Scott had ever heard from a preacher at a church. Could it be that this uneducated, kindhearted man somehow had an understanding of God that all the others had missed? Could he afford to put his trust in a stranger and a chance meeting in a gas station convenience store? The cab seemed to be bright, much brighter than the dull sky outside. He had a clarity and freedom of thought that was not normal. He could see the choice and the opportunity before him. He looked at the man who was offering him a lifeline and once more saw the depth of compassion that made no sense in their brief encounter.

"What will it be, Scott? God wants to give you life." A picture of the kind nurse flashed across Scott's mind. His imagination started to see a future with her, a home of his own, a peace in his heart, a job, and a purpose. In that moment, he examined his heart and chose to let his fleshly urges—his addiction—make a rebuttal to God's offer. The counteroffer promised a feeling of freedom from concerns. Freedom from responsibility. Freedom from failure. All he had to do was get his next fix, which he was an expert at doing. Out of the window by Chris, he could see a couple of people under the bridge and knew a dealer would not be far away.

Chris watched as the man's complexion in front of him turned from light to darkness, and he knew the moment had been lost. Scott's response was only the confirmation of what he could already see.

"Look, Chris, you have been incredibly kind to me. I appreciate all you have said, and I believe you believe it. But I just can't make my mind stretch that far."

Chris looked at him one more time with eyes of compassion. "My friend, never forget this. As long as you have breath, you have a choice. Scott, God loves you."

Scott shook Chris's hand, thanked him once more, and jumped out of the rig. Chris watched as Scott walked toward the underpass to the homeless man and woman with their shopping cart and all their earthly belongings in tow. He couldn't help wondering if there might have been a different outcome if he had parked somewhere else or at a different angle. He offered a heartfelt prayer to God on behalf of the damaged soul with whom he had just shared a ride. He asked God that another like himself would one day complete the job he was unable to do.

Chapter 28

Officer Smith

Sleep refused to come. Officer Smith couldn't get the conversation with Joey out of his mind. It sparked a chain of remembrance that he wished he could have avoided. Images swirling in his head. Images that could not be unseen. Atrocities committed by the person down the road. Not Hitler or Stalin or bin Laden but normal people leading apparently normal lives doing unthinkably evil things. He couldn't bear to go to the police department's shrink. Where would he start? To unpack the darkness and pain he had suffered in his fairly short life would be to go down a rabbit hole from which he may never return.

Officer Smith had never told anyone about his abuse, although he hinted at it with Joey. Just saying the words seemed to bring it back to life. It was always in the back of his mind. Every time he threatened or lashed out at a suspect, he drew on the seemingly bottomless reservoir of hatred for his abuser. However, now it was taking a new toll on his life. He could see the faces of every child he had interviewed and every offender he had put away. His other emotions were becoming secondary to his anger, as if they played supporting roles to the new lead actor on the stage of his life. *No, dude, no shrink can fix the mess you call life. The only thing you can do is dull the noise.*

This late-night outburst in his lonely apartment was a signal flare to the One who watched over him and vowed to save him. *Not yet, tormented friend. Not yet. You are still beyond My reach, for I must wait until you denounce your allegiance to the one who wants to kill you. That day must come, but until then, I can only fight to keep you alive.* The unheard voice would have fallen on deaf ears anyway, but the vow was real nonetheless.

Officer Smith reached for the vodka bottle next to his bed and unscrewed the top. He stared at the ceiling one last time to see if, by any chance, he could summon the courage to try to wrestle back his imagination, but that kind of courage was not in his arsenal. He took a large swig of the powerful spirit and choked it down. A mixer would only dilute and delay the process. The second swig went down more easily. He knew partial relief was within sight now, and he turned on the TV to pass the moments while he waited for the spirits to do their job.

A movie caught his attention. It was an old Western, the kind where the hero stood for all that was right, and even the bad guys seemed to have some form of moral code. As he took a couple more mouthfuls of vodka, the voices in his head seemed to ramp up instead of abate.

Your life is a waste. You are a worthless human being, just something to be used and thrown away. All you do now is watch other people prey on the weak. You don't make any difference whatsoever. Why don't you do something to make a difference? Nothing will stop those predators. They never change. Locking them up doesn't fix anything. Another monster takes their place. They are not afraid to steal the innocence of their victims. Prison is not enough of a deterrent. Someone needs to go on a killing spree and take out those vile life forms in a way that strikes fear in the heart of anyone even contemplating abusing a child.

His mind was filled once more with images of torture, images of inflicting the worst kind of pain on the perpetrators of evil. He wanted to keep playing the pictures in his head and enjoy the thought of finally exacting a fair punishment, but something inside him still resisted. Something still longed for goodness. He hated that weakness in himself. He wished he could completely sell out and take revenge on all the monsters he had convicted.

He stumbled out of bed toward the cabinet above the microwave in the kitchen. He pulled open the door. He couldn't read the label, but he didn't care. He dumped several sleeping pills into his hand. They hit the back of his throat before he could process the implications of such a large dose. The prescription allowed one pill as needed, but one pill was never enough to quell the voices or dim the images.

He shook the bottle before putting it back in the cabinet. He knew the doctor wouldn't prescribe another bottle without an evaluation. As he lay back in bed and waited for sleep to rescue him from his miserable existence, he contemplated ways to get more pills without going to that quack. The last thought that lodged in his mind was of a weak-willed pharmacy tech who was desperate to get a job in law enforcement. *He will do it. If I dangle the right carrot, he will get me a new prescription.* As sleep finally came, he didn't realize the shifting in his paradigm that was taking place. He was heading down the path to become like the object of his hatred—the abuser.

Chapter 29

Scott

Jackson had been Scott's friend for almost 30 years. Three kids and a devoted wife had kept Jackson on the straight and narrow while he watched his friend self-destruct. Now he was back in a familiar place with his old friend, sitting on his porch waiting for the usual pitch for money.

"Scott, man, we've been friends for so long, and you know I think of you as a brother. You saved my skin so many times when we were kids. You were always so big, and I was always so small. Dude, you would jump to my rescue at a moment's notice. There were several bullies who eventually wrote me off as a target just because they heard you might beat the crap out of them like you had done to others. When we were on the football team together and I finally found out I could throw a ball and became the starting quarterback, you always blocked whoever came at me. You got me my first job when I had to drop out of college, and you were the best man at my wedding, dude."

He looked at the man sitting in the seat across from him, and he had to force himself to see the friend he once knew so well. "I can't help thinking if I had been there for you when you fell on hard times, you never would have gone down this road." Tears welled up in his eyes as genuine regret filled his heart.

"It's not your fault, Jackson. I've had a wild ride, man, and to be honest, a lot of it was very enjoyable."

"Do you ever wish you had kids and a family?"

"When I look at you and Emily, I do, but I would have destroyed their lives, too. I'm on a slippery slope to destruction. I don't deserve to have friends like you."

"Don't say that, Scott. If it was not for Emily, I would be right there with you. I was headed down that road, too, remember?"

"Well, it sure feels that way, and I don't have any fight left in me. I've been from couch to couch, and everyone is sick of seeing my face. I'm broke, and it's been more than a day since I had my last fix. My body is starting to freak out, and I just want it to be all over."

"Don't talk like that. There is always hope. I'll pay for you to go to rehab—whatever it takes. Emily and I will take you into our home and help you get back on your feet again. Please let us help you, Scott."

"You're the only true friend I have left, Jackson, but to be honest, I know I'll only mess it up. I've been through the rehab process three times, and each time I get clean for a while, and then I end up crashing even harder. I can't do that anymore. I'm going to die an addict. I realize that now. Some folks have the fortitude to stop, but not me. This is my death sentence. Sooner or later, you're going to hear that I was found dead in a ditch somewhere."

Jackson wanted to reject those awful words, but he knew there was a lot more likelihood of that happening than he could bring himself to accept. If he gave his friend a fake response, he would be dishonest with him. The one thing these men always had was honesty.

During the pause in their conversation, both men looked at the ground and processed the painful reality that Scott's life had become. The darkness that now seemed to permanently camp around Scott embraced the self-destructing proclamation of their captive and agreed they could turn his words into a self-fulfilling prophecy. The darkness, as it often did, reminded him of the time clock attached to his addiction. *Just ask him for the money. You'd better get a fix soon or you won't be able to think straight. You'll start to make stupid choices again. Ask for the money!*

Scott broke the silence. "You know, I'm not going to lie to you, Jackson. I need cash to get high. If I don't get a fix, I'll get desperate. If I get desperate, I'll get stupid and do stupid things. Can you give me some money?"

"Scott, I would give you every penny I had if I thought it would help you, man, but I don't think I could live with myself if you ended up taking your own life."

"I get it. The truth is, I'm probably more likely to cause myself harm if I wait too long." The two men had this conversation more than once, and it always ended the same way.

"Scott, you know I can't leave you like this. If Emily knew I gave you money to get high, she'd kill me, so will you at least think about my offer to send you to rehab?"

"I'll think about it, Jackson, but it's very unlikely I'll change my mind."

That was the closest Jackson would come to lying to his friend. He thought about it for two seconds and then released himself from the obligation he had just made. "I don't have much money, but will fifty be enough?"

"That'll do me for a day. Do you have any more money, man? I could really do with some relief from living day to day."

"I'm sure I can scramble together some money from the kids' piggy banks and replace it after I hit the ATM."

Jackson came back with a little more than $100. He hugged his friend as he left the house, and then Scott walked down the driveway. *This may be the last time I see Scott.* He didn't want to dwell on it, but that was the most honest thought he could have right now. As Scott got into the beat-up old Ford sedan, Jackson noticed someone else in the car. A girl had been waiting there the whole time they were visiting. He knew his friend well enough to know that the extra few dollars would help get them both high. It was probably her car, and they probably had just met the night before.

Scott picked up speed as he raced to the dealer from whom he thought he could get the most bang for his buck. He spent every penny he had and then went to the woman's apartment to get high. He knew he could ration the drugs and make them last two days, but he also knew rationing was not in the scope of an addict's abilities. He knew he had no self-control when it came to drugs. It was already late at night, and he convinced himself that the drugs would last two days. As he injected the drugs into his arm, he gladly let his worries about his next fix disappear. He watched as Amanda, his new acquaintance, shot herself with the smaller dosage he had apportioned. For a brief moment, there was clarity without the incessant stress. Looking at his companion slipping into her altered state, he felt the compulsion to share his revelation.

"I feel like I'm constantly driving through a storm, and the rain is pelting my windshield while I'm moving at ninety miles an hour. When I get a fix, it's like I go under the overpass for a moment, and just for a few seconds, I can relax before it all comes back full force. I have been doing that for years now, and I don't think I can take it anymore. I just want it to stop, but I can't kick it." His heartfelt confession fell on deaf ears as Amanda only cared about her own relief.

Scott watched as she passed out quickly. The drugs did their job, and in that moment, he didn't care if she lived or died. The voice in his head was louder than usual despite the drugs that typically quieted them. *You need more. Get more. Check her place for a way to get more.* He went through her kitchen and then her bathroom looking for money, something to sell, or some prescription drugs. He found some jewelry that looked real and a prescription bottle he couldn't read. He took one last look at the woman spread out on the floor, grabbed her car keys, and left. He slammed the open pill bottle into his mouth and swallowed several of the unknown pills as he got into her car and drove off.

The pawn shop was closed, but he knew a low-life street hustler who came out at night to take advantage of folks desperate for cash.

"I'll give you fifty dollars for the ring."

"Come on, man, the ring is worth at least two grand."

"Look, dude, it doesn't matter what it's worth. If you want more, then wait for the pawn shop to open, and they'll do an appraisal and maybe give you more."

"You don't think I know that? You and I both know you're a parasite feeding off the weaknesses of addicts like me. I oughta kick your ass."

"Try it, big guy. I have a Beretta with your name on it, and the cops won't care if a drug addict dies. They won't even investigate your death if they find drugs in your system." He was close enough to the truth for Scott not to push the issue.

"Give me seventy-five dollars, and we can call it a deal."

"It's your lucky day, cowboy. I'm feeling generous. Here's sixty-five dollars. Take it or leave it."

"I'll take it."

It was the middle of the night, but this was his hometown, and Scott knew where to go to get some drugs. He drove around several spots before he finally found another night crawler feeding on the most desperate. He bought as much as he could, stuffed the drugs under the seat, and found a safe spot to take them. He was feeling weird and figured it was the prescription pills he had blindly swallowed. But he didn't let that slow him down. If he had been in his right mind, he might have tried to sleep it off, but the sun would be coming up soon, and something urged him to get the new drugs in his system while it was still night. He already had a dangerous quantity and an unstable concoction of drugs in his system, but he tied an elastic band around his arm anyway and slapped his forearm to find a vein.

The drugs hit him like a ton of bricks. He lost the ability to process decisions and subconsciously started up his car and pulled out onto the street. The car swerved erratically for 100 yards before he drove it over the shoulder and into the ditch on the side of the road. The airbag deployed and smacked him in the face. He fumbled around for the door handle and managed to push the door open. As he stepped out of the vehicle, his legs couldn't hold him up, and he fell backward into the ditch. He could feel the drugs overtake his body, and he knew he was overdosing. He thought he could hear someone laughing, and the last thought he had was his own words from earlier with Jackson: *Sooner or later you're gonna hear that I was found dead in a ditch somewhere.* He could hear his heart beating out of control. It felt as if someone or something had reached into his chest and squeezed his heart so tightly that it felt like it would burst. With that, his body started to shut down, and his heartbeat slowed. Darkness closed in on him. He could hear the voices of hell calling his name. Terror gripped his soul as his narrow hold on life slipped through his hands. Deep regret swept over his consciousness as he realized he was not as ready to die as he thought, nor was he ready to face the consequences of a lifetime of bad choices.

Chapter 30

Officer Smith

Officer Smith was on his way to see the pharmacy tech when he saw he had a message on his phone. He had already called Pete to set up a time to meet and plant the seed for the promise of a potential law enforcement job. "I'll do whatever it takes, dude. It's my dream to be a cop." He knew he could manipulate that enthusiasm. *That craving will be your undoing, Pete, and it will open the door to get all the drugs I need to stop the torment in my head.* He didn't care that he might ruin a young man's life or that he would be breaking the law. He only cared about himself and was blind to the transition he was making.

He was surprised to see that the message was from his captain, and he knew he should check to see if it was urgent before meeting Pete. The message said to check in at 9:00 a.m. for a meeting with the captain from SWAT. It was already 8:45 a.m., and he was 20 minutes away. He figured they probably needed some back story on a case they expected could go south and wanted to cover as many angles as possible. It was rare, but occasionally sex offenders or pedophiles led an extravagant criminal lifestyle and had only a small penchant for the sexual element of their deviant behavior. In those cases, the more proactive units would branch out and seek help from the more reactive child abuse investigation units. There was certainly no glamour attached to his department, and very little prestige followed his thankless task. Everyone was glad the work was getting done, but it was treated like the department's redheaded stepchild. He decided he'd better show up since he had been missing more time than usual lately. He didn't want to be seen as unreliable, but more importantly, he didn't want someone to start keeping a closer eye on his behavior.

Both captains were chatting when he entered the meeting a few minutes late.

"Sorry I'm late, Captain Halliday. I got sidetracked on the way here with a case file." It was a lie but one that would excuse tardiness in any circumstance with any superior, and he knew it.

"No worries, Smithy. You know Captain Kerrigan who heads up our vice team and SWAT, right?" He looked at the burly captain whose red whiskers epitomized the Irish heritage coursing through his veins. He was a modern-day warrior and carried the reputation of being fearless on the job. Officer Smith had admired him from a distance for quite a while.

"A pleasure to see you again, Captain Kerrigan. I hope things are going well in your unit. What can I do to help you?"

"Now that's the kind of attitude I like, Halliday. We need more men in our units whose first question is 'What can I do to help you?'"

"Like I told you, Captain Kerrigan, Officer Smith is one of the best officers I have on my team and, quite frankly, one of the best officers I have ever had the privilege to lead." The compliment caught him a little by surprise, and his heart was genuinely touched by this man who had mentored him for the last six years and taught him every legitimate thing he knew about child abuse investigation.

"Son, I will get right to the point," began Captain Kerrigan. "Our town has been expanding, and crime has grown right along with it. My unit has been working around the clock, but we need to hire someone right away. We cannot afford to have men and women who are not able to perform at their best day in and day out. When I sent out word to the other units about recruiting experienced talent, your name was the one that kept coming up."

Officer Smith wasn't sure who from the other units would have recommended him, but he was not about to question the source and motive of his own advocates. "I'm flattered, but am I understanding it right that you are actually offering me the job?"

"I said he had the right attitude, but I didn't say he was too sharp." Captain Halliday laughed at his own joke, but the other two men were locked in a gaze wondering what the other was thinking. Officer Smith was the first to break the stare and the silence.

"I accept the offer."

"You're not even going to ask what the job entails, the hours, or if the pay is any better?"

"Everyone knows what you guys do and how you put yourselves in the most dangerous situations every day. You can't dictate when SWAT will be needed, so I imagine those hours will be on call. Since you are at risk day in and day out, I'm guessing the position carries a base risk pay and extras for certain risk categories."

"Well, your powers of deduction are right on, but I bet you have built up some relationships in this department and may want to take the time to consider if it's worth leaving those behind, not to mention Captain Halliday's mentorship." Kerrigan was a captain who understood that an officer was a man first and that any relational loss could lead to loss of performance.

"In my six years," Smith chimed in, "more than 200 cases have come across my desk. We've identified the offenders in more than 60 percent of those cases. That equates to more than 120 cases in which I have looked into the face of evil and been compelled to find justice for the victims. In that time, I had a confession rate of 92 percent, while the average in the state is only 59 percent. Quite honestly, I have given the best part of myself to these cases, and I'm ready to take on a new challenge. In fact, I relish the chance to be proactive—to contain the development of crime and stop some in progress rather than chasing the crumbs from an already damaged life."

Smith's mind was on overdrive. He could feel in his core that for the first time in a long time, there may be a light at the end of the tunnel, and this time it was not another train headed his way.

"I hear you, Smith. If I'm honest, I'm not sure I could do what Captain Halliday has done so well for so long. I need to be on the forefront when it comes to stopping crime. You can start training next Monday."

As Officer Smith walked away from his new boss, his mind was still trying to take in what had just happened. His rescue would come at a cost to his colleagues, no doubt, but they could handle it. *I have played my part. It's time for me to move on.* He sat at his desk and logged on to his desktop computer. For the next 30 minutes, he read and reread the same information over and over without comprehending anything on the file he was building. He couldn't keep his focus on the task at hand, so instead, he spoke prophetically to the computer screen that was temporarily providing cover for his distracted mind. *You will be my last case in this department. Never again will I chase down offenders like you and put my mind into the sick, dark place you create. I won't need drugs to provide an escape. I'm free from your daily torment.*

A deeper look at the state of his heart would have revealed that his job was not the source of his struggle and he could not be freed by just a change in position. The other forces at work in him would make sure he would never find the freedom he was craving.

Chapter 31

Diesel

The lights went out in the cell block at 8:30 in the evening. As he had done almost every other evening, Diesel was reading his Bible. It had been a few years since that faithful day when he had come down from the top bunk and fallen to his knees before the Lord. Everyone who crossed his path knew how emphatic he was about the good news of Jesus and the bad news of hell. Lately, though, he had been mulling over a concept he had encountered in his recent reading of the Gospel of John and had been stuck on that page ever since. Jesus was just hours from His betrayal, and He was having one of the last conversations He would ever have with His disciples. As the Savior of the world, He was highlighting the most important elements of His message before He would sacrifice His life for them and everyone else who had ever lived or would ever live. Verses 12 and 13 of Chapter 15 seized his heart:

This is My commandment, that you love one another as I have loved you. Greater love has no one than this, than to lay down one's life for his friends.

He had always seen the first part of verse 12—"love one another"—and had then grabbed hold of verse 13—"Greater love has no one than this, than to lay down one's life for his friends." Ever since that day when he had accepted the free gift of salvation, his life had been his best version of living out those two verses. On many occasions, he had been spit on. He was ridiculed daily, but he knew Jesus didn't just lay down His life for His friends; He laid it down for those who were His enemies, and Diesel refused to predetermine whom he would lay his life down for. Just like the story of the Good Samaritan, everyone who was not saved was his friend for the gospel's sake. Even through the rejection he experienced at the hands of his fellow inmates, he still spoke boldly of Jesus out of loyalty. He did it out of commitment. He did it out of reverence and respect. He did it out of a sense of duty and a need to do at least something to repay the One who had paid so much for him.

But tonight, this Scripture had more to reveal to him—more than he could have ever bargained for and more than he could have ever dreamed. A new reason, a primal reason, a better and more powerful reason was knocking at the door of his heart, but his brain was getting in the way. What was he missing from these verses that would bring his whole thought processes to a halt? As the lights went out and he closed his Bible, he could still see the two verses as if they were open in front of him, and a life-altering inner conversation began to redefine his purpose and his ability to live the life of a believer. *What is it? Why is this passage getting my attention without saying what it wants me to know?* He decided to ask the author of the verses rather than his own soul for the answer. He closed his eyes, and the verses were suspended in front of him. All of a sudden, five words were highlighted and stood out from the rest—five words that had been there all along, but he was noticing for the first time. Those five words—*as I have loved you*—were about to rewrite his whole understanding.

They were sandwiched between the two verses, and the parallel message of the other two lines must have hidden those words, but not anymore. Now, the rest of the verses, the rest of that conversation, and maybe even the rest of the Bible seemed to frame this statement and find its power from those five words.

Jesus. I am not sure what I am reading, and I definitely don't understand what You are saying about this verse, but I want to wholeheartedly accept Your love. My mind is exploding with the revelation of Your unconditional love, and I feel it unraveling and reworking everything I have ever believed. All this time, I have been living to honor what You did for mankind. I have done everything I am doing out of obligation to You. If I am honest, I can say that I am often fearful that I won't please You, and that fear drives me on.

When I get tired or afraid, I remind myself that You laid down Your life for me and that I should do the same for You.

Then the revelation fell into place. As the last sentence completed in his mouth, his mind had pieced together the conundrum he had been trying to solve.

Wow, Lord! So You are telling me that all this time I have been living for You, I have been doing it to earn *Your love? That is contrary to these five words. According to these words, You already love me. Love is meant to inspire me to work because it has been freely given. Instead of feebly trying to earn something that can never be earned, I can only receive it?*

The revelation pinged around his brain for the rest of the evening. In wave after wave of realization, he recalled futile attempts to win what he already had, ignorant efforts to accomplish what was never asked with a motive that could never succeed. Instead, a glorious truth that his small mind had been unable to process before now painted colorful scenery on his once-bland canvas of a mission. He leaned over his bunk and excitedly shared the moment with his cellmate.

"Hey, Charlie, are you awake?" He had no intention of waiting for a response. "Charlie, I just read a Scripture that showed me how much Jesus loves me."

"Diesel, man, I'm trying to sleep here. You tell me every day that Jesus loves me."

"Not like this, Charlie. I have never told you this before. Heck, I have never told anyone this. We don't have to live a certain way to be acceptable to God. We don't have to tell others about Jesus." Charlie couldn't help interrupting his flow.

"Then why are you telling me? Go to sleep."

Diesel had no intention of stopping. "We don't have to do anything to get God to love us. In fact, the very reason we should do all this is because we are already loved. I should do all the things I do because He loves me. Do you get that, Charlie? He loves me already, whether I do good or bad. And He wants me to love you that way, Charlie."

"Well, if you love me so much, can you let me get some shut-eye?" Diesel finally realized Charlie wasn't quite sharing his exuberance.

"I'll be quiet now, Charlie, but don't expect me to be quiet when the lights come back on."

Diesel spent the next several hours plotting in the dark how to bring this greater revelation of the gospel to as many as he could in his current home.

Chapter 32

Officer Smith

The adrenaline generated by facing a perpetrator with a gun and live ammunition coursed through the veins of everyone on the team. Training had been a breeze, and Officer Smith's first six months on the job had provided the distraction he craved. He and his team were not in a big city, and most calls were for locals pushed over the edge for one reason or another or drug addicts desperate enough to step up their crime exploits to armed robbery. Today was no exception, but as usual, the bullets were real, and so was the adrenaline. The rush he felt from the danger was better than any narcotic.

Initially, this new career path seemed to satisfy his need to make his life count and feel alive, to take retribution on the evil in the world. However, he was immune to the fact that he was transferring one addiction for another, and, as with all addictions, he needed more and more danger to get the high he craved.

"I can go through the front door, Captain. He's been quiet for 30 minutes, and I bet he has passed out from whatever he was taking." Captain Kerrigan had seen the courage in his new recruit become a great asset to his team. He needed men who would take initiative in these situations. It takes an exceptional person to keep a clear head in stressful and dangerous situations, and Officer Smith never seemed to get rattled.

"We don't need to force the issue just yet," Kerrigan responded. "He hasn't fired a shot for a while. Often, offenders just need some time to see there is no way out, and then we can talk them out of doing something stupid that gets them killed."

"The longer it goes the more we drop our guard and the more likely we are to get sloppy." The statement was true, but Kerrigan was on top of that, and the team was still appropriately engaged. He didn't want to curb Officer Smith's enthusiasm since he saw in him the potential to become his successor. Retirement was looming, and he needed a good man to take his place. "Look, Smithy, why don't you take the lead and hail him on the megaphone. Just use the textbook approach if he answers. If not, we'll wait a little longer and try him a couple of more times before we consider the risk of going through the front door."

A few hours before, a neighbor whose kids had been in the old man's yard had called the Sheriff's Department. "It's a trailer park," she said. "What does he expect? There are no fences. He is as crazy as they come, and he is always strung out on something." The mom of the two teenage boys wanted to paint them in the best possible light and make a case for their innocence. "My boys did nothing wrong. They were playing football, and the ball landed in front of his place. The next thing we know, he comes out with a gun and starts shooting in the air. He could have killed my boys."

When the first squad car arrived, the man came out of his door with his rifle aimed at the two officers as they got out of the car. The officers did not engage, got back in their car, and called SWAT for backup. Now, they had been in a standoff for several hours, and if it had not been for Kerrigan's cool head, it could already have turned into a shoot-out. The perp's initial round of shots came through his living room window. They were aimed at the ground about five feet in front of the perimeter line the SWAT team had set up. Kerrigan realized they were probably warning shots and that lives could be spared with the right approach. The initial dialogue through the megaphone had calmed the situation, but the threat was nowhere near neutralized.

Smith's attempts to hail the offender were unsuccessful, but he waited another 30 minutes as the angst inside him rose. Drugs never failed to provide a high, but unrealized adrenaline was worse than no adrenaline at all. He felt the need to push this to a conclusion to avoid dealing with the low that would follow. He didn't realize it, but his new drug was even more enslaving and dangerous than his previous one, and he was flirting with developing an all-out death wish.

"Captain, I think we should try to flush him out with gas. I can shoot a penetrating round to fill the trailer with the gas, and he'll come running for the nearest exit."

"Good idea, Smithy. Avoid the area where the shots came from. I don't want to accidentally kill him with a gas round." Captain Kerrigan had a wry smile as he gave the instructions. It was highly unlikely they would hit the man, let alone kill him, but it was a general warning to extend some caution in their approach.

"Yes, sir!" Officer Smith ran to the back of his trunk and grabbed the gas gun and the penetrating round. He assessed the best location and fired the round. *Phuut! Phuut!* The round cleared through one wall and right out the other. "It went right through, Captain. I'm going to try a non-penetrating round." *Thud!* The round bounced off the exterior wall. Officer Smith thought for a minute. The only option left was a midrange gas can that cost a pretty penny. Small-town sheriffs' departments don't have a big budget, and cost is always a factor. "Hmm, the midrange should do the job." The words were barely out of his mouth when he was launching the shot. *Phuut! Phuut!* The walls were painfully thin, and the rounds again went right through and out the other side. Both men realized they needed another approach.

"Try him again on the horn, Smithy." Malcom Harlen, the angry man inside, owned the trailer. Police records showed he was a Vietnam veteran and had a history of violent and erratic behavior. Officer Smith tried to create a personal connection.

"Mr. Harlen, we want to make sure no one gets harmed today. Please, come out of your home with your hands in the air so we can resolve the problem. I know you are a veteran, and we appreciate the sacrifices you made for our country. My dad is also a Vietnam veteran, and I personally know some of the terrible things you have had to deal with. Just make your way to the door. All our weapons are lowered, and it is safe for you to come out." Their weapons were barely lowered, and each officer had positioned themselves out of the line of sight just in case. There was no response, but there was movement in the trailer, and they expected the old man to come out the door at any moment.

Captain Kerrigan noticed movement at one of the windows and intu-itively told his team to take cover. Shots were fired. *Pop! Pop!* A couple of rounds buzzed over Officer Smith's head after he ducked under a small wall around the dumpster.

"The rounds sounded like a .22, Captain."

"That's what I thought, too." Both men were relieved it was not an assault rifle, but it was obvious that Harlen knew how to use it and was not in the mood to negotiate.

"The shots came from the opposite end of the house from the front door. We could have a team approach from the other end and break through the door." Officer Smith's head was playing various scenarios, and all of them had higher levels of risk than his captain would allow. This option seemed like it may have a chance.

"Well, one thing is for sure," Kerrigan reasoned, "this standoff has a much higher percentage of going south than I thought five minutes ago. If we don't neutralize the threat, we run the risk of one of us getting killed, and I am not willing to wait on that scenario. Get two guys to go with you. As soon as you enter, stay low. You'll need to use the element of surprise to your advantage. Don't hesitate to take him out if you feel threatened." The orders were just what Smith wanted to hear.

The team advanced unnoticed to the door. It was unlocked. Officer Smith signaled to the two other men that he was going in. He pulled open the screen door, but when he had the front door half open, it made a loud screech. *Crap.* "Get back!" he shouted to the other men and dove low into the trailer on the linoleum floor.

Pop! Pop! Pop! Shots were fired in his general direction. He flipped over an old wooden table and took up a position behind it. He knew it would not be enough to protect him if the old man got off the right shot. His adrenaline was racing, but his mind was crystal clear. *Stay low.* Shots were still coming from the opposite end of the trailer. There was only one way Harlen could get a clear view of him and that was through the hallway.

Officer Smith processed the scenario in his mind and optimized his options. *He can't see me, and I will see him first if he tries to come down the hall. Even if he fires several more speculative shots, the chances of getting hit are slim. I can probably make my way closer to the hallway without being seen and get a better angle to take him out.* That last thought rang in his consciousness and took him by surprise. Up until that moment, he wanted the old man to get out of this alive. Not only was that last thought one of the worst options available, it was also aggressive and provocative. It seemed out of place with his previously dangerous but at least measured thoughts. In the room, there was another element to this equation that he was unaware of. The man was not alone. There was an unseen master manipulator inside these walls who had orchestrated much of the troubled veteran's madness. He was the one who tormented Harlen's thoughts day in and day out and made his life unbearable. It was the tormentor who jerked his emotions from one extreme to another as he replayed over and over in his head all the war atrocities he had been forced to participate in. It was he who had ruined his marriage, destroyed his relationship with his kids, and alienated him from his community through paranoia. It was his whisperings that made Harlen pull out his .22 and fire warning shots at the two teenage boys who were getting on his nerves. It was he who wanted to use this old man to impose maximum carnage before he would self-destruct. And now, he was pulling the strings on both men's emotions.

The two men at opposite ends of the trailer also appeared to be at opposite ends of society's acceptability spectrum. However, that tormentor who was still there scheming in the darkness knew these men were vulnerable in much the same way. Both had been damaged by life, and both were harboring a death wish. He planned to give them what they wanted by killing two birds with each other's stones.

I'm not a killer. Officer Smith wrestled with the suggestion that was becoming more compulsive by the second, and he needed some strong self-control since the urge to move seemed almost involuntary. *No. Don't fire unless you have to. He is just a lonely, bitter soul suffering from PTSD. You can reason with him now that he will see that his options are limited.* Smith gripped the edge of the table to regain control of his instinct. He thought about his own dad and how he would feel if another officer was in a standoff with him. *What would I want someone else to do if this were my dad?* The thought seemed to neutralize the murderous passion growing in his mind. He decided to try talking to the old man again. There was a risk he would be alerting him to his location, but it would take a very lucky shot to get him, even if Harlen narrowed down his position.

"Mr. Harlen. We are in your house. We want to end this now if you will put your gun down and come out." There was silence for a few seconds, and then a round of bullets tore through walls and furniture throughout the trailer. A second and third round of bullets followed at a swift pace, and the trailer was starting to resemble a war zone as cushions exploded and pictures and ornaments scattered all over the room in hundreds of pieces. Officer Smith stopped counting the bullets. It was obvious that the old man had stocked up. But this kind of physical encounter could be brutal even on a younger man. He was sure that after being holed up within a police perimeter for hours, the old man must be exhausted. The compassionate side of Smith's thinking won out once more and reflected in his surprisingly calm voice.

"Well, Malcom, are you done?" No reply. "I'm sure you are tired. Listen, if you put your gun down and come on out, this will all be over. What do you say, Malcom? You wanna call it quits?" Seconds of silence seemed like an eternity, and Officer Smith knew that Malcom Harlen's life hung in the balance of his next choice.

"I guess so. I'm tired." Officer Smith was surprised how clearly he could hear the offender.

"Come on out then where I can see you." He hoped the guys outside could hear him so they would know he was okay and not open fire when they saw Harlen walk through the trailer.

The old man was spent as he made his way down the hall. He had been in an old metal bathtub, shooting through the window and then ducking back inside the tub for protection. Officer Smith put him in cuffs and led him peacefully out the front door. As he debriefed Captain Kerrigan, both men realized the level of danger was even higher than they first realized.

He was a wily old guy and probably could have stayed alive in that bathtub long enough to hurt one or more of them.

"Good work today, Smithy."

"Thanks, Captain. All in a day's work, right?"

"I certainly hope not, son." The captain's words highlighted the gulf between their mentalities. Kerrigan had a family and a community he belonged to. He had a purpose to live for, while Officer Smith desperately wanted to feel alive—desperate enough to put his life on the line. Today, he almost crossed a line and took a life unnecessarily. It scared him how close he was to using deadly force, and he could not help but wonder how that line might present itself again. Would he have the self-restraint the next time? For now, he comforted himself with the adrenaline high that still hung around in his veins as he recounted the story to the guys and they made their way back to the station.

Chapter 33

Diesel

In the months that followed, being in prison took on a new meaning for Diesel. No longer did the fear of harm or the limitations and indignity of sharing a nine-by-seven cell and a latrine with a stranger bother him. The revelation of the love that God had toward him that he had received in the darkness of his cell made it seem like the best place on earth. It had unlocked something deep inside him, and an ocean of love, forgiveness, and unconditional acceptance by God was transforming his environment into his own piece of heaven. Charlie became the primary beneficiary of those changes.

"Hey, Charlie, have I told you today that God loves you?"

"Sure did. About five minutes ago."

"He loves you so much that He sacrificed His own life to pay for your sins. Isn't that amazing?"

"Just as amazing as the last time you told me, dude." Truth be told, Charlie desperately wanted to believe that God could love him, but his sins, as Diesel called them, loomed large in his mind. He had more faith in the power of his wrongdoing to condemn him than in God's desire or ability to forgive him.

"I'm telling you, bro, He will wash away everything you ever did. The Bible says that Jesus removes our sins from us as far as the east is from the west, which technically is an infinite distance unless you are talking about just our planet, and then it is still the farthest possible distance we can go on the earth. The best part is that He did it to remove anything and everything that could stand in the way of us choosing to accept the forgiveness and new life He offers."

"Listen, Diesel, you don't know the things I have done. I am the most selfish man I know. Dude, I even stole from my own family, from the people I thought I loved. How can God forgive that? I am convinced that there are some sins God won't forgive, and I am damned sure I have done them all."

Diesel pondered his cellmate's response. He could tell there was a tugging on Charlie's heart. He sent a silent prayer up to heaven, waited for direction, and then phrased the answer the best way he knew how. "You know what I think, Charlie? I think the only sin that is unforgivable is the sin of not accepting God's forgiveness." He paused to let the conundrum of his statement settle into his listener's mind. "Can you imagine paying the highest price possible on a gift for the ones you love, and then they won't take it? A gift can do you no good until you choose to receive it. You could get a presidential pardon from this place, but you would still have to receive that pardon to walk out a free man. With God, He offers so much more than just a pardon. He offers relationship and purpose and the ability to partner with Him to complete the work He prepared for us to do while we are on this planet."

"So are you saying that God planned for you to be in prison?" Diesel was forced back into the same asking-and-waiting scenario for assistance from God.

"Hmm. That's a fair question, but I think the better question is whether God had the foreknowledge to see if and where we would turn back to Him and then the ability to fit our wrong choices back into His good plan for us. I believe God knew I would end up in prison and that it would be in a nine-by-seven cell where He would finally get my attention. He did not plan *for* me to be here, but he did plan *on* me being here." The words came out more quickly than he could filter them, and in the silence that followed, doubt about their correctness or even their theological validity crept in. He had no real way of knowing if that answer was correct. What he did have was a sweet confidence that God would use his words in whatever way was needed to help men like Charlie with whom God had given him the privilege to share the good news.

Charlie pondered the answer quietly. Diesel wanted to give him some space, but the minutes that followed felt like an eternity. Finally, Diesel's desire to help the lost soul sharing the cell with him got the better of him, and he broke the silence.

"Charlie, I have never told you some of the things I did in my former way of life. You know that I'm in here for armed robbery, but that is just what they found me guilty of. Truth be told, that was just the tip of the iceberg. I have done things I am too ashamed to speak out loud. I was a son of hell, if ever there was one. The day I repented of my sins and made Jesus lord of my life, the foundations of hell shook, brother. Hell would have patented the rights to my life if it could because I was so far in that camp. I had given my soul over to the influence of demons, and I had cursed Christians. I grew up in church, and I ended up hating every single one of the people there. I hated everything to do with them. I thought they were the weakest and worst people on the planet. I used to plan mass killings of Christians in my head. Have you ever done that, Charlie?" Diesel gave a respectful five seconds for him to answer before he launched back into his testimony. "The guy you see before you today is not the man I was for the first four decades of my life. Bro, you would not have recognized me, let alone wanted to talk to me. I was an abuser, a manipulator, a drug addict, a thief. I had murder in my heart. I lied like it was my first language. I cursed God and people, and I would have thrown my own family under the bus to get the things I wanted. I had so much hate and deception in my heart that I used to fight people for fun and take their money after I beat the crap out of them." This sparked something in Charlie's heart to hear more.

"What do you mean? How did you get their money?"

"You won't believe it, even if I tell you, man."

"Try me."

"Dude, I am not proud of that stuff."

"Just tell me, man. I really want to know."

"Well, I worked with a couple of criminal profilers I got to know from hanging out with some law enforcement buddies of mine."

"How did you have friends in law enforcement with the life you lived?"

"Long story for another day, but these two were brilliant at understanding human dynamics and anticipating human behavior in stressful situations. They would go into a bar and pick out the alpha male who had a macho complex—the kind who clings to their glory days as high school football heroes and are still living through that filter. We knew our victims had a reputation to keep, and even though they were usually the biggest men in the bar, we knew they didn't have the anger and hatred I had inside of me. I had a death wish. You don't want to fight someone who doesn't care if they live or die. Then we would provoke a fight.

"One of the profilers was a woman, and she knew how to pick a fight. She would purposefully bump into the guy they had identified as the one most likely to get sucked into a confrontation and would have the backing of the locals to win. She would tell him that her boyfriend would whip his ass for touching her and then bet him he could. The other profiler would give the impression that he was the boyfriend. He was only about a buck fifty and was obviously a pencil pusher. The guy would take the bait, and then I would walk out of the bathroom claiming to be the boyfriend. We knew that the guy's pride and reputation wouldn't let him back down in front of his fans. Before you knew it, we had a few grand on the line in bets. I would strip away my opponent's confidence right off the bat. I would offer him the first hit for free. My head is made of cement, and I stuck it out there for him to hit. Many of those shots hurt, but they just got me riled up and even madder than I already was. I liked the pain, and it fueled my hate." Diesel stopped. Charlie waited a minute for him to start up again but then thought he could hear crying. He stepped out of his bunk to see what was going on.

"What's wrong, Diesel?" Charlie grabbed hold of the edge of his bed and pulled himself up so he was eye to eye with the bigger man. He saw tears rolling down his face. Diesel couldn't help but lament the way he had used and hated people. "Sorry, man," Charlie said. "I didn't mean to make you emotional by telling that story. My buddy got into a fight with a guy in a bar once, and he took me and my friends for over a grand and left him seeing stars. I can't remember much about the guy he fought, but he was a big, bald bad ass, and I just thought you might know something about it."

Diesel thought about the irony of the possibility that the guy he was trying to encourage to accept the forgiveness of his Savior might be one of the people he swindled in his past life.

"I don't know, man, but if it was me, I wish I could pay you back twice what I took from you and take back all the hits I put on your buddy."

"He was an asshole and deserved a good beating. Don't worry about it, man. Tell me one of the worst things that happened to you in the bars. You must have taken some beatings, too, right?"

Diesel thought about his response. He didn't want to glory in his past and certainly didn't want to try to build a relationship with Charlie around his prior sinful lifestyle, but he felt a prompting to keep talking. It was as if the Lord was giving him a green light to continue, and he felt he may finally be getting closer to a breakthrough.

"There are lots of things that I regret, and I don't want to build up a reputation for the man I used to be. I was just telling you so you would know that if God forgives sinners like me, He will certainly forgive you, too."

"C'mon, man. You never talk about this part of your life, and I never knew you used to be like that. I just figured you were basically a religious guy who got into drugs and lost your way for a while. I never knew you had a dark side."

"Dark side is an understatement. I think hell itself inspired some of those fights."

"What do you mean?"

"Well, one time there was a guy at the bar telling me who to fight. He was a biker and looked like he was full-blooded American Indian. He didn't say much and just pointed at another biker who had been talking trash all night. He told me I needed to humiliate him. I knocked him out and then looked back at the Indian standing by the bar motionless. It felt like I could hear his voice in my head telling me what to do. I took my knife out of my pocket, leaned down, and cut off about two feet of the guy's pony tail. The joint erupted in anger and laughter. The bartender pulled me out through a side door and told me to go out back. When I asked him if he knew the Native American at the end of the bar, he looked at me as if I had two heads. He told me there had been nobody of that description anywhere in the bar that night."

"Did you get away? What happened next?"

"I walked through the delivery door out back, and the next thing I knew, I was seeing stars. The girlfriend of the guy whose hair I cut off had run around back, picked up a two-by-four, hit me square in the face, and knocked out four of my teeth." Diesel pulled back his lip and popped down his false teeth to show Charlie the proof. "Yeah, my buddies restrained her until I came to, and we got out of that place as fast as we could. It was the weirdest feeling having someone else in your head, someone you thought was a real person, but I guess that is what the devil does all the time. In fact, Charlie, I think it is the devil telling you that God can't or won't forgive you for the things you have done. God can and will forgive anything you have done if you will only allow Him to become Lord of your life.

"Let me ask you a question. Who do you want running your life? You; a demon who has plans to destroy you; or God, who has only good plans for you?" The question jarred Charlie. It rang true in his heart more than ever before. He knew he didn't want to run his own life. He had made a mess of it so far. He definitely did not want the devil to have his way with him, but he was not yet ready to yield control of his life to God, no matter how good Diesel said He was. Sensing his struggle, Diesel decided to leave one last nugget of wisdom with his friend. "Charlie, you can't afford to sit on the fence on this one."

"Well, that's where I am, dude, firmly on the fence."

"One thing I have learned in my short time with God is that there is no middle ground, and to be double-minded about something is the same as being on the wrong side. You see, Charlie, when it comes to issues of the soul, there's no middle ground. God wants you to be all in. What that means is the devil owns the fence!"

Both men knew no more words needed to be spoken, and they both knew that significant ground had been gained in Charlie's heart.

Chapter 34

Officer Smith

Officer Smith stood on a stage next to his captain. It had been more than two years since he had joined the vice division and SWAT and transferred to Captain Kerrigan's leadership. It had been a two-year roller-coaster ride with spiked adrenaline and high-risk situations, and he excelled at them all. He was being promoted to the rank of detective and being awarded a commendation for bravery in the line of duty. He had built a reputation of having the coolest head in the history of the unit, and his bravery matched if not exceeded that reputation. His future was very bright as far as everyone on the outside could tell. In the minds of all attending, he would undoubtedly become a legend and have opportunities to mold the future of SWAT in the same way he had raised the bar in child abuse investigation.

As Kerrigan made a long-winded speech with plenty of platitudes, Smith couldn't help but feel a powerful sense of nothingness, an empty dissatisfaction in the bottom of his gut. He couldn't explain it and desperately wished it were different, but the more he heard his name mentioned in glowing terms, the more he just wanted to get drunk. All he could think of was going back to his solitary apartment and emptying the bottle of Jack Daniel's he had started the night before. He could no longer go to the bar since his professional reputation was now under greater scrutiny. But the added pressure made it more of a necessity to seek refuge in the bottle.

Smith had hoped that becoming a detective on Kerrigan's team would fill the void again like it had the first year he was part of his unit. As he took to the podium, he heard the right words come out of his mouth as if he were an observer of the whole occasion. He was on autopilot at the greatest moment of his career. *Maybe I am just having a bad night. Maybe when I start functioning as a detective, it will change. Maybe things will change. Maybe.* His attempts to rescue hope fell by the wayside as feebly as they had begun.

"Congratulations, Smithy."

"Thanks."

"Well done, man."

"Thanks."

"I know you are going to do great things."

"Thanks."

"Most promising talent on the force that I have seen in years. Keep up the good work, Smith."

"Thanks."

"So glad for you, man. You deserve this."

"Thanks."

Detective Smith felt like he was about to explode by the time the evening was over. He couldn't wait to get out of uniform and into a pair of shorts and seek refuge with the only friend who understood his woes: Jack Daniel. Something was different, though, or maybe something was the same again. *What is wrong with this bottle? Did someone water it down?* His voice longed for a hearing ear to absorb the pain inside. He looked at the bottle, assessing if it had enough left in it to put him to sleep. At that moment, it seemed like all the whiskey in the world couldn't offer him the sweet escape of sleep. *Where are those pills? Where did I put them?* He frantically looked all over the bathroom and then the kitchen. *What the heck were you thinking, you idiot?* In a moment of strength and at a time when the adrenaline high masqueraded as an appropriate savior, he had put them away somewhere safe. They were to be his trophy when he would finally kick his addiction, but now he needed them to rescue him from reality one more time. He did not have sufficient clarity to recall where he had hidden them, and his frustration grew. He threw the now-empty Jack Daniel's bottle at the wall and cursed until the neighbor in the apartment below started banging on the ceiling.

"Who do you think you are? Come up here and tell me to my face what your problem is. Call the cops, why don't you, and see how that backfires on you." The expletives rolled off his tongue until he eventually got tired of yelling at a neighbor whom he couldn't even put a face to.

He walked into his bedroom and fell facedown on his bed with his head landing near the only other piece of furniture in the room. The small black nightstand had a narrow drawer at the top with a little compartment at the back. Staring at the nightstand, he remembered. *That's where you are. I put you in the nightstand to remind myself each night that I don't need you. I stopped talking to you a long time ago. I stopped telling you that I don't need you anymore. But that was a lie; I need you now.* He pulled the drawer out and dumped the contents on the floor. There it was. A clear, zippered bag with about 20 blue pills inside. He poured out about half the pills and stumbled into the bathroom. Grabbing a red plastic cup, he launched the pills into his mouth, followed them up with one mouthful of water, and swallowed hard.

Just the feel of the pills going down his throat gave him the peace he needed to lie back down on the bed. The dark figure who had been shadowing him so closely for so long was enjoying the powerlessness of his subject. As Detective Smith was succumbing to the effects of the pills, he heard a voice in his head—a voice he had drawn courage from in the past but now only scared him. The figure couldn't contain his glee at his long-sought victory and prophesied to the helpless form in front of him. *One day you will end it all this way. One day I will make you do terrible things that you will wish you could take back. You will beg me to help you take your own life, and I will be there to oblige you.* For the final moment or two until he fell asleep, those words terrified him more than anything he had ever heard. He knew he was powerless to withstand the presence that had at first promised him significance when he felt powerless to change, the presence to which he had willingly submitted. The presence that seemed for so long to guide his success. The presence that now seemed to be enjoying his demise. The only consolation was knowing that he would not remember any of this when he finally woke up.

Chapter 35

Scott

The driver saw his usual turning point just ahead. He was ahead of schedule and bored with his normal routine. The sweeper truck moved at such a slow pace that his mind had way too much time to process all the useless information he fed it. Something urged him to keep on going straight instead of turning around at the usual spot.

Why the heck would I go farther than I am being paid to go?

Just do it. Change is good for the mind, right?

Whatever. I will go down this road a bit more than usual and then turn around.

Go down to the next road sign at least and then turn around.

He had many conversations with himself this deep into the night shift. He never knew who would come out on top, and he certainly didn't care. He took the truck about 200 feet past the turning point, and in the far reaches of his headlights, he saw a car in the ditch. *What's that car doing in the ditch? It looks abandoned.* He had no explanation to offer himself. A lone car in the ditch warranted no particular attention. He drove a little closer, but when he couldn't see anyone inside the vehicle, he decided this was a waste of time. As he turned the steering wheel to get back to his normal route, his headlights swung in the direction of the ditch and reflected on what looked like the side of a shoe. His brain processed in slow motion what he just saw. The truck had almost completed the turn before he realized that the shoe may have been attached to something else, more specifically a leg. He turned off the sweepers, put the truck in park, and jumped out of the cab. He expected his eyes had played a trick on him, and his desperate need to break his brutal

143

monotony was behind his petulant reaction. *You are wasting your time.* As he rounded the cab, he couldn't make out the shoe anymore. The lights were now pointed straight ahead, and there were no streetlights anywhere in this area. *Aw, man, I'm going to have to go over there in the dark. I'll probably get sprayed by a skunk or something. If I get sprayed again, I'm going to be pissed, and my old lady isn't going to let me in the bedroom for a month.*

As he approached the car, he looked toward the area where he thought he had seen the shoe. He rounded the trunk of the car and jumped when he saw the body of a large man attached to the other end of the shoe. "Dude! Are you okay, man?" The limp body offered no response. "Don't be dead, man. Don't be dead." He put one hand on the man's wrist and the other on his neck. "No, no, no! You don't have a pulse, dude. Your body is still warm, so you haven't been here long." *Crap! Crap! Remember your CPR, dude. You were a dumb lifeguard for four years and never had to perform CPR, and now here in the middle of the night, in the middle of nowhere, you have to do something you haven't practiced in years.* He racked his brain for the steps he used to know by heart. *Call 9-1-1 and put the phone on speaker on the ground. Then start compressions. You got this.* The phone rang as he was finding the sternum. "Man, you are one big dude. I'm going to have to push extra hard."

While the dispatcher took details of his location and instructed him to continue compressions until the ambulance arrived, this unsuspecting hero kept Scott's heart beating artificially until the ambulance crew stabilized him. His body had crashed, and the doctors immediately put him on life support when he arrived at the hospital.

Scott had a bad reputation at his local ER, but that night, one of the nurses on duty was an old friend of his from high school. He recognized his former football buddy and rushed over to check on his old friend.

"Scott, what happened, man?"

"You know he can't respond, right?" The attending physician walked up behind him, gave him a questioning glance, and checked his name tag as if to make a mental note of a potentially incompetent nurse.

"The intubation tube kind of gave it away, Doc. My question was more rhetorical."

"You know this guy?"

"Most people around here know him, but we were buddies in high school."

"He is lucky to be alive, but he isn't out of the woods yet. He overdosed on God knows what, and he had no pulse when someone found him."

"How long was he without oxygen?"

"No way to tell, but it was a complete miracle that someone found him. A road sweeper saw his foot sticking out of a ditch and almost didn't stop. He just happened to know CPR and kept him alive. If he lives, he will owe his life to that guy." The doctor walked away with little or no emotion. A drug addict saved from an overdose usually meant the inevitable had just been delayed.

"Scott, man, what happened to you? You were such a good guy back in the day. I really thought you were going to do something significant with your life. I thought you had such great potential." He grabbed his friend's arm and spoke to him as if he could hear his words.

"Listen to me, Scott. Don't give up. I promise you that life has more meaning than drugs. It doesn't matter what has happened in the past. There are still good reasons for living. Don't give up! Fight! God has a better life for you than you could ever know. Don't give up. Just don't give up." He bowed his head and offered a heartfelt prayer on behalf of the half-dead man he once knew as a popular, talented football player. The intensity or sincerity of his prayer must have had an impact because the grip of death the grave had on his seriously damaged heart loosened sufficiently, and the big man made it through the night.

Chapter 36

Detective Smith

The paint was peeling off the walls, and the chipped mirrors added to the raw, industrial feel of the local powerlifting team's hangout. Nearly every square inch of the room was covered by a bench, a squat rack, or a dead-lift station. Specialized equipment to reinforce the muscles and joints during heavy lifting hung from racks on the walls. Lifters grabbed what they needed for each lift, placing massive strain on their bodies as they lifted several times their own weight over and over again. A punching bag looked out of place in the corner of an otherwise cardio-free environment until a six-foot-four monster who failed his last dead-lift attempt took out his anger on the defenseless bag. He continued until he was either out of breath or his anger had subsided. It was impossible to tell which came first.

Every man and woman in this place had an ax to grind. They channeled that anger into a fight against gravity and the glory of setting a new personal best at whatever competition was looming in the never-ending cycle of train-compete, train-compete, train-compete. Detective Smith's drinking had become an issue with Kerrigan. Smith's eventual promotion to captain was contingent on his being able to keep his alcohol dependency under control. The fire inside him became murderous at times, so he threw himself headlong into the subculture of powerlifting and a new set of drugs that fuel some unique addictions.

"Smithy, man, you are becoming a monster. You seem to set a new personal best every time you come into the gym."

"It's the only place on the planet where I can blow off steam, Jake."

"You were strong when you got here, man, but with the numbers you posted at the last competition and what I saw you doing today, you could be close to winning at regionals in the spring."

"I've always been blessed with strength, but I'm gonna need some more of those supplements you hooked me up with last time. The stuff you got from Mexico." For a moment, he saw the double irony of being aware that strength was a blessing from a supposedly good God and his status as a detective being complicit in the illegal procurement of steroids from Mexico. His desire to maintain control on his job and in life was utterly dependent on finding a way to handle his anger and addictions outside the workplace. That necessity overrode any tinge of guilt he may have been tempted to feel.

"Some of us are headed to Cancun next week if you want to come. You can buy your own stuff and even sell some to help pay for your own supply."

"What is this? A multilevel marketing scheme?" The two men laughed, and with the awkwardness he felt in his facial muscles, Detective Smith realized a smile had not crossed his lips in a very long time. "Maybe I'll go with you next time."

"Sure thing, Smithy, but get with me before you leave today, and I'll give you a fresh supply. You've been packing on the muscle."

"I'd better be. I spend every free moment here."

"What do you weigh now?"

"I'm not sure, but last time I checked I was over two fifty."

"You're looking leaner, too."

"I've been eating right and using those fat burners you recommended."

"Did you get your body fat percentage checked lately?"

"It was at fourteen percent last time, but I think it has dropped a point or two."

"Dude, if you keep going this way, you could do some competitive body building, too."

"Prancing around in a thong in front of a bunch of men who are examining your body? I don't think so."

"Well, if you change your mind, I think you have the genetics to compete, and I can get you the right supplements to cause your body fat to plummet and get you ready for competition. It's a different kind of adrenaline, dude. Don't knock it until you've tried it."

Detective Smith didn't say a word to another person as he threw weights around the gym for another hour and a half. The release of endorphins coupled with physical exhaustion provided him the daily release from the nuclear reactor that was threatening to explode inside of him every day. He paid Jake for the steroids he had become dependent on and realized his new addiction was costlier than his income would support long-term. The figure in the shadows was constantly ready to give his advice on how he could solve his problems, and today was no different.

You should go to Cancun with the guys. You can have a good time and get enough steroids to sell and get the extra supplements you need to win in the spring. They do it all the time and don't get caught. Call Jake and tell him you'll go with them. Smith had become accustomed to obeying the voice. It was easier than debating and much easier than trying to run his own life. Without thinking, he pulled out his phone and hit speed dial. Within minutes, his flight was booked.

The closest he ever came to hope or optimism was when he could win at something, when he could distinguish himself as better than others. That fueled his ability to compete, but it was also his Achilles' heel, and Kerrigan could see it. His boss hoped that with time he would learn to temper his courage with wisdom. The phone rang. Kerrigan was on the other line.

"Hey, Captain, what's up?"

"I need you to come back in, Smithy."

"Sure, but what's going on?"

"I have a situation on the north side of town that local PD just told me is developing into a violent standoff. I'm on the other side of the state in a training session, and I'm concerned this may get out of hand. I know you just finished a shift a few hours ago, but in my absence, I would rather you lead the team if you feel up to it." The feeling of being needed fed the basic human desire for personal worth in all but the outliers in society, and Detective Smith was no different. He was weary from work and the gym, but the knowledge of being needed gave him the boost he craved at that moment. He ignored common sense and the proper self-evaluation protocol and jumped at the request.

"I'll be on site inside the hour, Captain. Just send me the location."

"Sergeant Price will be there to bring you up to speed."

"I'll contact you once the situation is resolved."

"Thanks, Smithy. I appreciate your commitment to the team. Think before you act, and don't stick your neck out for a maverick call."

"No neck-sticking. Got it." Both men hung up, and both knew that the man in charge didn't have the proper grid to evaluate if a move was truly maverick or not. Kerrigan knew he had to trust his potential successor or cut him loose, and the latter was not an option given his level of talent.

Detective Smith pulled up in his unmarked car and approached Sergeant Price. The scene before him didn't make much sense. There were furniture and appliances all over the front yard. Windows were broken where smaller appliances had been forcefully thrown out. The family was sitting by the ambulance, and although they had calmed down, they were still borderline hysterical and, thus, an escalation threat.

"The guy inside has snapped. He's threatening to kill everyone here."

"Have you seen a weapon?"

"He has some kind of shotgun in his hand, but he has shown no intention of firing it—not yet, anyway."

"Why is his family still out here?"

"He sent them out and told us to protect them from him but not to take them away."

"That doesn't make sense. What do you think is his end goal?"

"I think he's lost it, but to be honest, I don't think he's a killer. One of the guys knows his family and said he lost his job about six months ago and hasn't been able to keep up payments on the house. We suspect he was also paying for the furniture and appliances on credit."

"Where is he now?"

"He hasn't been out for about 10 minutes, but we heard him moving around inside a minute ago. Oh, by the way, his name is Bubba." Detective Smith checked his expression to make sure he was serious and then responded.

"Okay, Sergeant, I'll take the lead if you'll provide backup."

"You got it, but I forgot to mention one thing."

"What's that?"

"He's huge."

"You mean fat?"

"Not exactly. He's about six foot eight and must be at least 500 pounds. With the way he's been throwing around the furniture by himself, my guess is there's plenty of muscle mass underneath his overalls."

"Maybe we'll need to call in an animal tranquilizer." His attempt at humor was lost on the sergeant.

At that moment, a behemoth of a man ducked as he came out the front door. His head was shaved, and he had thick ripples of fat circling from the back of his neck to the front with sweat dripping out of every pore. He was carrying a washing machine like it was a toaster, and he threw it out past the porch and about 10 feet into the garden.

"I think you underestimated his size, Sergeant."

"It's all yours now, Detective." This time the humor was lost on the detective.

For the next two hours, Detective Smith tried to engage the beast of a man as he systematically ripped every appliance and pulled every piece of furniture out of his house. He was yelling the whole time and threatening to hurt them if they took his family away. However, Detective Smith didn't believe he had any intention to hurt anyone. He knew what it was like to have a raging anger on the inside. He could only imagine how hard it would be to control that anger if you were unable to provide for your family.

It looked like Bubba was running out of steam and furniture. The threat was low-grade in Smith's opinion, but it needed to be brought to a conclusion sooner rather than later. The family was ramping up their hysterics every time he threw out a piece of furniture or some of the kids' toys. This kind of situation can go south unexpectedly. Smith had seen it before. All it took was for something small to send someone over the edge and make the situation as well as the threat of harm escalate. Two hours of trying the standard negotiation and de-escalation tactics had not given him any breakthrough, and he knew he had to try something else.

"Listen, Bubba. I know what it's like to be so angry that you want to rip the whole world apart. I know you love your family and want what is best for them. What can I do to help you deal with this?"

The giant on the front steps with a shotgun at his side had paid little or no attention to the officers who had been trying to get him into a dialogue for hours. But Smith's ears perked up when he heard Bubba's offer.

"I want *you*, big boy."

"What do you mean?"

"You and me. Let's fight it out right here in my yard." Smith could still hear Kerrigan's words in his head as he evaluated the damage a man like this could do to him. *No maverick calls.* He knew that engaging this guy could end the risk to the others and to Bubba, as long as he survived the encounter. The figure in the shadows shared his opinion as well. *He may be bigger than you, but he is not stronger. You are the cop. You are the trained professional. You can take him.* His pride swelled as he once again embraced the voice of darkness. He took off his belt and his tactical jacket and came out from behind his car.

"I'm here. Drop your gun."

Bubba threw his gun to the side and grinned like a clown in a Stephen King movie. He started down the porch steps, and by the time he hit the bottom step, Detective Smith was halfway through the yard and gaining speed. When he was about 10 feet from his opponent, he instinctively ducked his head and launched himself close to chest height in an attempt to take Bubba by surprise. The big man barely had enough time to lean over before their shoulders and heads collided. Both men fell from the force of the impact. They lay there motionless for a moment, and fortunately for Smith, he was the first to stir. His colleagues observing the circus were stunned by the events they were watching until Price barked at his men.

"Go help him!"

"Yes, Sarge." Two officers ran to help Detective Smith get up off the ground.

"Are you all right?"

"Are you kidding me? No, I am not all right. I feel like I just got hit by a truck."

"Let me get a paramedic over here."

"No, I can get up. Nothing is broken."

While he was trying to stand, he saw the giant on the ground breathing but not moving. The mental mist of almost being knocked unconscious cleared, and he couldn't help but feel invincible. As they took Bubba away in the ambulance, the guys in the local PD started calling their shaken hero Goldberg. His reputation grew that day, but so did his carelessness. With the notoriety, his healthy fear of death and his desire for self-preservation took a permanent back seat to his ego. He was on a dangerous path, and most of his remaining natural warning signs had been rendered ineffective.

Chapter 37

Joey

For a season, Joey's life seemed to resemble a normal childhood. The dark clouds that had hung around for so long after the winter of abuse seemed to eventually dissipate. The desire to defend the weak was still present, but normal friendships and school sports provided the kind of distraction a 12-year-old boy needed. Tom lived next door, and both boys could throw a football back and forth between their yards for hours. Joey's mom was staring at him from the kitchen as she and her husband cleaned up after dinner.

"Honey, you know what?" She was still looking out the window.

"What?"

"I think Joey has finally come around again."

"He does seem to have brightened up, that's for sure."

"For a while, I was very concerned that something serious was wrong with him or maybe worse."

"What do you mean by that?"

"Oh, nothing. I am just glad to see him back playing with his friends."

"He said he made the middle school football team."

"That's good news. Coach McKenzie will be a good influence on him."

"Coach is a good man. He works those kids hard, but he cares about their well-being first and foremost."

"Thank you, Lord, for helping our little boy when he needed it."

"Amen."

They both went back to their chores, grateful that life appeared to be on an even keel for the first time in years.

The boys continued to call Heisman-worthy plays against imaginary defenses.

"Hey, Tom, do you ever get a pain in your crotch when you play football?"

"Not normally. Maybe when I tackle a guy and my cup isn't in the right place." Tom appeared to wince at a particular memory that he preferred not to rehash.

"No, I mean, like, are you ever in pain from your balls swelling?"

"Uh, no, not really, I can't remember that ever happening. Why do you ask?"

"I think there may be something wrong with me."

"Did you tell your parents?"

"No, are you kidding me? It feels way too embarrassing every time I try to tell them. I'm afraid my mom is going to freak out and insist on taking a look."

His counterpart didn't catch the football because he was laughing at that mental picture. "Dude, that would not be cool. But seriously, maybe you should let your dad know. You might need to go to the doctor or something."

"I'm not sure if Dad is a better prospect than Mom. He's super weird about all that stuff."

"As bad as it may seem, you just might have to accept your fate on that one." Tom's perfect spiral pass careened out of control, his arm distracted by his friend's struggle and the dilemma he faced. "Sorry, Joey, that was a horrible throw."

Tom noticed Joey wince in pain as he bent over to retrieve the football from the street. "It can't be good if it hurts just to pick up the football."

"Yeah, it's been hurting a lot lately, especially since we had tryouts for the football team. I'm worried they won't let me play if I have an injury or something.

Joey had struggled through preseason training, but the pain was getting out of control. He stood in front of the full-length mirror on his closet door and stared in disbelief. His testicles looked twice their normal size. Fear of what might be wrong overrode the fear of what his parents might think, and he finally told his dad about his problem. Dad said he was taking him to the doctor, and within an hour, the young teenager was sitting in the waiting room dreading the imminent conversation and humiliation. This was one time he didn't mind waiting his turn. When his name was called, he swallowed hard.

Dr. Madison was a kindhearted man with a pleasant disposition suitable to family practice. He had a way of making his patients feel at ease, and nothing ever seemed to be a big deal. Nothing until today. He took way more time than Joey would have liked and looked concerned as he addressed his dad.

"It's too hard to tell what's wrong by just looking at Joey's affected area. I will have to send him for some tests, but I suspect I will have to do a biopsy to determine exactly what it is."

"Will that hurt?" Joey wasn't being addressed directly, but he was the one most affected by the conversation, and he was not going to be silent.

"No, Joey. The biopsy won't hurt." The doctor realized he needed to rein in his visible concerns since this may not be what he suspected. There was no point alarming the boy and his family until he knew for sure.

Two weeks later, Dr. Madison was sitting across the room from Joey and his parents. This time, there was no margin of error or false hope of a pending biopsy to cling to. The prognosis and outlook were even worse than the doctor had expected, and Joey could sense it before a word was spoken. Dr. Madison's soft heart was not made for doling out bad news. He wanted to look at the ground or stare out the window while he delivered the proverbial death sentence, but he forced himself to look right at Joey and muster up as much strength as he could to deliver the news.

"Joey, I have been taking care of you since right after you were born. I have watched you grow into a fine young man, and you seem as strong as an ox in every other way. However, your body is operating differently than it should. Mutated cells are reproducing at a rapid rate and forming a growth on your testes. The biopsy results came back and confirmed my concerns. This is a cancerous growth." Both of Joey's parents looked on in disbelief as they heard the words no parent ever wants to hear.

It was Joey's mom who spoke up first. "Surely, there is a mistake. How could he have cancer? He is so healthy. He plays football all the time, and he is one of the strongest and fittest on his team." She knew her reasoning was flawed, but she wanted with all her being to be offered a lifeline in this conversation.

"Doctor." Joey's dad cleared his throat as he was about to ask a question he knew he was not ready to hear the answer to. "What treatment is available?"

"Well, this type of cancer is quite aggressive, and it is fairly advanced already. We'll need to do several rounds of radiation treatment as well as chemotherapy."

"But he will be all right. Right, Doc?" Her eyes were streaming with tears as she jumped into the conversation again to regain some sense of control over the bomb that had just exploded in her lap.

"Of course, there is a chance he will get better. Otherwise we wouldn't consider treatment, but it's not something I can guarantee. To be honest, there is still a significant risk that the treatment will not be successful." She buried her head in her hands and sobbed. The anguished mother could not have realized the impact she was having on her son who was facing two things that were normally hidden from the thoughts of a child: his own mortality and his mother's grief. Everything seemed to become a blur from that moment on as his recently rebuilt world came crashing down all around him for a second time.

Chapter 38

Detective Smith v. Scott

Long hours at the gym and dangerous encounters at work provided a rhythm for Detective Smith to burn off steam and keep his need for self-medication satiated through the perceived less destructive drugs of pride and adrenaline. Those were supplemented by steroids and pain killers "only when necessary." That was the mantra he had convinced himself to believe. Fat burners, creatine, mass gainers, whey protein, and supplements that boosted results and could never be proved were all shoved into his system in an effort to get an edge, a better performance, a new personal best in competition. Winning the regional championship by a large margin had grabbed the attention of a nationwide publication, and he interviewed for a story that highlighted his recent success under this nickname: the Beast from the East.

His coworkers were proud of their colleague, but they only knew one form of compliment—making fun of one another.

"Hey, Smithy. I hear you're breaking all sorts of powerlifting records. Do they know about the stupidity records you broke last week when you chased down that drug dealer with the pet snake in his bag?"

"Funny, Cantrell, real funny."

"For real, Smithy. Do they know you are a few sandwiches short of a picnic? That you don't know when to back down?"

"The truth is you don't know when to man up, Cantrell. The Girl Scouts have more balls than you." These men were brothers-in-arms and as such were unoffendable, so he pushed for the knockout punch. "At least we would get some cookies if they took your place."

"You're a funny guy, Smithy. I'm not sure what the ladies see in you. Oh yeah, you don't have any ladies right now. Sorry. My bad." A broad smile stretched across his face as he reveled in his boyish humor a little too much.

"At least when I'm with a woman, she feels safe. I hear your old lady requests a security detail when you're at home." Both men chuckled, but once again, Detective Smith racked up the exchange as a win for his corner. No engagement between the two men was ever too small not to warrant an intense effort to win whatever it was they were warring about. His hubris was equaled by his now massive physique. At almost 300 hundred pounds, he eclipsed the next-largest guy on the local PD by more than 50 pounds and by at least 10 percent less body fat.

"You want to make a routine trip to the local pushers today? We could use some of your Goldberg moves to scare the snot out of them."

"Sure, I was just planning on doing some paperwork, but that can wait until tomorrow. Let's go." He was hooked when he heard the name Goldberg. It was meant to be derogatory, but it fed his powerful ego too much to extrapolate the original intent.

The drive downtown was filled with the usual suspects—pimps and prostitutes fighting over money, the homeless harassing drivers in an attempt to clean their windshields without permission, and drug dealers on the prowl looking for their next victim to seduce with their destructive products.

"We've passed several potential, arrestable candidates, Cantrell. Are you looking for someone specific?"

"Yes, I am. That's why I wanted you to come. The guy is huge, built like you."

"So now the truth comes out. If you want, I can call your mommy and see if she can come, too."

"For real, Smithy. This guy used to be a local nuisance, a user causing problems all over town. He moved away somewhere and just came back a few months ago. I'm hearing his name way too much as a new source for drugs. He's a psycho, though, and I wouldn't be surprised if he goes ballistic on us. I was hoping your presence might stop him from doing something stupid while we have a chat with him."

"Sure, Cantrell. You could just say you're scared, though. It's okay to be scared of guys who are bigger than you." Even Detective Smith admitted that was a heavy dose of sarcasm.

Cantrell was no pushover and could handle himself just fine. His wife and kids were a constant reminder to take an extra measure of precaution whenever possible. Smith knew his motivation but was not willing to give an inch in their verbal rivalry.

"For real, Smithy, I need you to bring your A game today since this guy is a nut job. A road sweeper saved his life a couple of weeks ago, and he threatened to kill the nurse at the hospital for putting him on life support because he wanted to die."

"Sounds like a dangerous nut job all right. What's his name?"

"I just know him as Scott."

"Do you know where he is?"

"He's parked himself at the corner of Archibald and Main for the last week. There's an abandoned building a lot of the junkies use to stay out of the elements. We're almost there."

The unmarked police car pulled up on the old abandoned building that used to be a feed store. Some men and women staggered around outside in the midday sun, escaping their reality through the drugs they procured inside. The two men parked the car and made their way inside. They immediately came upon two men who were unconscious on the ground, and Cantrell checked for a pulse. "They're fine. No doubt just sleeping it off."

They went inside to what used to be the storage room, and before they knew it, a 50-pound bag of rotten feed hit them in the head. That was followed by a second bag and then a third. Cantrell could see that Smith was pissed and reaching for his weapon. "Stop! Police! Stop!" The bags stopped flying as the assailant had second thoughts about harming the men who had invaded his new home.

"What do you want?"

"Are you Scott?"

"Depends who's asking."

"Officer Randall Cantrell and Detective Smith."

"Okay." He stared at the two men as if he had the right to be indignant as they stood in his make-believe living room.

"I've been hearing rumors about you, Scott, and I wanted to pay you a friendly visit."

"Nothing friendly about your visit so far. Do you have any gifts you haven't shown me yet?" None of the men were in a laughing mood.

"No, I just wanted to tell you that I'm hearing chatter about you, and I wanted to give you a chance to give your side of the story before I throw you in jail." Scott was unmoved by the threat and walked right over to Cantrell. Both men were about six feet tall, but Cantrell looked like a lightweight compared to the heavyweight stature of his suspect. Detective Smith stepped between the men and made his presence known. For the first time, Scott locked his gaze on the detective and stared at him for what seemed like five minutes before he allowed a grin to surface on the left side of his face. "I know you."

"I have never met you before in my life."

"Yeah. I remember now. You are that dumb-ass cop who thought he would be treated like a hero for getting injured in the line of duty. We shared a room together while you recovered from your surgery. Well, was I right?"

"Were you right about what?"

"That you were just a commodity to your profession, a number that could help them reach their goal, and *you* didn't matter to them one bit."

Detective Smith was caught off guard by the deeply personal nature of the discussion. "You don't know anything about me." A memory of the hospital room flashed through his mind like an unwelcome guest at a wedding.

"That's where you're wrong, Detective. I know you like the back of my own hand. You're not as content with your life as you pretend to be. You don't know what's missing, but you wake up with a big hole in your soul that torments you. You try to fill the hole with a persona, an image that you portray to others and yourself that you are some kind of tough guy, but you and I know the truth. You're scared. You're scared that you have no value. Scared that your life won't amount to anything and that you're wasting every moment doing something you were never meant to do."

"Listen, man, you don't know jack, and if you don't shut up, I'm going to permanently shut your mouth for you."

Scott maliciously continued, "I know way more than you think. I know people, and I know you."

Detective Smith was visibly shaken, and his partner could see this conversation was going nowhere fast. He would have to rescue the man he brought with him just to keep him safe.

"Don't listen to him, Smithy. He doesn't have a clue what he's talking about."

"You're wrong, Officer Randall Cantrell. I do know what I'm talking about. So, Smithy, have you developed a death wish yet? What drugs have you started taking? Have you graduated from the pain pills yet?" Detective Smith stared in disbelief as the suspect in front of him continued to taunt him. "Ask me how I know. Ask me. I dare you to ask me. Come on. Just ask me, dude."

Detective Smith had had enough. He broke off conversation midstream and headed for the exit. "Come on, Cantrell. If you're done here, I would like to leave."

Cantrell knew what had just transpired was not healthy, and he figured it was best if they just left. "Okay, let's go."

Detective Smith had just stared into the eyes of the only man who seemed to know what was going on inside of him. He wanted to ask him how he knew these things, but his pride wouldn't let him. "You're a waste of space, man," Smith shouted back as they were leaving. "If we catch you dealing dope, we're gonna lock you up and throw away the key."

Scott just smiled at his accusers and went back to whatever he was doing before they arrived. As the two men were leaving the building, Scott decided to fire one more shot at Smith. "When you're ready to find out the truth, come ask me. Better yet, if you decide you want to take something a little stiffer than your pain meds, just let me know, and I'll give you the hookup."

For some reason, the offer appealed to Smith on many levels, and perhaps that was why he craved to hear more from this hardened deadbeat who seemed to understand him all too well. He resisted the last opportunity to engage Scott and headed out the door. He felt more tired than he should have and wanted nothing more than to take a rest. Detective Smith tried in vain to wash away the last few moments from his consciousness, but a deep wound had been opened up in a way that could not be swept under the table. Another meeting seemed inevitable.

Chapter 39

Scott

"I need to get out of this place, man. The cops are onto me."

"I can't help you out, Scott. I just came here to get a fix."

"Come on, Stu. I know you have a house, and I just need a place to crash for a while."

"It's not my place. I just rent it with a few other guys."

"I'm not looking to buy the place. I just need a couch to crash on while I work out my next move." Scott's wheels were turning. He had no doubt that he would get his drug-dependent acquaintance to give up his couch. Scott's impatience demanded that he do it in the least amount of time possible.

"Look, Stu, I've taken care of you time and again, and now it's time for you to return the favor. If I get caught selling, I'll have to give up the names of my customers." He stared hard at Stu to let him know that meant him and there was no room for bargaining."

"Look, man, I don't want any trouble. You could probably stay for a day or two."

"Don't worry, Stu. I'll be out of your hair before you know it. You won't even know I'm there."

As he pulled his stuff together, Scott wrestled with the remnants of his conscience. He had promised Jackson he would never become a dealer. They had both agreed there should be a line you don't cross in life. You don't hit women, you don't steal from your momma, and you don't deal drugs. It was said with humor, but Jackson had made him promise not to deal. Jackson seemed to know he would inevitably wind up in this place and hoped their bond of friendship would be enough to prevent him from going over the edge.

Sorry, buddy. I've let you down. I used to say I'd rather be dead than a lowlife, but I've even failed at that. I don't know what to do, man. I wish I could end it all. I wish we could be teenagers again. I wish I could have the strength to give up this life. I wish I could have made my marriage work and had a family like yours. I wish I hadn't thrown away my career. I wish you were here, dude. I feel so alone. His regret turned to anger. He had no other choice but to continue on the path he had taken. He determined to push past the promises he had made to a friend long ago, a friend who could no longer help him. He felt something harden inside. If he were going to go down this road, he was going to go all the way. He would become twice the son of hell that he had ever been.

He made Stu's house his base of operations for the next month. He was on a short leash from his supplier, and his clients were getting shadier. He wanted to prove he could move drugs faster than anyone else, that he could increase the amount of his supply. It was the first time he had tried to manage his own drug use from a business perspective. He had a pattern. He would use in the morning and sell in the evening. He found his sweet spot for dealing was when he was lucid but not yet in withdrawal. He had to be careful not to go over his limit.

He was wasted every day by midafternoon. Stu's roommates were afraid of the psycho-hulk he had brought home a month ago. Josh had always taken the role as leader of the group, and he was self-elected as the spokesman for the dissenting trio.

"Listen, Stu. We can't have him here anymore. We'll all have our asses thrown in jail. The cops are watching our place now, and every night when we come home, he has some low-life, strung-out thief or prostitute in our house."

"He won't leave, Josh. I've asked him to leave, but he won't leave."

"You gotta tell him to leave, dude." Byron had a look of fear in his eyes as he shared his convictions.

"Have you seen the guy, Byron? He doesn't listen to a word I say."

"Then you need to use this." Byron pulled a gun out of the bag slung over his shoulder.

"What the heck, dude? I have never used a gun in my life."

"Tell him to leave, or you will make him leave."

"Is it loaded?" Stu was not planning on taking the gun, but in the moment, his curiosity got the better of him.

"Yes, it's loaded. If he doesn't respond, fire a warning shot into the floor, and he'll know you're not messing around. You won't have to shoot him. You just have to scare him out of here."

Josh was feeling his influence waning, and he wanted to re-exert his authority as the alpha male.

"Look, Stu. If you don't take care of the problem, we'll kick you out, too."

"You can't do that, Josh. My name is on the lease." Josh looked like that was a revelation to him.

"Simple solution, then. We'll move out, and you and your buddy can take over the rent."

"No. No. I'll get him to leave." Stu centered his thoughts and took a deep breath. He pulled together as much courage as he could muster and grabbed the gun from Byron. He went into the living room, which had been completely taken over by his unwanted guest.

"Hey Scott! Scott!" He looked unconscious on the couch. Stu kicked the couch to wake him up.

"What? What time is it?"

"It's almost noon. We need to talk, man. You gotta leave the house today." Scott was trying to get his brain to catch up with the words he was hearing, and all he could manage was a blank stare.

"Look, you said it would just be for a few days, and it has been a month. You've been doing drug deals in my living room for the last couple of weeks, man. You're going to get me sent to prison."

"Slow down, Stuey. Nobody's going to prison."

"Really? Then why have I seen unmarked police cars on our street for the last two nights?"

"Just give me another week, and I'll be out of your hair. I promise."

"No, Scott, you have got to go now." Scott's head was pounding from his premature arousal, and he was losing patience with his host. He stood up from the couch and approached Stu. He knew his size was even intimidating to large men, but Stu was smaller than average and dwarfed by Scott.

"Are you going to make me go, Stu?" Stu backed off, but something snapped inside of him. Every man has a breaking point. It doesn't matter the size of your opponent or the odds of winning. Sometimes you just can't take any more. He pulled out the gun and pointed it at Scott. The hand holding the gun was shaking, so he grabbed it with his other hand to steady it. He hoped he didn't appear as weak as he was feeling.

"Yes, I'll make you leave, Scott. You're a piece of trash who takes advantage of everyone around you. I'm sick of you taking advantage of me." Scott knew the young man in front of him meant business, but he also knew Stu had a conscience he could exploit. He wasn't angry or offended by the things Stu said. He knew what he had become and had long ago let go of any pride or care about what people thought of him. He walked closer to the gun. Stu backed up until his back was flush against the living room wall.

"Scott, don't come any closer. I'll kill you, man. I promise." Scott made eye contact with him and communicated the closest thing to compassion he had left in him. Stu's resolve instantly weakened. Scott walked closer to him until the gun stuck into his stomach. He grabbed Stu's hands and raised the gun to his own forehead.

"Stu, I am what I am. I cannot change. Not now, not ever. The only way to stop me is by killing me. I give you permission to kill me."

"I'm not messing around, Scott."

"I know. In fact, I want you to kill me. I'm tired of being like this. I'm ready to die." The mood switched in the room, and Stu felt compassion for the broken life in front of him.

"I don't want to kill you, Scott. I just want you to leave."

"Do it, Stu." Anger rose in Scott in a way only someone with a death wish can invoke.

"Do it, Stu. Pull the trigger. Shoot me and put me out of my misery." Stu tried to lower his hands, but Scott had not let go, and he forced him to keep the gun on his forehead.

"Just squeeze the trigger, Stu. Be a man, for God's sake!" Stu's arms were squirming to break free, but Scott's massive hands held them in place like an adult playing with a three-year-old.

"I'm not going to do it, Scott."

"Yes, you are." A normal man would have a hard time holding a gun to his own head and pulling the trigger. But Scott was no normal man, and his resolve to die had just crossed a line he had never crossed before. He held the gun firmly against his forehead and straightened up the barrel. Fear gripped Stu as he realized he was powerless to change what was happening. Scott put his thumb over Stu's finger that had been on the trigger the whole time. Scott took a second to look into Stu's eyes—a parting gift to warn Stu not to become like him. Terror fell on Stu as he understood he was about to play a role in killing the man who stood in front of him.

"No, no, no! Please, Scott, don't do it." Scott squeezed Stu's finger slowly. Time froze for Stu as he could feel his finger go to the point of no return.

Click! Both men looked surprised. Scott knew his way around guns. The gun had not jammed, and he had heard the hammer strike. He recocked the gun and squeezed again without Stu's consent.

Click again.

Click again.

Click! Fear now made Stu lose control of all non-primary functions, and his bladder released its contents in the midst of the scene unfolding before him. Scott could see the fear in his eyes and the dark patch on his jeans. He grabbed the gun out of his hands.

"Did you even put bullets in the gun, you spineless piece of crap?" The adrenaline from his commitment to killing himself caused an explosive anger to rise in him, and he smacked Stu across the head. Stu fell to the ground in pain as blood poured from his ear. Scott popped open the cylinder, and every chamber had a round in it. He looked in disbelief at first and then in dismay as he realized he was not in control of his own life. *What kind of cruel God won't even let a man end his misery?* He looked at the man on the ground. He had humiliated him and reduced him to tears. Scott grabbed his backpack with his drugs in it and stuffed in a jacket and some clothes that were lying around in the room. Then he walked out the door.

Chapter 40

Diesel

Eight men sat on the transportation bus as the guards chatted among themselves. The mood of the guards was lighter than usual, and the inmates relaxed as they began to gaze at the beautiful Tennessee landscape gracing both sides of the road. It was early in winter, but snow had already blanketed the fields and hung from the trees as the sun tried in vain to resist the inevitable advance of the deadness of the season.

"Hey, Charlie! I can't help thinking about what heaven looks like. If the earth can be this beautiful, even in the dead of winter, how incredible do you think heaven will be?" Diesel was being unusually contemplative. The men rarely got farther than the yard, but those who had demonstrated good behavior occasionally had the opportunity to do some work on the outside. Diesel was relishing this opportunity.

"I only ever imagined heaven as being a bunch of clouds and harps and babies with wings." Charlie was pulling his cellmate's leg, but in the process, he exposed his stereotypical understanding of heaven.

"No, dude, heaven is a place like earth is a place. It's described as having streets of gold and buildings with foundations of precious stones and gates made of massive pearls." He could see this was news to Charlie.

"The Bible describes heaven in that kind of detail?"

"Yeah, and Jesus even says that He has gone to heaven to prepare a place for those who have put their trust in Him for salvation."

"Like a house?"

"Exactly. In fact, the Bible calls it a mansion. I even heard one preacher say the word for *mansion* is more correctly interpreted as *estate*—a mansion with lots of land, in other words."

"Dude, you are blowing my mind." Both men laughed. Diesel was laser-focused on helping others know God the way he did, but he had not lost his sense of humor and enjoyed the lighthearted interaction.

The guards gave clear instructions to the men as they left the bus. They all knew they had to follow the instructions to a T or else their future opportunities to be part of an outside work team would be lost. Escaping was a deadly prospect, and the thought had not crossed any of their minds. The air was bitterly cold in the shade as they made their way to the makeshift work station the owner of the dairy farm had prepared. However, the sun still held enough heat to make the conditions comfortable enough to work.

The farmer was on hand to direct the men into two teams. The recent winter storm had damaged some fencing, and their task was to lug the logs that would be used to make the replacement fence up the hill to a small mill at the top. The gravel road had been washed out by the storm, and the tractors weren't able to safely traverse the large gully that almost split the road in two.

"Why did he build his mill at the top of a hill? Would it not have made more sense to put it at the bottom of the hill?" Charlie seemed to be asking a genuine question.

"I think it used to be at the bottom of the hill, Charlie. The tree line is way above the mill, so I'm guessing these logs were delivered before the storm and it's easier to use them than cut down new trees." Diesel was just speculating, but as with everything else, he spoke with the kind of conviction that made others think he was right or at least convinced he was right.

"Were you a farmer in a previous life?" Charlie chuckled as he made fun of Diesel. He thought the explanation was reasonable but didn't want him to know it.

Most of the logs were too big for one man to carry, and each of the four-man teams would carry one log at a time. It was overkill and inefficient, but they wanted to pace themselves to comfortably last the six hours of work that were ahead of them.

"C'mon, guys. Two of us can get a log each and do this work in half the time." Diesel had always prided himself on his strength, but he also wanted to work hard to prove himself to the guards in hopes of getting another chance at being part of a work team.

"Okay, smart-ass. If it's so easy, you can carry one by yourself."

"Yeah, Diesel. You think you're so strong. Put one on your shoulders and show us how it's done."

Charlie was intrigued to see what his cellmate would do, and he decided to sweeten the deal a little.

"Tell you what, Diesel. If you can carry the log up the hill by yourself, I'll give you my Mountain Dew I've been saving in the cell." Diesel thought about the offer for a moment. A carbonated drink is like contraband when you're locked up. He was surprised Charlie was willing to part with it. Maybe he felt like there was no real risk given the task he was betting against, but Diesel was not about to turn down the chance.

"You're on, man, but I pick the log." They were all fairly uniform in size, but there were some that looked less bulky and a little lighter than the others. None of them seemed manageable for one person.

"Whatever, dude, you're not going to be able to do it."

The logs were more than eight feet long and weighed at least 350 pounds each. The ground was flat for the first 30 yards and then had a 30-degree incline for more than 500 feet to get to the mill. Diesel selected the smallest log he could find and muttered to himself as the full weight of the log landed on his shoulders, *You can do this, Diesel. You're going to look like an idiot if you don't.*

By the time he made his way to the incline, the log felt like it weighed twice as much as when he first put it on his shoulders. *You can do this. You can get this log up this ridiculously large hill.* Each step whittled away his conviction as the men below taunted him. With his arms draped around the log, he stopped about a third of the way up the hill. He closed his eyes as he contemplated the humiliation he would feel if he put the log down. The pain was starting to burn in his shoulders, but he was more concerned about his legs that were already threatening to turn into jelly if he didn't stop.

He could feel the sun warming his back. He closed his eyes and soaked in the comfort it brought him in the moment. As he opened his eyes, he was caught off guard by the shadow that had formed on the ground in front of him. The log across his shoulders perfectly resembled how he expected his Savior looked as He bore the weight of the cross. It was his accusers' cruel prelude to their mode of execution—up the Via Dolorosa to Mount Calvary where He took upon Himself the sins of the world.

Sadness and joy swept over his finite emotions. He had never been more grateful to his Savior than at that moment. He closed his eyes and prayed to the King who had once bore so much more weight than he now had on his back.

"Lord, I would do anything for you. I don't care about a soda, but I ask you to give me the strength to carry this log to the top of the hill so I can experience in that small way some of what You did when You gave your life for me."

In that very moment, Diesel felt power surge through his limbs, and a supernatural force started pulling him toward the mill. His feet picked up pace as the men's taunts turned into astonishment. Faster and faster he moved until he was only 50 feet from the mill. He almost sprinted to the finish line. He could hear the men below cheer him on, but all he cared about was the sweet whisper in his heart: *Well done, good and faithful servant.*

Chapter 41

Joey

Mom and Dad stood before the doctor in disbelief as the latest prognosis brought with it their greatest fears. Mom needed to lash out at something, and the man sitting across the desk was her only option.

"You have given Joey radiation and chemo for more than a year, and you are telling me that the cancer has spread to his lymph nodes and chest? He has been nauseous nonstop, and his body has been falling apart from all the radiation. I can't accept that we just give up and take him home to die. I can't believe there is no more you can do. This can't all have been for nothing." She was beside herself with worry and grief. She looked at her husband, hoping he could make sense of her pain, hoping he could somehow make it all go away. Her eyes filled with tears as she realized he was as powerless as she was.

"We will continue to give Joey steroids to boost his immune system, but his body cannot take more radiation without causing irreparable damage. His intestines are already badly damaged, and he is no longer responding to the treatment. From here on, the best treatment is your continued prayers. If Joey is going to make it, he will do it by the grace of God alone."

Somehow, the doctor's words brought comfort to Dick. He had four sons whom he loved more than they would ever know. Even though he had been a strict disciplinarian, his boys never doubted his commitment to take care of them. He had been a lay minister for years, and his faith in God had not waned. Joey's cancer had tested that faith, which had weathered the storm so far. In a strange way, being thrown on the graces of God was the one place—maybe the only place—he could handle right now. He turned to his wife, held her face in his hands, and wiped away the tears flowing down her cheeks.

"Honey, it's not the time for grief. If God chooses to take our son, then we can grieve. I refuse to grieve until there is no more hope. The doctor just told us that we still have hope, and that hope is Jesus. I promise you, I will fight for our son until his last breath, but I need you to be strong, too. Can you do that?"

She looked him in the eye as if to examine his resolve, to make sure those words were not meant for the benefit of the doctor. When she was satisfied that he was speaking from his heart, she responded.

"We have three other boys the Lord has blessed us with. I am not sure I can have the same hope you have in Him right now, but I believe that you believe. I don't know if that is enough, but it is the best I can do right now."

"That will be enough."

They took Joey home from the hospital with a bag full of medicines and supplements. He was 14 now and had become accustomed to the cycle of nausea and the regimen of taking drugs. All he wanted was a chance at a normal life, a chance to play football again.

"Dad, I know the doc said I won't be having any more radiation and I just have to wait and see. But I am going to get better at some point, right?" Dick pulled the car over on the side of the road. He turned to face his son, and a boldness came over him that he didn't know he possessed.

"Son, I am not going to sugarcoat this for you. The doctor is not confident that you will make it, but he gave me the best news I could have asked for today. He told me that you were in God's hands now, and if I know anything, it is that our God is a God of miracles. He is the same yesterday, today, and forever. If He healed the lepers and the blind and deaf, He can heal you. I promise you that I will pray to God like I have never prayed before. I refuse to believe cancer is bigger than our God, and I refuse to accept that prayer won't make a difference. The doctors don't want you to get your hopes up, son, but I do. I want you to get your hopes up—hopes of getting well and playing football, hopes of getting married one day and living a full life." He almost choked up on the last thought. He squeezed his son's hand, and for a moment, all three felt the confidence that could only come from a force more powerful than their physical reality.

The days that followed saw Joey stabilize, but there was no discernible improvement. Dick could be heard pacing the floor all hours of the day, intermittently yelling at the devil and the sickness and then beseeching the favor of heaven. It did something on the inside of Joey, something that gave him the will to live as normally as he could, no matter how long he had left.

"Mom, now that I'm not having the radiation treatment, I don't feel nearly as nauseous as before. Can you call my school and ask if I can go back to school?"

"Sweetheart, you have been out of school for so long, I'm not sure it is a good idea to jump back in so close to the end of the school year. Your dad and I were thinking we would hold you back a grade if, I mean, when you get better."

"I know, Mom, but something inside me just needs to be around my friends again and feel normal for a while. I'm not going to try to catch up. I just want to forget about the cancer for a bit and act like I have a normal life." His words surprised her, and she intuitively knew he was right, even though she was concerned that his immune system was not ready for public exposure. As any mother would, she was afraid he might pick up a life-threatening illness at school. She fought back those fears with everything she could.

"Okay, I will call the school in the morning." She committed her son to the Lord and put a note on her chalkboard in the kitchen to call the school. In less than 12 hours, the arrangements were made.

For the first time in a very long time, Joey made the trek up the hill in his backyard to the ledge where he had spent so much time contemplating life. He was glad to have a chance to do something normal again. As his thoughts wandered, he found himself talking to the One he knew had all the answers. He had avoided this conversation for a very long time.

"I am so confused. I don't know why you would want me to die." He let the words linger in the air for a moment. As the thought hung around his consciousness, he searched his heart for an answer.

"Is it because of the bad things I did when I was seven? I told you many times that I was sorry. I don't know why I did those things. I didn't really want it to happen, and I don't know why I went back. I know I probably deserve to die for that. Please don't punish me this way, though. I am so tired of being sick. I just want to get well."

He thought about making a promise to his Creator that he would dedicate his life to the ministry—like his dad—if He would let him live. But deep down, he knew he could not serve a master who punished people the way he had suffered in his short life.

Joey didn't know that he wasn't alone on that ledge. The Creator, who fell under his accusations, had sent One to protect him. One who had been by his side from the moment he was conceived. One who had kept him alive when he was so close to death. One who had on so many occasions interrupted the plans of the devil to destroy his life. One who had stopped him from stepping off this very spot when all seemed lost and the darkness threatened to become too great. One whose commission entitled him to direct access to the face of the One his charge was now accusing. This One who had spent many lifetimes protecting countless innocents and defenseless children could be silent no more.

You possess no guilt for the harm that was done to you. You are beloved in the sight of our Master. The day will come for you to return to His domain, but it is not yet. Your illness is in no way your fault but rather the result of this broken and fallen world. I have vowed to be by your side until your dying breath. You are not alone, Image-Bearer. His proclamation charged the air with faith and gave the young man the steely resolve he needed to hope again.

The next morning, he rode in the truck with his dad, and they both reported to the principal's office. Having his dad with him felt weird, but so did everything since he had gotten sick. It felt like the first day of junior high school all over again. This time, however, he was the only kid having his first day, and everyone else looked like they had it all figured out. He would not admit it, but he was glad he was not alone.

"I bet this is what it feels like when you move to a new school in the middle of the year." His dad did not respond but hoped he wouldn't feel this way the whole time he was back. It was already May. He could have waited until August to return when school started again, but Joey doubted he would ever be well enough to come back. He desperately wanted to feel normal for a while.

"I hope they can get me back in my old classes."

"I'm sure they will, son."

He didn't have to wait long before he got the green light and a note to bring to the science lab where he would rejoin his class. His dad was not particularly affectionate, especially since Joey had taken his last growth spurt and they now stood at roughly the same height. Still, he grabbed his son and gave him a hug that lingered. Neither was in a hurry to let go. His dad grabbed his shoulders and looked him square in the eye. "I am proud of you, son, for not giving up. I am proud of how you continue to fight this sickness. I want you to know that I am right beside you in this fight. I believe in the power of prayer, and I believe God wants you well."

They embraced once more, and then Joey made his way down the hall to his class. A long-term sub had taken the place of his former teacher. Mr. Silva was from Brazil and a breath of fresh air in a normally dull class. He had grown up in a small rural village in the Amazon and took every opportunity to share stories of his former way of life. Providence ensured the timeliness of this day's tale.

"I know I have told you many stories from my homeland, but I want to tell you the story of the day that changed my life and set me on the path to becoming a teacher here in the US." All the students seemed to come to attention, which made Joey even more intrigued to hear what he had to say. He listened closely as Mr. Silva continued in his thick Portuguese accent.

"When I was just a young boy, we had missionaries from America come to our village. We believed in spiritual forces and in the power of the gods of our land. We had known them to be demanding and cruel. We always seemed to be making amends for some wrong we had unknowingly done, but these missionaries told us all about a different God—a God who was kind, forgiving, and merciful. A God who walked the earth as a man and went about healing the sick and casting out evil spirits. A God who had power over all other gods. We were amazed at their stories but found it hard to believe that a God like that existed. It seemed to be too good to be true, and we did not want to risk angering our gods by abandoning them for the God of the foreigners.

"One day while playing in our barn, my best friend and I were jumping off bales of hay. My friend fell on top of a pitch fork that was hidden under some hay. It pierced his body, causing life-threatening injuries. The missionaries had medical supplies but explained to his parents that he would die without more extensive medical attention. There were no medical facilities within 100 miles and no transportation, even if he could survive the trip. They told my friend's parents that without the intervention of their God, he would not make it through the night. They called the elders of our town to come to his bedside and told them once more about the good God who came to save mankind from bondage and loved to heal the sick. They laid hands on him and prayed for his healing. They prayed with such boldness that we all expected something supernatural to happen. His body was so pale, and there seemed to be almost no life left in him.

"The missionaries told everyone to go home and return in the morning. It was a long night for the whole village, and many were tempted to ask our former gods to intervene, but our elders would not allow it. When we came back the next day, my friend was not dead. His color had returned to his body, and he was able to sit up. It took a few weeks before he was able to get back to his normal life, but we all knew he had been rescued from death and that the God of the missionaries had the power to bring the dead to life. Many in the village put their trust in Jesus that day, as did I. I told my new God that if He would let me, I would tell the stories of His greatness back in the land of those missionaries. That is why I became a teacher, and that is why I am before you today teaching the truth of science and telling you stories of the God who created the very objects of our studies."

The class was riveted, but none more than Joey. Something resonated inside him. His paradigm about the reason for his illness began to shift. The testimony of this man who had come from the Amazon in Brazil to teach science at his school and who decided to tell that very story on Joey's first day back in class sparked into life a new possibility. *This can't be coincidence. It just can't be. God, if You want me to believe You will heal me, then I will, but I need help.*

Spring had melted away all vestiges of winter and was beckoning the summer heat that would soon make everyone wish for the cooler days of winter. As Joey sat in the backyard after school, wiping away the beads of sweat, he thought of the best way he could get God to confirm the message he believed he had just received. He considered the best way to ask for an indisputable sign, something that would be impossible except by the power of God.

"Lord, if there is frost on the ground tomorrow morning, I will know it was you speaking to me today, and I will believe I am healed like the boy in the story."

As simple as that, the matter was settled. A sense of peace came across him since he no longer had to struggle with his doubts. It would all be settled tomorrow morning by forces outside of his control.

Joey went to bed, exhausted from his first day back at school. It had taken more out of him than he had expected. The plan was to go back every other day until he felt well enough to go back full time. He had originally fought his mom on that plan but was now glad he didn't have to go back tomorrow.

The sun was already pouring through the curtains in his bedroom as his eyes opened to the new day. For a moment, he grappled to remember something he felt was important and that he should remember, and then it hit him. He jumped out of bed and ran downstairs and out the front door.

"No, no, no! I couldn't have missed it." He ran back in the house looking to unload his frustration.

"Mom! Mom! What time is it?"

"It's after 11:00."

"What?"

"What's the matter, Joey?"

"Why didn't you wake me up earlier?"

"Because you were fast asleep, and you need as much rest as possible if you are to have any chance of getting better." He knew her logic was sound, and she could not have known how his getting better was, in this instance, dependent on *not* sleeping in. He wanted to lash out at her, but he was more frustrated with himself for not setting an alarm to get up. He got control of his emotions and asked the question he had hoped to find the answer to firsthand. Now he could only hope to get a secondhand confirmation.

"Mom?"

"Yes."

"Did you notice if there was frost on the ground this morning?"

"Sweetheart, it's May. We don't get frost in May unless we have a late-season cold front come in, but the weather has been beautiful lately."

"So you were out this morning, and there was no frost?"

"No. I made breakfast and did some chores around the house and didn't go out until around 10:00."

"Is Dad around?"

"I think he's out in the shed working. Why?"

"I want to ask him if he saw a frost this morning." His mom shook her head and went back to work.

"Dad, are you in there?"

"Yes, son. Is everything okay?"

"Yes. I just have a question." Joey didn't wait for his dad to respond and launched into his investigation.

"Did you happen to notice if there was a frost outside this morning?"

"Funny you should ask, son. I always start my day reading my Bible and praying in the den before everyone else gets up. Then I get some work done inside, and the sun is usually well up before I ever venture out." He paused, like he was confused by his own actions.

"But this morning, I decided to go for a walk while I was praying. I was pleasantly surprised by how cold the air was, and I noticed that the whole yard was glistening white. I was really surprised to see a frost this late in the spring, especially since it has been so warm lately. It disappeared as soon as the sun came up. Thirty minutes later and I would have missed it. Why do you ask?" Joey had a look of astonishment on his face that his dad had missed while he was relaying the events of the morning.

"Are you okay, Joey?"

"Yeah, Dad," Joey replied with a smile on his face. "Never better." His dad wanted to ask more, but something inside told him to hold off.

"Let me know if you need anything, son."

"Sure, Dad. I think I'm going to go for a walk."

Joey skipped up the trail to his so-called prayer ledge with a strength that had been absent for a long while. The scene before him was breathtaking. He never got tired of admiring the handiwork of his Creator, but for the last seven years, he couldn't understand how the Creator of such beauty could also allow the darkness in his life. Like the morning sun melting a heavy frost, hope had finally melted away the coldness of his fears.

"Thank You for the sign, Lord. Thank You for hearing my prayer. I don't understand Your ways at all, and I don't know if You are still mad at me for all the things I have done. But I believe you have given me a sign that I am healed. Thank You for giving me my life back."

Joey sat silently before creation and its Creator for another hour. Tears of joy from being released from his death sentence flowed down his face, and each one was counted and appreciated by the One who had granted this miracle.

Chapter 42

Detective Smith

It had been months since the encounter with Cantrell, but Detective Smith couldn't find a way to shake Scott's words from his thinking. They had entered deep into his subconscious and emerged without warning, unsettling him at the most inconvenient times.

"Detective Smith, are you listening to me?"

"Sorry, Pete, I was miles away."

"I just want to confirm that you are absolutely sure I will get into the academy. You know, before I start getting you your, uh, you know."

"Yeah, of course, Pete. I just need a little time."

"Well, I don't mind helping you out as long as I know I don't have to be a pharm tech for the rest of my life. I want to do something meaningful with my life and bring some value, like you."

"I do know, and that's why I will work to make sure you get your chance." Once again, the irony of the nature of a conversation like this wasn't lost on him. Here he was, bribing a pharmacy tech to give him illegal drugs to supply his habit under the guise of helping him qualify for a job in law enforcement.

"I just need time to work my contact in the department and wait for the right opportunity to drop your name. If I ask when they have no openings, it will be shot down, but if I wait until they ask me, you will be a shoo-in."

"I understand, man. I can wait as long as I know there is a light at the end of the tunnel."

"Sure. When will you have my order ready?"

"Order?"

"My, er, prescription?"

"Oh yeah. Sorry. I have it in the drawer under Rogers."

"Why Rogers?"

"As in Mr. Rogers."

"Why Mr. Rogers?"

"No reason, it was the first name that came to my mind." Detective Smith could see why Pete's previous interviews with the various police departments didn't yield a positive result.

"Well, I guess it doesn't matter what name you use as long as it's not mine."

Pete handed him the drugs and in doing so broke at least five laws. Detective Smith's actions left him vulnerable to the limited intelligence of his accomplice. There was now a paper trail that could be traced if someone ever put the pieces together. He knew he was crossing a criminal line and putting his own career and freedom in jeopardy.

As he stared at the medicine bottle on his kitchen table, he debated how much of the drug he could take and still function undetected. *Well, Smithy, you are reaching a new high in your career. You're using your abilities as a detective to calculate how to become a functioning drug addict. Scott was right. You are a loser.*

His self-esteem hit a new low, and in the midst of his self-loathing, he overshot his first dosage. He couldn't drive in a straight line and spent the morning looking for an excuse to stay out of Kerrigan's sight. His colleagues could see the strange look on his face and chose to seek an alternative reason rather than the obvious explanation.

"What's up, Smithy" Delany Frances had trained under his guidance and looked up to him as a cop and role model.

"Nothing."

"You look like you're out of it. Is everything okay?"

"I told you, nothing!" He knew his comment would end the conversation, but in his intoxicated state, he couldn't calculate the damage he would inflict on a friendship he valued. Officer Frances looked shocked and quickly turned and walked out of the room.

Later that morning, it was Officer Cantrell's turn to see the change in his colleague.

"Dude, have you been taking one steroid too many lately?"

"What the heck, man? Can't a guy get some peace?"

"You're just looking a little rough, Smithy. No need to bite my head off." The drugs had removed his ability to process thoughts and, therefore, the consequences of his actions.

"Just give me some space, man. I'm just a little out of it."

"Have you been drinking?"

"No. Nothing like that. I just need to get some fresh air." He picked himself up out of his chair and stumbled toward the door, crashing into the edge of his desk on the way out. It took him several seconds to realize he had hit something, and the pain never registered. Cantrell followed him.

"Okay, Smithy, we're getting out of here." He grabbed Smith's arm and tried to straighten up his 300-pound frame as they started to draw attention from the officers across the hall. Cantrell couldn't help letting his thoughts be known while focusing on navigating the most obscure route to the parking lot.

"I don't know what you took, but you need to get out of here before Kerrigan sees you and sends you for a tox screen." Smith offered no immediate response. Cantrell led him out the back door and helped him into his car.

"What are you doing, Cantrell?" Detective Smith was stirred by the change of environment.

"I'm saving your skin."

"I don't know what you're talking about." He was talking more slowly and starting to slur. "I'm fine, just fine. There is nothin', nothin'." His voice trailed off, and he closed his eyes as he slumped into the passenger seat.

"I know you haven't been doing well lately, but this is career suicide, man." Cantrell didn't expect a response and knew there would probably be no recollection of his intervention.

When they arrived at Smith's apartment building, Cantrell found Smith's keys attached to his belt. He left him in the car while he made sure his apartment was clear before trying to maneuver the man-mountain into his home. "You are a neat freak, Smithy, that is for sure." Everything was in its place, and the furniture looked like it had just been vacuumed. The kitchen was off to the side of the living room, and a half wall filled with cabinets separated the two rooms. Cantrell caught a glimpse of an orange prescription bottle on the counter and assumed it was the culprit.

"'John Rogers'? Why do you have a prescription for John Rogers?" Cantrell speculated out loud. At that moment, Detective Smith fell against the door.

"What are you doing in my house?" Smith was out of it, but Cantrell was glad he didn't have to try to carry him into the apartment.

"What are these, Smithy? The prescription says they are for a John Rogers."

"I don't know what you're talking about. They're mine." Cantrell had smelled a rat long ago, and he wasn't sure he wanted to find out the truth while his friend was not in control.

"Look, man, you need to go to bed and sleep this off and not come back to work until you have your story straight." He made sure Smith was sitting on the couch and left without another word being said. Smith's text message later that evening offered an explanation.

"Feeling better. The pharmacy gave me the wrong prescription by mistake." Cantrell's suspicion had been aroused, and despite the explanation, he couldn't shake the horrible feeling in his gut that his friend had a serious problem.

The figure in the shadows smiled as he watched the drama he had set in motion unfold as planned. He made a promise to his fallen apprentice. "Soon. Soon it will all be over."

Chapter 43

Scott

He couldn't get the incident with Stu out of his head. In an extremely rare optimistic moment, Scott tried to convince himself that his inability to commit suicide was providential. Somehow and for some reason, which he could not begin to fathom, he was being kept alive. *You're absurd. You're an idiot. That is a dumb fantasy. You are a piece of crap, and the only reason you're alive is because you suck at killing yourself, just like everything else."*

He stared at the last of his drugs. He owed his supplier 10 grand, but he didn't care anymore. *What's the worst they could do? Kill me? That's a laugh. Hopefully, they'll be better at it than I am.* As he waited for the drugs to take effect, he couldn't help but lament the train wreck his life had become. Every couch and every relationship had been exhausted. Even Jackson had told him he couldn't help him anymore. He had taken advantage of him one time too many, and his lifelong friend's final conversation haunted him.

"Scott, I can't believe you have started selling drugs. You promised me, man. You gave me your word that no matter how bad things got, you would never go that low. Why didn't you come to me? I would have done whatever was necessary to make sure you didn't go down that road. You don't understand, man, I promised Emily I would end our friendship if you did this. I agreed because I was sure it would never happen." Jackson paused and looked into his friend's eyes. All he saw was a lifeless stare. "You have to leave, man. You're not the friend I once knew, and I can't allow you to drag other people into this type of life. I will always love you, man, but we are done."

For the first time in his life, Jackson closed the door in his face. The effects of the loss of that friendship couldn't have been foreseen by either man. Scott lost the last vestiges of his dignity and became animalistic in his approach to life. He didn't care about anyone or anything except getting high. With the last of the drugs in his system, he took refuge in the mindlessness of his temporary savior. *If only I could stay high forever.*

He passed out for several hours before he regained consciousness. The brutal reality of having no more drugs set in. An unhinged drug addict with nothing to lose is one of the most dangerous creatures on the planet.

He was now reduced to living on the street under a bright blue tarp draped over a few boxes that created enough room to sleep and stay out of the rain. A dirty blanket separated him from the concrete, but the insects didn't mind sharing the space with their new neighbor. What little food he ate came from a nearby restaurant dumpster, and he smelled just like the discarded, rotting food he rummaged through to survive. He knew his only option was to steal to get another fix.

For the next two weeks, Scott observed as people failed to lock their car doors. He saw them leave their possessions unattended. People in general were too trusting, but in the commercial district of the city, they were especially easy prey, and Scott took full advantage. Purses, laptops, clothes, briefcases, personal effects of all kinds, jewelry, and a host of other things that were of no marketable value were easy pickings. The items he couldn't sell or trade for drugs he cast into the same dumpster that fed him.

It didn't take the police long to find the remains of the stolen items, and Scott noticed an increase in the presence of law enforcement in the area. One detective in particular caught his attention.

"Officer Smith?"

"Detective Smith!" His head was pounding, and he was in desperate need of a fix of his own, but he was waiting until he was off duty. The last thing he wanted to do was have a chat with a hobo. "What do you want?"

"Don't you remember me?" Scott had a full beard that was mostly gray, and he had lost some weight, but his large frame was still unmistakable. Detective Smith racked his brain for a minute to remember where he knew him from.

"You are that idiot who was selling drugs on the other side of town. You claimed you knew me from my accident." He didn't want to give Scott any rope to string out this conversation any more.

"I may be an idiot, but my offer still stands."

"What offer?"

"C'mon now, we both know I rattled your cage last time we talked."

"If you believe that, then you are more of an idiot than I thought."

"I told you back then how I knew your darkest struggles. I offered you the scoop on my uncanny ability to read your innermost thoughts."

"And I told you it was a bunch of bull."

The figure in the shadows derived great pleasure from watching two of his slaves taunt each other. He knew that hope is the glue that keeps people alive, and his specialty was destroying that hope. Now he was reveling in the hopeless lives of two of his masterpieces. One was a more complete work, but the other wasn't far behind. He couldn't hide his glee, nor did he want to. He sneered at his foe who stood facing him on the other side of the men. His face was full of determination, but it was also etched with anguish since the soul he sought to rescue was closer than ever to damnation. The tension between these age-old enemies was broken by the obnoxious nature and control of the provocateur.

"You are the one full of bull, Detective. You are the one who refuses to face reality. You are a sad excuse for a human being who needs others to give you self-worth. You are the one who hides his addiction so he can keep up the facade of approval. I can see it in your eyes that you are using more than the last time we met. Have you started taking big-boy drugs yet?"

"Shut your mouth, bum, or I will shut it for you."

"Go ahead and try. You can't hurt me. Pull out your gun and shoot me. You would be doing me a favor. I give you permission to do it. Go on! Do it!" Scott stared right into the detective's eyes and didn't flinch. He could see him reach for his gun, and still he didn't flinch. His willingness to die unnerved Detective Smith, who holstered his gun.

"You are not worth the bullet. Go ahead and kill yourself, 'cause I'm not going to do your dirty work for you. You're not the only one who can read people. You want to die, and you want me to pull the trigger so you can get some sick pleasure by sucking me into your train wreck of a life, but you're not going to do it." A whisper from the shadows fueled the next words out of his mouth.

"I bet you even tried to do it but failed at that, too, didn't you?" Scott was the one on the back foot now. He didn't have the desire to continue this yelling match. He looked at his opponent and thought about the one thing that might inflict the most harm. It was his turn to receive inspiration from the shadows. He reached into his pocket and pulled out a small baggie with a quarter ounce of heroin.

"Here it is, cowboy. The real stuff. This is what you've been craving. Forget that prescription crap you've been binging on." He threw the baggie at him. "You can arrest me, or you can take the drugs for yourself."

Detective Smith stared at him with more contempt than he had for any other soul alive. He hated him more than the man who abused him when he was younger. He hated him more than every child abuser he had ever interrogated. He hated him more than the monster who had cut his own son into pieces. Still, he reached for the drugs. Once they were in his hand, he felt powerless to give them back. At that moment, he hated only one person more than the lowlife standing in front of him. Himself.

Chapter 44

Detective Smith

Detective Smith sat in his apartment staring at the plastic baggie full of heroin. He had clocked out early and gone home for the day. It felt like his entire mistake-ridden life had been exposed by a drug-dealing bum, and he couldn't bear to look his colleagues in the eye. He couldn't hide anymore. It felt like every move he made was on display for the world to see. All people had to do was take a moment to look at him and they would know he was a fraud. *Just open the bag and take the drugs. Scott's right. What's the point in delaying the inevitable?*

He continued to stare at the bag. He pulled his chair up to the edge of the table where the drugs lay. He pulled the top of the bag open and stuck his nose in, inhaling the heroin-laced air. His subconscious started to play tricks on him, making him feel like the drug had already entered his system. He licked his finger and was about to stick it in the bag and ingest whatever stuck to it when the ring of his phone caused him to jump.

"What the heck? Hello. Smith here."

"You are needed at Ryan's Pharmacy on Cross Street. They've had a break-in, and we need an officer over there to take photos."

"I'm off duty. Can't someone else go?"

"Sorry, Smith. You're the only one nearby with a camera."

He looked at the bag and reluctantly sealed the top. "Send the address to my phone. Tell them I'll be there in fifteen minutes."

"You got it, Smith."

When he arrived, the pharmacy was a mess. It was a snatch-and-grab job, and judging by the mess and the valuable drugs still lying on the storage room floor, the thieves didn't know what they were looking for.

As Smith started taking photos of the crime scene, he noticed several hundred pills of his pain reliever of choice scattered across the floor. Thoughts flashed through his mind that should have raised massive red flags in his self-preservation mechanism. However, his recent interaction with Scott had recalibrated his conscience and with it his ability to follow any normal self-preservation protocol. There were just a couple of pharmacy techs between him and several months' worth of the prescription he could no longer get in legitimate ways.

"Clear the scene, please."

"What do you mean, Detective?"

"I mean you have to clear the scene. This is a crime scene, not a circus." The two techs looked at each other and tried to process the mental image of a circus and how their presence in the room provoked that thought.

"I need to have clear pictures of the whole room, and I don't want both of you showing up in the evidence." They shrugged their shoulders and left the room.

He paused for a moment to contemplate his next action. He was hoping for something within him to jump out and stop him, but that never happened. Instead, the familiar whisper inside his head was compelling him to pick up as much as he could without making it obvious that he had just raided a crime scene. He reached down and grabbed a handful of pill sheets and then another and another. He left around half of the medication on the floor. He figured that if anyone remembered seeing those drugs, the remnant would be sufficient not to raise any suspicion that some of the drugs had been taken. He stuffed them inside his camera bag.

He gathered all the remaining physical evidence and took the usual array of photos. He calmly completed his review of the scene and cleared the pharmacy to open for business. He was surprised by his lack of emotion. Over a decade of his career and a potential jail sentence were on the line, yet he didn't feel an ounce of fear or remorse. As he made his way back to his apartment, the absence of any strong emotion evoked a startling realization.

What the heck is wrong with me?

You're okay, said a soothing voice in his head. The nature of the words that drifted into his conscience surprised him. The voice was not new. It was the same voice he had followed for the last several years, but something was different.

The figure in the shadows continued to whisper calming words to his questioning soul. He had escalated his plan of destruction, but he needed his pawn to gain composure to make sure he didn't reach out for help.

The words had their desired effect, and Smith stopped his self-diagnosis. He swallowed several of his newly acquired pills and waited for the effects to kick in. As he did, he felt the urge to do something familiar, something routine, and he grabbed his gym bag. His regimen required that he take a powerful mixture of steroids and other supplements within an hour of his workout. The muscle-building, fat-burning concoction was in his glove box, and without thinking, he mixed it with his bottle of water and drank it down in just a few gulps. There was no way he could have known the lethal combination he had just ingested. It only took a few minutes of driving before the drugs started to react violently within his body.

What on earth! He reached for his phone to call Cantrell, but he couldn't remember the code to unlock the screen.

Oh no! Oh no! He struggled to cling to reality as his truck stopped at the next red light. He tried to roll down the window but couldn't remember which control operated it.

"Help me, please!" His voice was losing strength as his futile attempts to call for help couldn't be heard above the noise of the traffic. He slumped over the steering wheel, his weight shifting to his left side as he lost consciousness. His foot, which was already on the brake, was wedged in place, and the car stayed in its spot despite being in gear.

When the light turned green, two older ladies in their 1984 Cadillac Seville waited patiently for the truck in front of them to move. The light turned red, and they finally honked to get the driver's attention. They assumed he had heard it, and they waited for the next change of light. By this time, there were several cars in line whose drivers weren't as patient as the older ladies. After the light turned green and then red a second time, the passenger in the Cadillac opened the door and got out to check on the driver of the truck. She let out a screech when she found the overly muscular man slumped over the wheel of his car. He didn't appear to be breathing.

The ambulance was on the scene in minutes, but hopes were slim after the valiant efforts by the EMTs to save Detective Smith's life when he was still in the car.

"He's completely unresponsive, and I can't find a pulse."

"We need to get him into the ambulance immediately, or any chance he might have will be gone." They turned off the car's engine and together, with a Good Samaritan from one of the cars stuck behind Detective Smith's truck, pulled him out and onto a stretcher.

"His pupils are dilated, and his lips and fingertips are turning blue. He most likely has overdosed on something."

"Was anyone with him in the truck? Does anyone know what he took?"

"No, but I'll check and see if there's anything in the truck that might tell us what he's on." In the ambulance, they hooked up the respirator and the AED and started CPR.

"I grabbed his gym bag and a camera bag that were in the back seat. That's all he had."

"The doc is gonna want to know what he took." They found some of the steroids and fat burners in the gym bag. Then they found the pain killers.

"Wow! He must have a couple hundred of these pills."

"What are they?"

"There're various quantities of Oxycontin, but what is he doing with so many? There's no way he got these with a prescription."

"That must be the cause of his overdose."

"It's not our responsibility to work out where he got all those pills. We can give them to the local PD when we get to the hospital, and they can follow up with this guy—if he makes it."

They rushed him to the ER and shared their findings with the receiving doctor. He ordered his stomach pumped. His body had shut down, but the quick thinking of the EMTs combined with the machines in the ambulance had kept him alive. They were about to find out if he had enough life left in him to pull through. The ventilator was breathing for him since his body was unable to do even the most basic functions by itself.

His body looked like a lifeless form. The beeps of the machines and the furious attention of the hospital staff desperately trying to keep him alive all seemed surreal.

How am I seeing this? Am I dying? Can anyone hear me? Smith felt like he was hovering above, looking down at his own body. Fear raced through the core of his being. He wasn't ready to meet his Maker. He was afraid of his destination. In the melee below, there were two static figures intermittently staring at his body and then at each other. One seemed to emanate darkness, the other light. The dark one looked stoic and unmoved, while the other was deeply moved as He watched the scene unfold. Just about the time Smith saw himself flatline and the team grab the crash cart, he cried out for help.

Please, God. Don't let me die!

Hearing his prayer, the figure who demonstrated genuine concern for his condition reached out his hand and touched Smith's chest. A light flashed and flowed into the dying man's body. It happened simultaneously with the crash cart, so it was hard to distinguish what had caused it. Smith continued to watch from outside his body as his heart started beating again. He breathed a sigh of relief along with a second prayer.

Please, God. Let me live.

Chapter 45

Diesel

The two men sat in the cell after dark. Chapel was the following morning, and Diesel liked to prepare his cellmate for the weekly service.

"Charlie?"

"Yeah, Diesel."

"You know Jesus loves you, right?"

"I know you think He does."

"Well, that's also true, but why do you think Jesus would give up His life for you if He didn't love you?"

"He didn't die for scum like me; He died for good people."

"The Bible says He took upon Himself the sins of the whole world—the good, the bad, and the ugly." Diesel smirked at his reference and launched back into his pre-chapel message.

"The Bible tells us that we all have sinned. There is no one who is good, Charlie. Not even one. All you have to do is trust in Him and you can have complete confidence in your salvation."

"No, man, I just can't believe there's a chance of heaven for the likes of me. Not with all the stupid crap I've done. No man, I'm a lost cause."

"I don't believe you believe that, Charlie. Why do you even come to chapel if that's the case?"

"Well, there's nothing better to do."

"You might fool others, but you don't fool me."

"In all honesty, Diesel, I really don't see how Jesus would die for me. I can believe He would die for you because you do so much for Him."

"That's funny, man. I've told you some of my stories, and you still think I'm somehow worthy of His love and you are not? You believe I've earned my salvation? No, dude. I'm so far from that it's not even funny." Charlie wanted to get out of Diesel's spotlight and looked for an opportunity to redirect the conversation.

"Tell me some more of those stories, Diesel, the not-so-good days. Didn't you say you were married before? What happened to your wife?"

"Which one? I was married three times, and I messed them all up. You think a guy would get better with practice," Diesel said with a laugh.

"I guess the one you were married to the longest."

"I loved that woman, but it was a selfish love, and we were both a little crazy. She put up with my nonsense for a long time, but I finally pushed her over the edge."

"How so?"

"I had been off drugs for a few years, and her worst fear was that I would go back on them. I was in a car accident where an old lady T-boned my car and messed me up pretty bad. I was very careful to avoid addictive pain medication, but it was unbearable, and eventually I started taking something for the pain. Well, it didn't take long before my addiction was in full control again, and I was losing the ability to hide it from others. They caught on at work and were trying to help me, but it was too little too late. My wife put two and two together and knew I was back on drugs again. She lost it. I don't blame her. I think Mother Teresa would have lost it with me, too."

"What did she do?"

"We were cleaning up after dinner when she confronted me, and I admitted to her that I was using again. Something snapped in her. She grabbed a steak knife in the sink and stabbed me right in the abdomen all the way to the handle of the blade."

"What the heck?"

"I take full responsibility for her actions. I was brutal to live with, and it was the straw that broke the camel's back. She literally just snapped."

"Did they have to operate?"

"I told you I was a different person back then. I just went into my bedroom and expected to pass out and die. I refused to go to the doctor because

I was such a jerk. I got sick and had a fever for about a week, and then I
slowly got better. It's a miracle she didn't hit something inside my body that
would have killed me, but after two weeks, I was back at work."

"You're crazy, man. Did you guys get back together after that?"

"I wasn't a healthy person to be with, and she wasn't in a great place
either. We both realized we were toxic for each other, but she had the courage
to take action, and we went our separate ways."

"Did you stay off drugs then?"

"For a while, but I had so many issues that it was just a matter of time
before I was back using. I threw away a great career, financial success, family,
and friends. Basically, everything good in my life was sacrificed for drugs."

"All that from a car accident?"

"Charlie, I have lived with one form of pain or another for most of my
life. I have broken about a hundred things in my body, and I have had to
overcome cancer and all the damage it did to my system. Drugs become a
coping mechanism when you live with pain. When you use them as much as
I did, the body builds up an immunity, and you have to keep taking higher
dosages or get different drugs to cope with the pain. For me, it was only a
matter of time before the doc's solution didn't adequately solve the problem,
and I succumbed to the temptation to self-medicate."

"How did you keep doing your job and hide it from your wife so long?"

"You promise yourself you will be responsible. You only need a small
amount of the drug to get through the day. The drug doesn't just take away
your pain; it makes you feel better about yourself and life—the difference
between the times you have the drug in your system and when you don't start
to create a whole new problem. At that point, it's no longer about coping with
physical pain but coping with the pain of having to deal with the real world
when contentment was just a pill away. Then you just want to be high all
the time, and you take risks that you should never take. I would often drive
others in the car when I was high. It impairs all your decision-making, and I
promise you, I became one of the most selfish men to ever walk the planet."

"That is hard to believe knowing you now."

"I am a new man in Christ. Old things have passed away, and He has
given me a new heart. The fact that you have a hard time believing me just

goes to show how thoroughly the gospel works. I wish you would believe for yourself, Charlie. I really want you to know the kind of peace I've found through Jesus."

"I told you before, man, I am beyond saving."

"That's bull, Charlie, and you know it. You know what a horrible person I was and many of the horrible things I did. I broke my mother's heart. I put my father into an early grave. I tormented three wives and drove away every friend I ever had. I wasted every talent God gave me, and then I threw away my freedom by becoming a low-life druggie who would do anything to get my selfish needs met. How are you any worse than me, Charlie? The foundations of hell shook when I came into the Kingdom of God." Diesel broke into a smile. The tension in the room relaxed, and he leaned over the top bunk and looked down at his cellmate with nothing but love.

"My friend, Jesus gives you and me the incredible freedom to choose or reject Him. Don't let your rejection be based on a lie from the pit of hell. If you don't want Jesus, then He will honor your decision. But if the reason you're not accepting His forgiveness is because you think your sin is too bad, then you're greatly misunderstanding the immensity of the work of the cross. Hell itself couldn't slow down the work of the cross. Our combined sins would barely even register on the scale if we could measure the magnitude and power of the resurrection's ability to forgive the whole world of all their sins."

Charlie had no words. Once more, Diesel knew it was time to let the words that had already been spoken go about the business for which they had been shared.

Chapter 46

Detective Smith

Kerrigan stared at his protégé in the chair in front of him. He was heavy with the burden of the loss of the man he was planning to take over the unit, but more than that, he was saddened by the loss of someone he cared about.

"I don't know what to say, Smithy." Detective Smith was looking at the ground, and Kerrigan hoped it was because he was ashamed of what he had done. But the truth was, he didn't really know the man in front of him, even though he had worked with him for more than five years.

"I messed up, Captain, and I deserve whatever consequences are coming to me."

"The consequence for what you did is prison time. You realize that, Smithy?"

"Yes, Captain."

"What were you thinking, man?"

"I don't want to make excuses."

"Well, right about now, an excuse sure would help a whole lot."

"It's hard to explain, Captain."

"Try me."

Detective Smith sighed and his shoulders slumped as he prepared to expose his secret. "I've been suffering from depression or PTSD or something, Captain. I was too proud to get help. All the years of being a child abuse investigator broke me. Case after case after case of pure evil. When I joined your unit, I thought I would find some balance to my misery, that I would finally be able to stop evil before it happened. It worked for a while, but once I realized the old pain wasn't going away, it just seemed to get worse and worse. Alcohol worked for a while, and then the voices in my head just kept getting louder and louder. Being drunk didn't work any longer. I needed something to escape, something to help me cope, help me get up every day and still try to bring peace and order to our town while the whole time there was anarchy and chaos inside of me."

For the first time, Kerrigan could see the torment his number two was going through. His heart sank. "I wish you would have told me sooner, Smithy. Once the doctor filed his report on the drugs in your gym bag, my hands were tied."

Detective Smith had no fight left in him. "I understand, Captain. You gotta do what you gotta do. I understand. I'm sorry I put you in that position, and I don't blame you for sending me to prison." Those words were more than the veteran captain could take. He cared for all his men, but he had an unusual affection for the man in front of him. He was more like a son than anything else. Tears rolled down his cheeks.

"I pulled some strings. This was a crime of opportunity and not a premeditated act. The hard and often deadly life of a cop behind bars shouldn't be miscalculated. It should be reserved for those who really deserve it. I believe you're sorry for what you did, Smithy, and in part, I hold myself and the department responsible for not seeing the signs and offering help. I managed to keep you out of prison."

Detective Smith stared at him in disbelief. "I'm not going to do time for this?"

"No, but I couldn't save your job. I have to let you go. You won't ever be able to get another job as a cop or any other government job. This will follow you wherever you go." Kerrigan moved around to sit on the front edge of his desk, hoping the sincerity of his next statement could be felt. "Smithy, I believed in you, and I still do. One mistake does not define a man. You are a good guy and an outstanding cop, but now you have a hard road ahead. You won't have your team around you when you need them the most. You have to find a new path. You have to find something that will give you meaning, and you have to get help. I have two things to give you. Here is the contact info of the local Narcotics Anonymous group. I know that seems weird, but it will help. The other one is the number for a shrink I know who has helped me in the past. He's an ex-cop and understands what you're going through. Here is his card. I've already arranged for him to bill me personally for any session you have. Promise me, Smithy, that you will go see him. He can help you get through this."

Detective Smith was broken. He had expected to be put in an orange jumpsuit and hauled off in the back of a cruiser by a couple of the men he had trained. He would have said anything to get out of the office and not have to deal with the emotions that were starting to overwhelm him.

"I promise, Captain. I will get help."

As he left the office that day, he had sincere remorse. When he got home, he even flushed the drugs he got from Scott down the toilet. But in the days that followed, as he sat alone in his apartment trying to find the courage to call the name on the card, he was visited all too often by the figure in the shadows. The voices grew louder. Long gone were the promises of significance, of vengeance. The reel playing in his mind only consisted of sounds of self-loathing. *Failure, fool, idiot, scum, waste of space, addict, abuser, manipulator, taker, useless, loser.* Over and over as if on an endless loop, the voices never stopped. Darkness moved into his apartment, and the chain of events that had led to his dismissal and the subsequent shame that kept him locked up in his apartment prevented the One who wanted to help from breaking through the thick blanket of evil that shrouded him.

Smith was looking for a way to self-destruct, and he saw his opportunity a couple of weeks after he was fired. A letter from the Human Resources Department arrived. He almost didn't open it, but something prompted him to look at it. It was a statement that read this: "$79,247.51." It was the liquidated value of his retirement. The accompanying letter said he had the option to leave it in the retirement fund and draw a pension since he had more than 10 years of service. All he could see was a way to end the voices that were tormenting him. The only way he knew. The only way that ever worked. To find oblivion once more.

Chapter 47

Joey

"Sorry, Doctor, it sounded like you were saying that the cancer was all gone."

"That is exactly what I said."

"Last time we were here, you told me my son was going to die, that the cancer had spread to his lymph nodes and his chest and that you were sending him home to die."

"Actually, I said we were putting him in the hands of God and that He would decide the outcome, and it looks like your prayers worked." It was a strange response to get from a doctor, a man who dedicated his life to healing people through scientific knowledge, but it was no less sweet to the mom and dad who had endured two years of the worst type of fears any parent could face.

"Is he in the clear? Is the cancer gone for good?"

"The doctor in me has to tell you that we define Joey's state as being in remission and that medically he is still of much higher statistical likelihood of the cancer returning for the next five years. However, I have no medical explanation for the reversal of a cancer's progression at the point Joey was at, let alone the apparent complete disappearance of it from his body. So the believer in me is compelled to tell you to rejoice in his healing and take each day as a gift from God."

Joey spent the summer building his strength, and by August, he was training with the junior high football team. The steroids from his cancer treatment had prematurely accelerated puberty and muscle growth. At 15, he was the size of a fully grown man and weighed more than

200 pounds. By the time the season began, his reputation would precede him, and opposing coaches would insist that Joey produce his birth certificate before they would allow him to play. He was the not-so-secret weapon that propelled an average team to regional success. For a season, life seemed to have corrected course and offered Joey hope for the future he always dreamed of.

However, Joey couldn't shake the thoughts that once had carried him to the brink of stepping off the ledge when he was only nine years old. In a weird way, the battle with cancer had given him a reason to live, a reason to fight, and therefore, a reason not to think so much about his abuse. The thoughts of the sickness being a punishment initially vanished, but what if that actually was the cause, and life would be a never-ending process of payback for the price of his sins?

These thoughts weighed on his mind as he made the trek back up the mountain trail from his backyard. He couldn't shake his doubts and concerns that grew with every passing step. He approached the place that once was his retreat and then his confessional. Now it was where he deposited his bitterness toward God and the world. He stood on the ledge, and as a man would address his equal, he decided to address the deity that handled his happiness with such carelessness, or was it disdain?

"Am I just something for You to torment, to use up and throw away? Is my life worth so little that You play games to see how far You can push me without killing me?" He searched his soul, hoping for the God he was accusing to defend Himself, but there was no response or at least none he could hear given his current state of heart.

"I refuse to be a slave to someone who gets a kick out of the misery of others. I don't care that You have unlimited power. I refuse to bow down to You or do what You say. I am my own man, and from now on, I will take care of myself." His demeanor was defiant, but his heart and mind were in conflict. He deeply desired to make things right with his Creator. In his heart, he longed to hear God tell him it was all a cosmic mistake and He loved him and never intended for him to suffer as he had, that He did not blame him for the things that happened when he was just a young boy, and that his sickness had no connection with that whatsoever. But his mind was relentless in presenting and representing the case of his guilt, the cause-and-effect scenario that kept him on course for destruction.

Lashing out was the only way he could get relief, and the accuser knew it. So did the One who had watched out for him since birth, held back by the laws of cause and effect that had to be obeyed. Intervention was impossible at this juncture, and it would only be preservation until the time was right.

Fall turned to winter, and although the weather turned colder, Joey's anger did not. He refused to go to church and lashed out at any God-related comment. He was bigger than his dad now, and though he did not relish a potential battle with the man who had established the law of his house with a firm hand, he was no longer afraid of a face-off with him. In more ways than one, his dad was the very target of his anger. One Sunday morning, Joey's refusal to once again attend church was the start of a heated discussion. "You can't tell me what to do anymore."

"What? Of course I can tell you what to do. I am your father, and you still live under my roof." Joey snapped at what seemed like the threat of losing his home. He couldn't see past his anger and was in no mood for debate.

"Then I'll make it easy for you. I am done being part of this family, and I am done being your son. I can take care of myself." There were so many ridiculous elements to Joey's statement that his dad didn't know what to expose first. Something on the inside told him to try for his heart.

"I don't understand what has gotten into you, son. Your mom and I love you dearly and only want what is best for you. Since the cancer went away and you started playing football again, we thought you were finding your place, but you seem so angry at everything and everyone. We are worried about you, son."

Just like he had done with his heavenly Father, he tried to find a place in his heart to back down and say he was sorry, but wave after wave of unreasonable thoughts flushed through his system in a relentless torrent of teenage emotions. He could only stem the tide for a moment before it burst through his momentary conflict and unleashed again on his unsuspecting opponent.

"You just want me to be like you, to line up and do all the things the church tells you to do. It's all about appearances and making people think everything is okay. Well, it is not okay, and I am done pretending!"

His mom had heard the shouting match from the kitchen and walked into the living room. "What's wrong, Joey? Why are you and your dad fighting?" Her appeal to Joey knocked his dad off guard. He felt like she was defending Joey. He knew she was not, but his hesitation opened the door for Joey to take advantage of the situation. He knew how to push his dad's buttons, and he was too deep into his tirade to even care to hold back.

"I'm done with your rules. I'm done playing your games. I'm done presenting the perfect image to the world. You and Mom are so hypocritical. You care more about what others think than about your own son. You tell me that I have to shape up because you provide for me. What kind of person holds that over someone else's head? Are you going to starve me because I have a mind of my own?" Joey released the anger that had been building up for years, and as he did, he felt a shiver run down his spine. What was that moving across the back window?

"That is not what your dad was saying, Joey. Please calm down and stop fighting with him." Joey didn't bother to look at his mom but kept his steely glare aimed at his dad.

"Well, I won't let you down anymore. I'm out of here. I am done with you. I can take care of myself, and there is nothing you can do to stop me." Joey was about to storm from the house, but something held him in place.

His dad was about to come unglued. He wanted to yell and scream. He had lost control of the situation, and he could do nothing to regain the place of influence that had just been relinquished. The powerlessness he felt to influence the dreadful choice Joey was making threatened to manifest physically. Instead, he turned his battle inward and wrestled his thoughts rather than his son. *Don't say anything. He doesn't know what he is saying. You will only make it worse*, he pleaded with himself. Then he offered up a prayer. *Please, Lord, help me not to do any more damage today than has already been done.* His silent prayer helped him calm down until he was ready to speak.

"You are right, son. We do care too much about what others think, and you are capable of making your own decisions. We don't want you to go, but if you really want to move out, you can. In fact, if you tell me where you want to go, I will drop you off." Joey wasn't sure what to do. This was not the response he was expecting. Just as he began to waver, a chill swept into the room as if someone had cracked the back window. A whisper from the back of his mind assured him that this had to be some kind of trick. He was not backing down. He said the first thing that came to his mind.

"Just drop me off downtown."

True to his word, his dad pulled out the car while Joey packed a bag and grabbed whatever cash he had saved up. Regret was already trying to set in, but his resolve was still too strong to listen to reason. His dad parked the car down one of the many side streets that fed off the main thoroughfare downtown. Joey and his dad walked silently together down the cold alleyway, and to his dad's surprise, Joey didn't insist that he leave him alone. He would stay until he was told to leave. Both of them were breaking new ground. They continued to walk in silence, and Dick noticed a homeless guy trying to stay warm under a blue tarp positioned at the corner of a dumpster. He suddenly felt a prompting to speak to the man.

"Excuse me, sir. Are you okay?"

"Do you have any money?"

"No."

"Then get lost!" The man sat up and turned in his direction. Dick could see this wasn't the type of character he wanted to start an altercation with. He wanted to back out of the conversation as quickly as he had started it, but the prompting kept coming.

"I am wondering if you could do me and my son here a favor. He wants to leave home and live on the streets so he can have more freedom and not have to live under the tyranny of our home." He immediately regretted using that inflammatory word, but it seemed to connect with the homeless man in front of him.

"I was once like you, kid."

"You are nothing like me. You don't even know me."

"Ha! That's where you are wrong. I once stood in your shoes, and my father brought me to the streets of this very city and introduced me to a bum—just like the one you're looking at." Dick wasn't sure where this was going but continued to feel a prompting to let it play out.

"So, here's a piece of advice for you. You can choose to be free, to abandon society's expectations and your parents' tyranny and live a life of complete freedom just like me. But just like me, you must be willing to pay the price that your choices demand. I have lost everything I ever thought dear. I have destroyed every relationship I ever had, and I am always one bad deal away from an overdose or being shot and killed. If that's what you want, then be my guest. I will even share my tarp with you and show you the ropes around here." He had called Joey's bluff, and his dad couldn't believe the sage wisdom coming from a man whose condition only a moment ago raised doubts about whether he could even speak.

"Uh, um." Joey couldn't find a response to the broken stranger's words of advice. This bum standing in front of him seemed to know him better than he knew himself.

"Uh, no thanks. I think I'll just go home with my dad." Dick couldn't believe his ears. He whispered a prayer of thanks in his heart to God for the man who did in five minutes what he felt was beyond hoping for. He couldn't help but wonder if the man was an angel in disguise.

"Excuse me, sir, would you tell me your name?"

"Scott."

"Just Scott?"

"I have nothing left to my name, and even then, I have been disowned by my family. So yeah, just Scott."

"Well, thank you, Mr. Scott. I appreciate all you have done for my son, and I know God does, too."

"That's some kind of twisted joke. God has nothing to do with it. I have probably done your son more harm than good, and you should just pray he forgets everything I said. I tend to mess up everything I touch."

"I will pray, but it will be that God restores what drugs and the devil have stolen from you. I can see a good man inside of you, Scott, and I am going to ask the Lord to bring that out of you." Scott felt the urge to rebuke the stranger standing in front of him, but something about the love the man had shown his son touched him deeply. All he could do was watch the two walk away with the father's arm around his son's shoulders. In that moment, he mourned the pain and hurt he had caused those he loved in his lifetime, especially his own dad. Despite the chill of the evening air, Scott felt a warmth course through him that he no longer thought existed.

Chapter 48

Smith

Three months of decadence and debauchery had exhausted Smith physically and emotionally. He had blown his entire life's savings on a nonstop drug binge. When he had sucked his pension funds dry, he sold every valuable item he possessed to liquidate funds and feed his self-implosion. The binge was a culmination of his damaged life and the perfect storm of circumstances that drove him to this train wreck of a journey. Everything that once provided restraint had been removed. Not even the threat of prison or worse could hold him back. There was no pleasure he didn't afford himself in his pursuit to escape the intolerable pain he was suffering. Life became a nonstop pursuit of escape, and under the influence of whatever drug he could get his hand on, it seemed bearable—until all the money was gone.

In a cheap hotel room in a seedy part of town, he stared at his final eight ball—his last bag of cocaine. It represented the end of the ride that had kept his pain at bay for the last few months. He knew what awaited him on the other side of those drugs. He looked out the window at a world that only seemed to cause him pain, and he made the decision that he was not ready to make in that hospital room just three months earlier. He processed the options internally, but he was not as alone as he thought. The two who had shadowed his moves for years looked at each other as Smith considered his and their battle.

"I have to kill myself. The only way this pain is ever going to stop is if I die. These are the last drugs I possess, and I have nothing left to buy any more." He talked to himself like a parent instructing a child to do a new chore.

"There are enough drugs here to kill five people. If I put them in my system fast enough, I will overdose to the point that my heart will explode, and it will all be over. I will go to sleep and never wake up."

You will finally be free, something whispered in his head.

"Why didn't I think of this before?" He was genuinely curious why this simple option had never presented itself so clearly before. Why had he fought dying so much in the past, especially during that bizarre out-of-body experience in the ER?

What were you fighting to save? You were an idiot! Your life is worthless and useless. It will be better for everyone who ever knew you if you kill yourself and spare the world the hassle of having to deal with your messes.

His thoughts continued to spill out into the seemingly empty hotel room, giving the opposite but unequal forces a chance to hear and assess the likelihood of accomplishing their very different goals pertaining to the life over which they now battled. One was dedicated to his death, and the other was under a vow to save him and effect heaven's change in his life.

He is mine. It ends today. You have no right to interfere. He has rejected you and your God and embraced my will for his life. The one who lived in the darkness of the shadows had pure contempt for his adversary and the life in the balance. His grotesque form was revealed as he left the fortitude of the darkness to defend his rights over his slave.

You are always so over-confident. The battle is not over yet.

You are delusional. He has started a chain of events that will inexorably lead to his death. You can't change that now. His will is his own, and I own his will. You might as well leave and let me finish the inevitable.

Go to hell, you murderer.

This worthless soul can fill that request today, but as for me, I have a whole world to corrupt. The detestable being cackled at his own words.

His opponent's resolve escalated as he considered all the lives that had chosen the wrong path and ended in destruction. He was committed to doing absolutely everything possible to save this life, even if it meant going beyond the normal reaches of his power.

Their attention shifted back to the actions of the man at the center of their fight. He liquefied the first dose of cocaine and applied the tourniquet to his arm. Then he searched for a vein in which to insert the needle. The impact was almost instantaneous as the drugs took hold of his consciousness. It was the last time he would feel that surging release from the bondage of reality. Over the next few hours, he shot himself up with a volume of drugs that would have lasted a normal person a whole week. His body had already surpassed normal human limits as he prepared the last hit.

He sat on the edge of the bed with the syringe in hand. The vein was well worn, but he had picked a spot that he knew would work. The syringe contained four times the maximum dosage needed to end a life and would be combined with the massive amounts of the drug already in his system. *I should feel something. I am about to end my life, and I don't even feel anything.* He grabbed the syringe and prepared to insert it into his waiting vein. He took one last look around. The hotel room contained two dingy twin beds, and Smith was sitting on the one closest to the door with his feet between the two beds. He rested the syringe on his arm and looked at the faux wood linoleum flooring separating the two beds. If he was not so committed to ending his life, he may have reacted more strongly as his eyes landed on a pair of black boots. They were biker boots that were connected to a pair of jean-clad legs.

As he looked up, he saw a man sitting opposite him. Smith turned to check the door. He had been very careful to turn the lock and latch the chain at the top of the door. It was still in place. Once he was satisfied that no one could have come into the room without his knowledge, he looked again at the man in front of him. A leather vest covered a black T-shirt. His face was strikingly handsome and contained the features and coloring of Native American heritage. Smith suspected he would be more than six feet tall if he stood up. His physique was large and well defined, and the muscles on his neck and face were well developed. His face was without emotion, but his presence was instantaneously intimidating. Smith expected the man to attack him at any moment, but they sat staring at each other for several minutes.

When it became apparent that his presence was delaying Smith from taking the massive dose of cocaine in the syringe, the man looked at his prey and spoke firmly but slowly, almost in a tone of compassion but somehow lacking any genuine emotion.

"It is okay. It will all be over soon. It will all be over soon." The dark man repeated himself until Smith yielded the need for any explanation for his presence and raised his hand. He applied the necessary pressure to the syringe that was already resting in place on his arm, inserting the lethal dose into his drug-saturated system. He lay down on the bed and waited for death. A perverted peace from a twisted perception of reality settled on its host, and he believed he would soon find freedom from this miserable life. He hoped that death would finally engulf him and ultimately be the savior that he longed for. And with that final thought, he lost consciousness.

Chapter 49

Scott

It had started raining, and Scott pulled his cardboard box as far inside his duct-taped tarp as it would go. Water dripped heavily from the roof of the buildings. He could feel it slide behind the tarp and seep in through the small holes in the old plastic. As he listened to the sound of the rain, he couldn't get the encounter with the young man and his dad out of his mind. It was like he was staring into the eyes of his younger self, and not for the first time in his life, he longed to take back all the pain he had caused those who loved him. He felt the dichotomy of two different people inside of him, one who truly wanted to have a meaningful life and one who wanted to indulge in every desire he could imagine. That part of him never warned the other part of the cost of following its impulses. He had no one to blame anymore but himself, and now, in a more sober moment, his broken spirit languished at his loss.

You are an idiot, Scott. You destroyed every good relationship you ever had. Jackson, even Jackson, has disowned you. Is this how you want to die, living under a tarp in an alley and becoming an object of ridicule and a warning to wayward teenagers? As he marinated in his pain, a thought came to his mind—a thought he would have dismissed any other time, but at this moment, his heart was ripe for the suggestion.

Go back home. Mom will take you back. His mother had ended up kicking him out once before when he showed up on her doorstep. Her heart had been broken too many times by her son who cared for no one other than himself. He didn't want to hurt her again. *I can be there for her. I won't pretend to be off drugs, but at least I can help her around the house and help take care of her.* It was a delusion of the highest order, but having failed on so many occasions to end his own life, the pain of having no significance in life and the indignity of living as a bum on the street was becoming unbearable.

Darkness had descended by the time he reached his childhood home. He stood outside the small house, staring at the front door for what seemed like an eternity. The prospect of being rejected by his mom was harder than he had expected. In the end, it came down to one simple equation. *What have you got to lose?*

He knocked loudly and could hear his mother shuffle from the kitchen to the front door. There was a glass window in the top third of the door, but his mom was barely five feet tall and had become hunched over in her old age. Scott knew if he stood back a little from the door, she wouldn't see him until she opened the door. He had warned her before of the danger of opening the door without knowing who was there, and now he was taking advantage of it.

The door opened slowly as she reached for the screen door handle without looking up. She was moving much more slowly and looked like she had aged 10 years since the last time he had seen her. Feelings of guilt flooded his heart as he saw the effects of the torment he had inflicted on his mother. He didn't wait for her to look up.

"Mom. It's me. Scott." She was startled to hear his voice. Fear threatened to dominate her thoughts, but as only a mother's heart can, she chose to remember the baby she had carried in her womb, the boy she had taught to read and write and the young man who had so many good ambitions before darkness had overtaken him.

"Oh my, Scott, you look awful. Come in, son. Come in." These were not just the concerns of a caring mother. Life on the streets had been rough to say the least. Scott had lost almost 80 pounds and was just a shadow of the man his mother had last seen.

"Let me fix you something to eat. I'm sure you are hungry." His body had grown accustomed to being without food. Eating was a function to keep his body alive so he could keep finding his next fix. But right now, the thought of having his mother's cooking again had an appeal far beyond sustenance.

"That would be great, Mom."

There were few exchanges while she pulled together the ingredients to make an omelet, using the ham she had boiled for her dinner the Sunday before. Both of them seemed reluctant to spoil the moment and discover the motives for the unexpected visit. Scott realized she wasn't going to ask. He took a deep breath and poured out his heart to the only soul who still cared about him.

"Mom, I just want you to know that I am sorry for all the pain I caused you. I don't expect anything from you, and I am not here to ask for anything except a chance to make things up to you." She held her breath. This was not the first time she had heard this speech, and she wasn't ready to allow hope to rise in her heart. But having a repentant son in her kitchen was not in the plan when she woke up today, and she was not about to abandon the gift before she had time to unwrap it.

"It's just good to see your face and know you are still alive, son. I heard reports from one of your friends who works as a nurse at the hospital that you nearly died a while back. The news shook me to my core, son. Is that true?"

"Yeah." He felt like a five-year-old getting caught with his hand in the cookie jar again, but this time it was his life or death they were dealing with.

"If I am honest, Mom, I wanted to die in that hospital. I felt I had caused more harm in my life than I could ever make amends for."

"Well, God obviously had other plans."

He was not about to refute her beliefs, and somewhere inside of him he wanted to believe she was right. "I don't know, Mom. It feels more like God wants to punish me than save me."

"I raised you to know better than that." The rebuke brought him comfort, for only someone who really cares chooses to correct a wayward soul.

"You did, Mom. You did."

The omelet tasted even better than he had expected, and the coffee sharpened his thoughts. Both of them began to feel more at ease, and he shared some of the things he thought she would like to know.

"I met a girl. A nurse. Her name is Jennifer."

"Is she a churchgoing girl?"

"Don't nurses get a pass because of all the good work they do?" His playful humor disarmed her emotions but not her religious convictions.

"It's not just what you do but what you believe that matters."

"I know. I was just teasing you. I felt like we made a real connection, but I had to leave town before I could find out if she felt the same."

"Well, once you get back on your feet, you can go back and ask her." He couldn't tell her that there was a hit out on him and that he had only made the connection while recovering from an attempt on his life. He had to dilute the facts to a point that would save her from the painful details.

"Maybe I'll do that when I'm back on my feet."

"Scott." Her voice sounded ominous, and he knew he was about to be asked a question he didn't want to answer.

"Yes, Mom."

"I need you to be honest with me about your drug use. I can't have you stay here if you are still using or at the very least trying to get off of them." He wanted to tell her the truth. He wanted to tell her that he could never change, but he desperately needed to matter to someone, and she was the only person left who would care. But he knew she wouldn't let him stay if she knew the truth. He sighed as he processed the most truthful lie he could tell her.

"I want to change. I hate the life I have been living. I don't have the strength to do it on my own, but I am willing to try." And there it was. The lie to begin all other lies. The manipulation of a soul who was too weak to see the truth. It didn't matter how good his intentions were. As long as there was the need for drugs, there was the dependence on manipulation. He tried to convince himself it wasn't really a lie as he concocted a plan he had no intention of keeping.

"I'm still using, Mom. I need something that will get me free, but I have to start somewhere. I can't get off drugs while I'm living on the streets."

"Jesus will set you free, Scott."

"I want to believe that, Mom, but it has never happened, and I have asked him a million times."

"You have to give your heart to him, Scott. You have to repent your sins and give him everything. He will forgive you even more than I ever could, and He will set you free." The words sounded so promising, and his mother's faith almost compelled him to start hoping, but the urge to get his next fix was building in him. Just like Dr. Jekyll and Mr. Hyde, he needed to end this conversation sooner rather than later before he transformed into the out-of-control drug addict he really was.

"I promise I won't get high when I'm in the house, Mom. I just need a place to gather my thoughts and lay my head while I get my act together."

"I can't take it if you lie to me, Scott. It will put me in an early grave. I would rather you tell me now if you are lying to me. I can't watch you kill yourself. A mother should never have to go through that."

"I know, Mom. I know I have lied to you in the past, but I really do want to change."

"Okay, son. Okay. Your room is just as you left it last time you stayed here. It's late, and I need to go to bed. You should go to bed, too. Maybe tomorrow we can visit the new rehab that just opened up. It's a faith-based program, and I hear they are having a lot of success helping people get free of drugs."

"Sure, Mom. We can check it out if you have time."

Scott watched TV as his mom got ready for bed. The normality of being at home seemed surreal, but he needed to play this right in order to continue the illusion as long as he could. Getting an anonymous fix in his old neighborhood this late at night would be almost impossible, and he needed to try to get some sleep before the withdrawal kicked in. He wanted to savor feeling normal for a little while longer and figured he was tired enough to fall asleep watching TV.

Chapter 50

Smith

In the hours that had passed in the dreary hotel room, there unfolded a great battle for Smith's very existence. Hell had called upon its hoards to violently rip the soul from the body of their latest victim, but his guardian had shielded his charge from death until the critical volume of drugs diminished in potency. The battle had remained at an intensity that only a supernatural being could sustain. The flashes of light from his sword kept the advances of the evil ones at bay.

Wave after wave attacked as the protector fought valiantly for his charge to have another chance at life. It was still unclear how he could turn Smith from the wicked path to which he clung, but all he could think of now was keeping hell's parasites at bay. Numerically, the fight seemed completely one-sided as the lone protector fought hundreds of advancing foes. He could feel the power of heaven course through his veins as his blade sliced through demon after demon. Each time Smith looked like he would succumb to the overdose, the protector would reach inside, touch his failing heart, and impart the strength he needed to stay alive.

The room came to a stop as the attention of all returned to the man who lay across the small bed. Somehow, he had survived the effects of the overdose and started to stir from his unconscious state.

You had no right to keep him alive! hissed a demon, angry that he had been denied his prize.

No, but I had a right to stop him from dying prematurely. Long ago, a prayer was recorded on his behalf that gave me the legal grounds to intervene. A woman of strong faith prayed diligently through times of great loss for her children and her children's children for generations to come. He is of that line, and this gave me the right to defend him.

That's just semantics. His life is mine. You only delayed the inevitable. You can't keep playing that card.

He was right. As much as he hated to admit it, he was running out of options. He could fight the demons for a while longer, but he would not last the night if something drastic didn't happen. He had to leave the room in an attempt to secure more help, but in doing so, he knew the unsuspecting one at the center of this battle would be more vulnerable than ever to the manipulation of the evil ones who remained.

The sound of the TV blaring caused Smith to wake with a start. Why was he still alive? There was no way he could have survived the effects of the drugs. He was furious that he was not dead. He was not the only one.

You need to end this now. There are other ways to end your life. Drastic times call for drastic measures. The effect of the drugs coupled with years of listening to this voice caused him not to even question the command.

What can I do?

Find something sharp and cut your wrists. He wanted this over with before his opponent returned and caused any more complications.

Smith searched the whole room, but there was nothing sharp enough to cut to the depth required to sever the blood vessels in his forearm.

Open the door and look outside.

There was nothing in sight except a half-full dumpster in the corner of the hotel parking lot.

There will be something in there.

Smith hesitated. He was measuring up his desire to die with the risk of meeting someone he knew or, worse, a cop who would catch him rummaging through a dumpster.

You need to end this now, the voice demanded, and just as before, Smith obeyed his orders.

He dug around in the dumpster but couldn't even find a bottle to break or a sharp object of any kind. As he got closer to the bottom, he saw some building debris from a remodel they had done on the exterior of the hotel.

In the middle of the debris, he could see a used box blade. He grabbed it and rushed back to his room.

What the heck is wrong with this thing? It's duller than a spoon. The blade had been used to scrape old mud off the wall until the edge of the blade was completely worn down.

Keep trying. It will work. There was a note of impatience that Smith detected for the first time. A hint of doubt about the instructions he was receiving might have broken into his consciousness if he wasn't so distracted by the prospect of having to use a dull blade to slice through his arm. He could tell this was not going to be an easy task, and he needed all the commitment he could muster.

Slash after slash left little more than a dull ache and raw skin around the area he was trying to cut. He was growing tired from the drugs and the marathon effort of trying to kill himself.

Pull yourself together, Smith. You just need to break the skin, and you can do the rest even if the blade is dull. He pressed as hard as he could and slid the knife across his arm. He managed a small incision toward the end of the stroke but away from the blood vessels. Again and again he applied pressure and pulled the blade across his arm. After 20 or so attempts, the cumulative pain from each stroke was making itself known. *Get this done, Smith, or it's going to be way more painful than you need it to be.*

He applied as much pressure as he could and broke through several layers of skin. The dull blade could only do so much, and it took several dozen more swipes until he eventually pierced a vein and the dark blood oozed out of his arm. A sense of relief came over him as he watched the white sheets turn red and his life drain away in front of his eyes.

He started to feel light-headed, but within a few minutes, the blood flow slowed down.

What the heck? The last thing he wanted to do right then was start cutting the wound open again with the dull box blade. The sinister voice came into his consciousness again to stop him from giving up.

Run the bath with hot water.

The wound had almost stopped bleeding before he climbed into the bath, but it quickly opened up again. The water started changing color as more and more blood mixed with the hot water. In a matter of minutes, the water was completely red, and Smith expected to lose consciousness at any moment. To his dismay, the water started cooling down, and he was still conscious. When he pulled his arm out of the water, the blood loss had slowed down. He knew he had too much strength to be anywhere near death. *This is ridiculous! What is wrong with my body that it won't bleed out? It can't possibly be this hard to die.*

Use the blade again.

No.

Use the blade again.

No! The voice stopped. He had not been challenged before. He needed to change strategies.

You are almost there. You cut the vein before, but you just need one more cut to the artery and you will bleed out.

That suggestion held enough logic to be considered, and he really wanted this nightmare to end. He searched for the blade on the blood-soaked sheets and stared at the wound one more time. There were at least 10 open wounds on his forearm where he had tried to find a blood vessel to cut. It looked like a piece of ravaged meat, and he didn't know where to continue. He could see inside his arm through one cut and saw what looked like a brighter colored blood vessel. He knew the blood in the arteries had more oxygen and were typically brighter in color. He picked up the blade and closed his eyes as he jammed the corner of the dull blade into his arm one more time.

The blood spurted out of his arm, and he knew he had struck the right spot. He sat on the bed and watched the blood jump several feet out of his arm and cover everything in sight. The sheets that were originally a dingy white were barely visible as the blood seemed to cover almost the entire bed. The room looked like a scene from a horror movie. Smith's eyes began to close as he finally felt the life drain from his body.

His protector appeared in the room as the last of his blood began to seep from his wounds. He looked at the evil monster standing over his victim, gloating at the termination of another needless life. As their eyes locked, the detestable being could not help but laugh with sick glee at his evil work.

You are too late. Not even your trickery can keep him alive now, the creature boasted. *You can't stop the bleeding, and even if you could, he has lost too much blood to survive. You lose.* The protector did not break the stare as they both heard a knock at the door. Receiving no answer, the woman unlocked the door and entered.

"Mr. Smith? Mr. Smith?" a voice called.

The gloater was the one to break eye contact first so he could confirm there was no threat to the completion of his plan.

"Aaaaaaghhh! Oh my God! Oh my God! Oh my God!" Frantically, the cleaning lady ran out of the room. In less than a minute, she returned with Smith's old friend who had seen him check in the night before and "out of the blue" had felt an urge to come and check on his friend at this late hour.

"Quick! I need something to make a tourniquet." He was trained in combat first aid and kept a clear head despite the dire situation around him. The cleaning lady gave him some linens from her cart. He tore a strip and quickly wrapped it around Scott's arm.

"Call 9-1-1." The cleaning lady grabbed her phone and within seconds was giving the dispatcher the location of the hotel and the number of the room.

No! No! No! Stop it! You can't do this! He is mine. I won him legally. His life is mine to take. You can't save him. You have no right!"

The protector had assumed an aggressive stance over the body of the almost-dead man and dared his opponent to fight him. *They can't hear your evil rants, and you have no authority over what they do of their own volition.*

The figure in the shadows defied the protector's dare and reached into his victim's chest and squeezed his heart, attempting to restart the flow of blood. The protector knew there was little he could do to stop him at this point. However, in one last attempt to save his charge, he reached down and applied pressure to the tourniquet, and it miraculously held, and so did Smith's heart. The aggressor stomped around the room screaming at the underhanded work of his nemesis and claiming rights he knew he did not have once the third parties got involved.

"He has lost a lot of blood, but I can get a faint pulse," the rescuer explained the situation to the EMT.

"We will take it from here."

Smith survived the trip to the hospital. In no time, they had intubated him and were replacing the lost blood in his body. His protector continued to stand guard. The look on his face showed his determination to do absolutely everything he could to save this life. He knew that if he could keep him alive, his Master could use him to reach those who followed the same destructive path. It was a slim hope but infinitely more than what he had just a few hours ago.

Chapter 51

Scott

Scott woke up, his head throbbing to the tune of a shampoo commercial. He looked at the clock on the wall. It was four in the morning. Before he could remember where he was, his body was shouting its need for any kind of drug. *Crap, crap, crap! What the heck am I going to do? I can't get any drugs around here at this time of night. I've got to hold it together until I can get into town. I can't let Mom know how bad I am, or it will break her heart.*

His resolve was honest but not strong. The next two hours seemed like two days. He was starting to sweat, and the cravings were unbearable. *Something. Anything. I just need something to take the edge off.* A prompting from inside his head made the one suggestion that he didn't want to hear. *Mom will have some pain pills. All I need is a couple to take the edge off. She won't even notice they're gone.*

He wrestled with the betrayal for another hour, but once the thought had been planted in his head, resistance was futile. He knew he couldn't stay in this state of withdrawal while a solution was at hand, no matter what the cost. He finally rationalized his plan to the point where he could justify the action. *If she sees me in this condition, it will break her heart. It's better that I ease her into understanding the struggle I have.*

Scott knew his mom never got up before eight, so he had time to take the pills and recover some normalcy before she woke up. *She's always messing up the days on her medicines. She'll just think she miscounted.*

On and on the argument went until Scott had hardwired the action into his brain. He opened the cabinet in the kitchen where she kept all her prescription medicines. She prepared her medicine for the week every Monday morning and put them in a seven-day dispenser. He could see the little blue pills in their respective days staring at him, begging to be taken.

He decided his only course was to take the pills directly from the bottle to raise as little suspicion as possible. He rummaged through every cabinet but couldn't find the bottles anywhere. *She must have hidden them before she went to bed last night.*

He racked his brain, wondering where she may have put them. In his desperation, he was getting increasingly stressed and was obsessing about the pills in the dispenser. Once more the voice in his head made the obvious and easiest suggestion. *Just take those pills, and then when you find the others, you can replace them.*

He fought the suggestion since he knew his chances of replacing the pills were limited, but all he could think about was taking the edge off the shakes and sweats that were getting stronger now. He relented and went back to the cabinet where his mom kept the pill container and stared at the two pills sitting in the Wednesday slot. He was committed now, but the voice was not finished giving him advice.

If Mom takes two and she's only half my weight, then I'll need at least twice that. His concern for his mother's feelings was dropping down in priority with each new thought. He grabbed three days' worth of pain pills and knocked them back. Even though they wouldn't take effect for several minutes, his manic thoughts began to ease, and he let his guard down again.

Smash! The sound of a coffee cup shattering into dozens of pieces startled him out of his self-contemplation.

"No, Scott. No! Please tell me you didn't just take my medicine. You lied to me again. You just came home so you could get my pills again, didn't you?" The woman who thought she could cry no more over the son who had broken her heart so many times wept profusely as wave after wave of realization swept over her mind.

"You told me you came back to take care of me, Scott, and I was stupid enough to believe you. I can't take this anymore."

"I can explain, Mom. I was only taking the pills so I wouldn't go into withdrawal. I didn't want you to see me like that."

"I would much rather see you that way. I would at least know you were trying. You didn't even wait twelve hours to steal from me."

The last vestiges of true humanity in Scott were shattered. It would have been infinitely better to have not gone home than to do this to his mother. Over the years, he had learned to numb himself to the pain he caused others, but looking at his mother's face dismantled any self-preservation he could muster. In that moment, the voice that had led him astray was on hand to offer an even more destructive and outrageous suggestion.

He walked into his old bedroom and pulled out the top drawer of the dresser. There, under several pair of socks, was his old switchblade. The blade wasn't even three inches long, but it would be enough to carry out the plan he was following, like a bird flying into a snare. He brushed by his mother who was bent over in the kitchen chair, weeping. If he had any doubt, his resolve was confirmed seeing her like that.

He walked the mile and a half to Cooke's Pharmacy and stepped right up to the counter. Several of the staff recognized him and greeted him as he got closer. There was an older man behind the counter who looked a little frail, and Scott made a beeline for him.

"What can I help you with, young man?"

"I need one hundred forty-milligram methadone.

In smaller towns where most everyone knows each other, some formalities are often dispensed with. The old man saw that the staff knew the disheveled man in front of him and went to get the medicine. He suspected he was not in a good place, but it was not uncommon for doctors to treat the short-term needs of their patients rather than take the hard road necessary for recovery. He returned with the drugs.

"I will just need to see your prescription, and then I can check you out." For a moment, Scott considered turning around and walking away without the drugs, but there was no other solution in sight. The drugs were merely an arm's length away in the hand of a frail man, and he knew he would have to commit a much greater crime than theft to get what he wanted. He only needed a moment to take the next step.

It won't matter. Once I take these drugs, it will be all over. I will take enough to kill five elephants, and then my miserable existence and this crime won't matter. I won't have to live through this cycle of drugs and pain ever again. He looked at the old man who was a little confused by Scott's non-responsiveness.

"Excuse me, sir, I just need the prescription." Scott pulled the knife out of his pocket and held it about 12 inches from the man's face.

"Look, old man. I don't want to hurt you, but I will if you make me. Just give me the drugs, and I will walk out the door, and no one will get hurt." The man started shaking, dropped the drugs on the counter, and took several steps back.

"What's going on, Scott?" The other employees noticed the look on the old man's face and realized something was not right.

Scott ran out the door. It was now a race against time, and he couldn't afford to get caught before he had a chance to ingest the drugs and have them accomplish their destructive mission.

I need to take these now, or I will be found, and they'll pump my stomach. He ran down the street about a block to an automotive shop where a childhood friend worked.

"Tom, I need you to drive me home. It's urgent."

"Scott? Scott, is that you, man? It's been a long time, dude. You look awful."

"Please, Tom, I can't explain, but I need your help." Tom knew his friend was in trouble, but as bad as Scott's reputation was, they had history, and he owed him.

"Hop in, man. Where do you want to go?"

"Home."

"That's only a mile away." He was confused at the urgency to get somewhere he could walk to in 15 minutes.

"Drive, Tom!"

There was no room for debate. By the time they were pulling away from the shop, Scott could hear the sound of the sirens in the distance. He knew they were coming for him.

"Faster, Tom."

"I'm already going way over the limit."

"I don't care. Just get me there as fast as you can." For the first time in their relationship, Tom felt unsafe and just wanted to get his old friend out of his car and never see him again. He sped up and pulled over by his house. The police car sped by them and pulled up to a house about two blocks away.

"They must not know which house I live in," Scott muttered as he jumped out of the car and slammed the door shut. Tom didn't wait around to see if his friend was okay. A second police car pulled up behind the first one, and Tom put two and two together and realized he had probably just aided in a crime. He left the scene and went back to the shop, hoping he wouldn't get dragged into whatever mess Scott had created.

Scott knew he needed to act right away. He ran into the house and straight to the basement. He thought he could hear his mother still crying, but there was no time to explain or say goodbye.

You wouldn't understand, Mom. You can't see that I really do love you. I hope you will realize that I'm doing this for you.

He locked the basement door, ran down the stairs, and dumped the drugs on the table. They were small but powerful disc-shaped painkillers. Five would be dangerous, and 10 would certainly be deadly. He had 100 pills, and he was not about to take any chances. He started swallowing as many as he could. *That's at least 20.* He took several more before he heard banging on the front door.

Crap! I need more time. He heard a quick exchange between the officers and his mom. He could tell she was still in shock, but it was a small house, and within a few minutes, they realized he was in the basement.

"Open the door, Scott. We know you're in there."

"I'm not coming out. Do you hear? It ends here."

"What do you mean, Scott?" One of the officers motioned to the one doing the talking.

"Scott, this is Chance. We used to work together, man. Look, nobody got hurt, so this doesn't have to get out of hand. Let us in so we can help you." He turned to his colleague and whispered, "Call for an ambulance."

Scott could feel the drugs taking effect, but he couldn't take the risk of getting his stomach pumped before the pills reached a lethal dosage in his system. He needed to buy some time.

"Chance, I remember yoouu." His words started to slur. "Just give me a...a...a minute."

The officers knew they needed to act quickly to save his life. *Thump! Thump! Thump!* They smashed their bodies against the door in an effort to break through.

Adrenaline started to kick into Scott's system and counter the effects of the drugs. He looked around for a weapon. All he could see was a writing pen. Without thinking, he stabbed himself in the neck hoping to hit the artery and bleed out. Blood flowed from his neck, but it was not from a main vessel. He slammed the pen into his neck again. The lock on the door broke loose as the officers made it through his first layer of defense. Scott tried to swallow some more pills, but the injuries to his neck made it more difficult. He was losing consciousness, but he had consumed enough, more than enough drugs to kill himself, and all he needed was a few more minutes for them to take effect.

"He's dying down there." Chance had looked up to Scott as a big brother when they were younger and didn't expect the wave of emotion that was compelling him to save his old friend.

Then they saw Scott slumped over the couch with blood flowing out of his neck. Chance ran to him to check for signs of life. "I can't get a pulse. Where's the ambulance? I can't get a pulse!" Chance started to administer CPR and pray silently for his friend.

"Please let me see my son." Scott's mom tried to push past the officers in the doorway.

"Ma'am, you need to stay outside and let us do our job."

"This is my house, and that is my son."

"Let her in." Chance removed himself from his professional capacity to feel the pain of his friend's mom. "You're Scott's mom, right?"

"Yes. Yes. Oh! My boy! Oh Lord, help my son. Please don't let him die. Please! Please! I don't think I can take it if he dies. Please have mercy on him." She desperately hoped her prayers fell on the ears of the One who could dispense supernatural mercy since she knew there was nothing deserving of mercy for her son.

The ambulance didn't arrive for several more minutes. The EMTs continued CPR until they got a faint pulse and loaded him up into the ambulance. One of the EMTs pushed a tube down Scott's throat and into his stomach and pumped out the contents. While they hooked him up to the machines, one of the EMTs tried to encourage the officer who was visibly shaken.

"What's your name, officer?"

"Broderick. Officer Chance Broderick."

"Well, Officer Chance Broderick, your quick thinking kept this guy alive. If you hadn't administered CPR, he would be dead for sure. The pump will get rid of whatever drugs didn't have time to get into his system." Chance knew the EMT was trying to be helpful, but he felt compelled to get more than just a glass-half-full response.

"Do you think he'll make it?

"It's not my place to say."

"Please, I need your honest opinion. I don't want to give his mother false hope."

The EMT could tell it wasn't just the mother's feelings the cop was processing. "If you want me to be honest with you, he doesn't look good. Those drugs are very potent, and he took a lot. If he wasn't such a big guy, he would have no chance at all."

"I've known him for several years. Drugs destroyed his life, but I can't help thinking that God has other plans for him."

"Well, prayer is about all that will save him now."

The ambulance raced to the hospital with the life of a very damaged man hanging in the balance. The fervent prayers of a good friend and a brokenhearted mother were the only opportunity he had to survive.

Chapter 52

Diesel

It was a clear, crisp day in early spring, and the usual suspects were lobbying for a position of influence or protection, whatever their circumstances called for. Big Red was surrounded by his posse. Polish Mike and the Aryan Nations contingent dominated the weights as their bald heads and intimidating tattoos glistened in the sunlight. The Black Brotherhood, which had the largest following, operated its own subculture of prison life. Their leader, known as Black Samson, matched Big Red in size but not influence. What Big Red lacked in numbers he made up for in his strategic use of resources.

Diesel observed the various groups and subgroups that existed to maintain a degree of control for each person. Prison in many ways was like a jungle, and survival of the fittest was the law governing who flourished and who got crushed. But Diesel knew his survival was solely dependent on the true King of the universe who reigned supreme, even in a place like this. He was primed for a divine encounter as he relished the opportunity to share the good news with anyone and everyone he came in contact with. That is, with the exception of the one person who was making a beeline toward him from across the yard.

Diesel never backed down, but he found himself examining his bladder for an excuse to avoid the inevitable mind-bending debate he was about to have.

"Hey, Diesel."

"Big Joe. Fancy meeting you here."

"How are you doing?"

Diesel was confused by the pleasantries and was on guard for what angle Big Joe would take in his incessant efforts to humiliate him. Once the discussion began, there was only one direction he would go with it.

"I'm doing great, actually. God is so good, and it's a beautiful day."

"Yes, it sure is. It sure is a beautiful day." The two men exchanged a few more meaningless comments about the weather and their health before Diesel realized his visitor was not there to harass him.

"Big Joe, you have never taken the time to make small talk with me before. I'm guessing you have some kind of agenda. So feel free to cut to the chase."

"Actually, you are right, I do have something I want to talk to you about." Big Joe paused. For the first time in all his encounters with his antagonist, the man struggled to form words. Diesel realized this was not a premeditated attack and there was something Big Joe needed help with.

"Whatever it is, Big Joe, just ask. I don't bite." He couldn't help but make a lightly sarcastic comment, but the invitation was genuine, and Big Joe knew it.

"Aw, what the heck. I need prayer, Diesel, and you are the only person I trust with that kind of request. I have watched you survive death threats and avoid beatings. I have seen you get favor with the various factions in this hellhole, and the only conclusion I can come to is that you have divine protection here. You should be dead. You should be dead five times over, but God is watching over you, and I am convinced that you have some kind of direct line to Him."

"I thought you didn't believe in God." Diesel was genuinely moved by the appeal of the man who had used his incredible gifted intellect to oppose so many of his gospel presentations, yet he couldn't help but be astonished at the request.

"In all our encounters, Diesel, I never actually said that I don't believe in God. I was raised in an Episcopal church. The minister was a good man, but he could never answer my questions to my satisfaction, even as a kid. The more I dug with my brain, the more questions I found. There were answers all right, but they never shored up all the angles. I've found that the truth requires faith, and that is the one thing I'm short of. It's the one thing you seem to have by the bucketload."

"I don't know if that's true, but I certainly do believe what the Bible says is true, and with all my heart I believe I am communicating with the author of the universe every time I pray." Big Joe felt a wave of unexpected emotion rise up inside of him at the sincerity and simple faith of this much-ridiculed and often despised man. He choked back the weakness in his throat and hoped the tears didn't roll down his face, but it was too late.

"Diesel, I don't know how you believe the way you do, but I wish I could. The only person I have left in this world who truly cares about me is my sister. She hated all the bad things I did, but she never stopped loving me and still to this day comes to visit me. She never got married, and she loves God like you do. And I ridicule her faith just like I do yours. She just smiles and tells me one day I will understand. She's smarter than I am and full of all the good things I'm not."

Tears were running freely down his face as he searched for the strength to say the words he had come to share. "Sarah is the only good thing in my world." He took a deep breath to fortify the words he desperately didn't want to say. "She just told me that the doctors said she has cervical cancer. Diesel, she only has three months to live. Please pray for her and ask God to heal her or extend her life. I only have nine months left before I'm released, and at least I could take care of her. Please, Diesel, use that direct line you have to help Sarah."

Diesel was blown away by the request and the unexpected emotion of his seemingly coldhearted opponent to whom he had lost so many minor arguments. He searched his heart for the appropriate answer. Although he believed in healing and had seen miracles in his short time as a follower of Jesus, he had never experienced a bona fide, verifiable healing on the level of cancer. He knew that faith required a declaration of truth, but it also needed to be believed. He needed a word from the God of healing, and he took a moment to examine his heart for instruction. A Scripture rose within him, softly at first, but then it reached a level he could not hold back. He instinctively grabbed Big Joe's hands and closed his eyes to avoid being distracted by what reaction this demonstrative gesture may cause.

"I am the God who heals you. I am the God who heals you. Big Joe, the Lord wants you to know that He is the same yesterday, today, and tomorrow.

When Jesus came, He healed all those who came to Him. I do not know why some people get healed and some do not, but I do know that God is the God who heals us. So, Lord, I pray for Sarah, and I ask that you minister healing to her body. Cancer, in the powerful name of Jesus, I command you to leave Sarah's body now. She belongs to Him and is a blood-bought child of God. The Bible says that by His stripes she was healed. Sarah, be healed now in Jesus's name."

Diesel stopped abruptly. He had prayed what he wanted to pray, and any more at that point would have been unnecessary amplification. He felt the need to give some extra insight to Big Joe since he knew he would have questions. When he opened his eyes, he saw that Big Joe's head was looking at the ground, and there was a pool of tears forming below him.

"Big Joe, as you know, praying is not a magical formula. It's not an incantation of words to get the desired result. It requires faith and truth to flow in harmony in the heart of the ones praying. All I can say for sure is that I heard the Lord saying that He is the Lord that heals us, and it resounded loudly in my heart as I was praying. It has been my experience that when God highlights His words like that, it is for a reason. He is not a God who taunts or teases us. He is a good God, even to the unrighteous. I encourage you to examine your heart and get right with God. I believe Sarah is healed and God is offering you an opportunity to redeem your life from the pit you are in."

"Thank you, Diesel. I know I can't take back all the hassle I have caused you, but please know I am sincerely grateful for your prayer and the faithful witness you have been in this prison yard. The men may not say it, but along with the slander and ridicule, there is an admiration that they do not want to acknowledge. I will take your words to heart, but I think I am too far gone for God to redeem."

Diesel couldn't help but laugh at the reoccurring objection and the ridiculously weak argument. "You know better than that, Big Joe. With all your theological reasoning, you know that the sacrifice of an infinite and eternal God can easily cleanse the sins of men like you and me." Big Joe managed a smile as he acknowledged the gaping hole in his conditional response.

"As usual, Diesel, you are right. I will do some praying of my own, and I promise I will never harass you again." He turned and made his way across the yard, wiping the tears from his eyes with a hope that one day there may be tears of joy in their place.

Diesel couldn't help but marvel at the amazing turnaround in Big Joe and the irony of his testimony that even the most hardened criminals harbor secret admiration for him.

All these months and years I have testified of Your goodness and salvation and received nothing but ridicule. The message has been changing their hearts, even when they didn't want it to. That is truly amazing, Lord. Imagine what you could do with folks who are willing.

In his heart, a thought interrupted his monologue. *It is also the messenger I have been making in my image that has changed them. Well done, my son. Your faithful witness brings me much pleasure.*

It was Diesel's turn to shed some tears as he sought a solitary spot to offer worship to the God who can turn even the ugliest environment into a reflection of heaven.

Chapter 53

Smith

The darkness had a faint light that seemed brighter at the center. It didn't illuminate anything; it just had a glow. But the darkness was penetrated by sounds, unrecognizable at first, and then they unscrambled in his head and resembled voices. He racked his brain in an attempt to remember how he got here and where *here* was. The confusion was hurting his brain. *Who is that? Where am I?* He listened more intently. He didn't know if it was fog in his brain or fear, but he had to know what was going on.

"He has been in an induced coma for three days, but they've started the process of waking him up."

"I heard he came within a whisker of death."

"Yes. It's a miracle he's still alive."

He tried to make sense of what they were saying. *Are they talking about me? Why would I be nearly dead?* Then it all started to come rushing back, the last three months culminating in the overdose and then the dull box blade. *I watched as I bled out and died. Is this heaven? I can't be in heaven. This must be hell or some kind of holding place.* The only way he could find out for sure was to ask. As soon as he tried to verbalize his questions, he was caught off guard by the object in his mouth.

I can't talk! I can't talk! His focus shifted from the questions he had to an intense anxiety. His mind started to panic and play tricks on him. *I can't breathe. I can't breathe. Somebody help me!* He was screaming on the inside, but no one could hear him. He couldn't move his limbs. Nothing would respond. The effects of his brush with death and his apparent paralysis were sending him into a full-on panic. The fear intensified as he was still unable to discern where he was and why he couldn't move or talk.

He heard one of the voices from before say, "His BP is rising fast. He's pulling out of the coma. He may be trying to piece together where he is."

"He's going to need a mild sedative." The nurses scurried around the bed checking his vital signs and ensuring the patient was ready to re-enter the harsh reality of the land of the living once more.

The doctor ordered the intubation tube to be removed and asked that he be restrained, given his propensity for self-harm and his obvious ability to harm others. "Call me when he wakes up and be sure to bring him back gently to reality. He went to great lengths to take his life, and although he may thank us one day, he will more likely be angry at us for saving him."

Smith could hear sounds again and quickly remembered that he was in a strange place. He checked again to see if he could move. It felt different. He was restricted, but he could feel his limbs and move them a little but not much. *Maybe I can talk.* The feeling of choking last time made him immediately wary of checking on his ability to talk, but his paranoia of not knowing grew more dominant than his fear. As he opened his mouth, the searing pain in his throat flashed across his consciousness like a burn from an open flame.

"Aaagghh." *I can talk. It hurts like hell, but I can talk.*

"He's coming to. Call Dr. Perry. He'll want to talk to him."

"Where am I?" His voice was hoarse but the pain in his mouth had diminished slightly. There was no mistaking that he was in the land of the living, but how and where?

"You are in Lafollette Hospital. You sustained some injuries, but you are going to be okay."

Okay? Okay? I don't want to be okay! The words stayed in his mind, but the reality of having failed in his attempt to end his life was hitting him like a ton of bricks. His anger started to manifest, and he wanted to make someone pay for keeping him alive. He moved his arm, fully expecting it to swing across his body and make contact with whatever was making those obnoxious beeping sounds. His hand shifted about an inch as the restraints did their job.

What is wrong with me? Why can't I move? He continued to question, but his eyes remained closed. The doctor walked into the room as his patient struggled to get a grip on his situation.

"Mr. Smith. Mr. Smith, can you hear me? I am Dr. Perry. You are in the hospital. Do you understand?" His words were delivered slowly, but with an air of authority. The patient shook his head. "Your arms and legs are restrained, and I am going to need you to stop fighting or we will have to sedate you again. Nod if you understand what I am saying." Smith found a degree of comfort in at least knowing what was going on and nodded. "You lost a lot of blood, and we had to intubate you to help your body while it tried to survive. As the drugs wear off, we will be able to tell you more, but for now, you need to rest. You are in the hands of two of the best nurses you will ever meet." There was a tone of humor in his voice, but Smith was in no state to be uplifted or encouraged.

He resented the doctor and his tone. All the reasons he wanted to die were still there, and all the pain he went through was wasted. His thoughts returned to the night at the hotel room. *Why didn't I die? What kind of torment is this that I can't even take my own life?* He couldn't face going through that again. Hopelessness gripped his heart.

The figure in the shadows stood in the corner of the hospital room still seething over his failure and the incompetence of his human slave to complete the simple task of taking his own life. The presence of the protector across the room only served to make his anger more intense, and it spilled into the subconscious of his victim.

Smith felt his anger rise. Raw anger. Murderous anger. The nurses had left, and he yanked against his restraints. He could hear the machine beside him start to beep faster, and he knew the nurse would be back in the room any second if he didn't get his heart rate under control. He fought to control his breathing and then focused his mind. *Get control of yourself, Smith.* His hopelessness began to turn toward revenge. He wanted to make someone pay for the fact that his miserable life had not ended. *If I can't die, then someone else will. They should have let me die. They will regret resuscitating me.* He visualized himself stabbing the doctor, the nurses, and the EMTs. He thought about finding the person who called 9-1-1 and slicing him with the dull box blade until he bled to death. The figure in the shadows wore a fiendish smile as he spewed his vile imagination into Smith's consciousness. Maybe this miserable human could still be useful.

No. I need to find the one responsible for getting me in this state. There is one person who needs to pay, that excuse for a human being that stole my life. He narrowed his focus on the one who had intersected his life at more than one critical point and repeatedly made his life go in a downward spiral. It was not the one who had abused him or the low-life child abusers he investigated. It was not even the spawns of hell who killed the children they were supposed to help. No one had stolen his confidence and caused him to question his existence, his value, his purpose, his future, his life more than the drug addict he had met as a 20-year-old cop—the drug dealer who taunted him during an investigation and introduced him to cocaine, the pusher who pushed him over the edge into insanity and made him attempt suicide.

You bastard, Scott. This is all your fault! I would still have my job, my relationships, my purpose, my life if it had not been for you. Wherever you are, I promise you, I will find you and kill you. If I cannot kill myself, then I will kill you. I will cause you so much pain you won't just regret the day we met, you will regret the day you were born!

The intensity and sincerity of his intent soothed his own anger and that of his dark master. He knew he would make good on his word and find a wicked redemption in his failed suicide.

Chapter 54

Scott

It was Monday morning, and the usual bustle transpired as the courtroom staff and legal representatives looked to close out any unfinished business from the previous week and get ready for the new cases on the docket. The attorney for the State of Tennessee and the court-appointed attorney representing Scott chatted about the details of his case. Each was trying to broker the best deal for the parties they represented, but they both knew this was a slam dunk for the state. All Scott's attorney could hope for was an attempt to introduce some mitigating circumstances for the judge's consideration.

The courtroom came to a hush as the bailiff called "all rise" for the entrance of the judge. It all seemed like a bad dream. Scott looked around the courtroom and saw so many faces he recognized from his childhood. It was a small town, and Scott was well-known from his high school football days. The faces he didn't know stared at him like he was a new attraction at a zoo, and those he did know avoided making eye contact.

Scott's thoughts couldn't help but express the deep bitterness he felt. *God, you are the cruelest being I know. I didn't ask to be saved, and You had no right to save me. It should be You I am standing before, not this courtroom. I should have been able to look You in the eye and tell You how I felt about the injustices of the world You created. You made us with weaknesses and addictions. You gave us the intelligence to create drugs and destroy our lives. You even torment us with guilt, all the while telling us we should be better and not giving us the help we need to live right. You are a self-righteous, egotistical dictator, and I would never choose to serve You. I would rather go to hell than serve You!*

His thoughts were genuine and only amplified as the doors opened and he saw the judge enter from his chambers. A cruel twist of fate meant that his case was to be heard by the Honorable Judge McIntyre. Donald McIntyre, or Donny, as Scott knew him, had been one of his closest friends from fourth grade all the way through high school. They had played football together and gotten into more mischief than the judge cared to remember. After high school, their paths had crossed less frequently, but they had remained friends. It was only in recent years when he had gotten into more serious trouble that Scott deliberately avoided seeing his old friend. Donny's life was the antithesis of what he had become. Although he was glad that Donny had found a good path in life, he couldn't help but feel guilt and shame whenever he thought about seeing him.

It took the judge a moment to make his way to the chair where he would preside over the hearings. He moved slowly as he contemplated what he was about to do. His face was forlorn as he took his seat and looked at his old friend standing in front of him in an orange jumpsuit. He wanted nothing more than to declare his friend not guilty and for Scott to find the solution to his addiction and the devastation that had become his life. However, this was armed robbery, and although he could sympathize with Scott's intention not to cause harm, the law was the law. Even the minimum sentence for this category of crime would see him put away for at least 10 years.

The men's eyes locked gaze for a moment, and each instinctively knew what the other was thinking. They couldn't communicate verbally as friends, but there was visible pain on each man's face as the magnitude of the circumstances and the appropriate punishment of the crime were about to be brought before the court. The observers in the room were well aware of the relationship between the two men, and whispers started to rise as they could see the emotion and strain show on Judge McIntyre's face. The bailiff made another call for order, and the court quieted.

The charges were read, and Scott entered a guilty plea. The case was now about the severity of the sentence. The damning evidence was presented over the next several hours as the prosecution sought to provide layer upon layer of evidence of premeditation and intent. They argued that he committed this crime without concern for the consequences of the law or the lives of the store clerks. One statement in particular stood out as they tore his character to shreds. "Your honor, this man had total disregard for the very laws that hold our society together, and it was this attitude that culminated in an act of heinous violence. This was not a single act of a desperate man trying to end his life but a premeditated act of an aberration of our society that must be quarantined for the good and safety of our law-abiding citizens."

To hear them talk about his actions and motives with the single purpose of causing his old friend to see him as an evil monster bent on destruction was more than he could bear. He looked away and distracted himself with an internal dialogue that only served to reinforce the feelings he was trying to escape. *It's all true. I didn't care about anyone else. I would have hurt that old man to get those drugs. I just want to stop causing people I love pain. No matter what I try, I can't even seem to do that. I deserve to be behind bars. They should lock me up and throw away the key. If they send me to Brushy Mountain Prison, I will probably leave in a body bag. They would be doing me a favor.*

As he listened to the weak attempts of his substandard attorney trying to propose excuses for his rampant lawlessness, he hastened the end of the process and the inevitable sentence that would dictate the time frame he would have in order for his death wish to be fulfilled. As all the proceedings came to a close and the moment he had been anticipating arrived, he could not have foreseen the impact the next few moments would have on him.

Judge McIntyre looked at his friend standing before him and waited to pronounce his sentence. He was visibly moved by the weight of the responsibility that the law put on him to perform an act his heart desperately wanted to avoid. After some cursory comments, he could put off the sentencing no longer. "Ten years in federal prison." The words came out of his mouth, but his heart longed to communicate a different future. He was moved to do something he had never done before, something that broke court protocol, but he did not care. He removed his glasses and reached for his handkerchief. He wiped the tears that by now were visibly staining his cheeks. The two men locked eyes as he sought to find the impossible words to give a guilty man the strength to pay back his debt to society and at the same time do all he could to reform his character.

"Scott, you are one of the strongest men I know. There is good in you, I know it. This is a hard sentence, but if anyone can make it through this, I know you can. You can come out of this a better man. Don't give up, Scott, and I will be here to welcome you when you get out." The words were sincere and heartfelt, and Scott could see the honorable intent of his friend. As much as he appreciated the sentiment, he was still facing 10 years in federal prison, and the hopelessness in the pit of his stomach was growing as he was led from the courtroom. He could only hope that another prisoner could do him the favor of finishing what he had failed to do so many times and give him the opportunity to make his case against a much higher authority.

Chapter 55

Joey

Dick stared at the kitchen table. His bride with whom he had shared the last 25 years was slumped over, sobbing. He felt helpless and out of control. He had to do something. He could hear her attempt to gather her emotions and knew she would at least be able to hear him now.

"I don't know what we did wrong, sweetheart. I thought I had done my best with Joey. I know I am far from being a perfect father, but I have always tried to show how much I love him, even when he blatantly disobeyed us."

She composed herself in an effort to respond to her hurting husband. "It's not you, Dick." She sniffed a couple of times, blew her nose in the wad of tissues she held, and tried to steady her voice. "I don't know what it is, but I can't help thinking that we let him down. I've been wondering for quite some time when and maybe why he changed. He used to be such a happy little boy, and then everything changed. It was like the light went out inside him, and we were left with some lesser version of the boy we used to have in our home."

Dick looked at his wife with the kind of intuitive understanding of her pain that only parents can share. "I don't know. I remember bringing him to see Officer Smith before his teenage years, before cancer, and before he got so angry." He looked into his wife's eyes and saw her mind straining to pinpoint the timing of the change that led him down this dark path.

"It was even before that. I can recall a change when he was only seven or eight. It was like a sadness came over him. He stopped letting me help him. He shut me out. I asked if he was okay, but I should have pushed harder and made him tell me what was wrong while he still wanted us in his life."

"It's not that bad yet. He does want us in his life. He's just lashing out at the ones who love him enough to not lash back."

"I don't know, Dick. When I look in his eyes, he looks lost. He doesn't want to connect with me anymore. We need to do something. We can't keep doing what we are doing. It's not working. We have to try something different."

"Last year when he threatened to move out and I brought him to the streets, he talked to a homeless guy who got in his face about throwing away the good life he had. It seemed to bring him back to his senses for a while at least. What if we did something like that again, but a little more severe?"

Just like any mother would, concern started to manifest on her face when she heard an idea that sounded like it may harm her son. "What do you mean 'more severe'? I don't want to put him at risk of being hurt even more."

"Of course I don't mean letting him get hurt. In fact, I'm not sure what I mean. It feels like the devil has gotten a hold of our kid and won't let go. Maybe if he meets someone who has been down the wrong road and has allowed the Lord to change his life, he will see there is hope. Maybe a story with a positive ending and not just a guy living on the streets will get to him."

The couple sat and processed the idea. Both of them searched their mental Rolodex to think who a good candidate might be. Maybe it was the desperate heart of a mom that caused her to be the first to think of a solution. When she grabbed Dick's hand, she had the kind of knowing look that only a woman can communicate.

"I know who we need to bring him to see. Remember that guy we heard about in church? The guy who is locked up for a long time but he gave his life to Jesus? I heard his mom share about how he repented and got radically saved in prison, and ever since, he has been on fire for Jesus. She said he doesn't even realize he's locked up. He treats prison like a mission field and talks about the Lord to everyone. I think all of us need to spend some time with him." She managed a smile for the first time in ages, and he acknowledged her breakthrough by returning it.

"Do you remember the guy's name?"

"I think it was Diesel. Yes, that's it. Diesel was his name. She said he grew up right here in our neighborhood and that he overcame some kind of sickness when he was a kid, just like Joey. I assume he is still in prison, right?"

"Probably, but I will check and see." A peace settled over them. A large figure shrouded in unseen light filled the room with his presence and imparted the comfort that only heaven can provide. Dick took the presence of peace to mean he was on the right track to helping his son. He needed that assurance, as did his wife.

Dick wasted no time, and after a couple of hours of calls and texts, he excitedly ran to find his wife and share the good news. "I've found it, babe. I've found Diesel's location, and I contacted his mother." His wife smiled in a way that communicated her satisfaction with his efforts. "I made an appointment to visit Diesel a couple of weeks from now. Hopefully, Joey can stay out of trouble until then." They both knew they needed help, and Diesel was as good a candidate as any to bring hope to their son. Now all they had to do was convince Joey to go to the prison, and they had to pray.

Later that day, Joey was lying on the couch watching TV. At the commercial break, Dick brought up the idea in a rather nonchalant way. To their surprise, Joey claimed he knew about Diesel or at least had heard of him. He didn't resist the idea, but his motive was still unclear, even to himself. He just felt like he should go. Something about the idea started to invoke the same type of feeling he used to experience up on the mountainside before the darkness had come to settle on his life. In his angry moments, he was driven to self-destruction, but deep down he just wanted to feel alive again, no matter what the cost.

Chapter 56

Scott

The sun beat down on the weights as Scott pumped another rep on the bench press. In the weeks that had passed since his arrival at Brushy Mountain Prison, he had regained his appetite for working out. His body quickly inflated to its prior dimensions, and his reputation grew as quickly. Cyril, doing Big Red's bidding, attempted to recruit the latest asset before he became a problem.

"Look, Scott, there's a hierarchy inside these walls, and it's run by fear. You have the ability to instill fear in most men you meet one-on-one, but you are still just one guy. Pretty much everyone in here makes some form of allegiance to a group or aligns themselves with someone who can give them protection."

"Eight. Nine. Ten." The weight rack clanged as he dumped the bar along with the 300 pounds of weight that he made look like hollow plastic rather than solid metal. "I can take care of myself, and you can tell Red the same thing."

"Big Red. You have to call him *Big* Red or he gets angry."

"I don't give a crap what he wants to be called. Just get out of my face, or I'll drop my next set on your skull." Cyril knew when a man meant business, and he backed away.

"Just think about it, okay?" He made sure he was out of grabbing range as he made his parting plea.

On the other side of the yard, the leader of the Black Domination Gang had closely watched the exchange. There were gang chapters all over the nation, but Brushy Mountain had one of the most notorious and deadly leaders the gang had ever known. Jeremiah stood six feet eight inches tall and weighed close to 400 pounds. His hated opposition was the Aryan Brotherhood. Scott's obvious strength, shaved head, and tattoos screamed recruitment to any of the white gangs, but especially the Brotherhood. Several of Jeremiah's men had either been moved or released in recent months. He was no fool and knew Scott could shift the balance of power in the prison if he united with his enemy. His only option was to put him down before his reputation grew. He approached Scott from behind and stood over him as he pushed out his next set of reps.

"I need the bench."

"You can have it when I'm done."

"You don't understand. I am not asking you."

Scott's energy had been depleted by his hard workout, but something inside of him had had just about enough of prison yard politics. He was on the verge of snapping.

"No, *you* don't understand. I have the bench, and I will be done when I'm done. Got it, asshole?"

Jeremiah moved to the left around the outside of the bench press and grabbed a 35-pound dumbbell as he positioned himself to slam the weight into Scott's skull. Scott rolled off the bench on the other side just in time to miss the swipe at his head.

"You are going down, you stupid redneck!" Jeremiah dropped his weight as he ran at Scott. The force of his 400 pounds slamming into his body would no doubt cause severe damage, but Scott saw an opportunity. As his opponent picked up momentum, he planted his right foot behind him, and at the last second possible, he launched a ferocious uppercut straight into Jeremiah's jaw. The one-in-a-thousand punch connected perfectly with Jeremiah's head, and he fell to the floor unconscious. Gasps could be heard from across the yard.

For a moment, it seemed like time stood still. Everyone in the yard had heard the interaction between the two men and had watched as the leader of the most powerful gang in the prison had been dropped by the newcomer. They all assumed he had signed his immediate death warrant, but the members of Black Domination stared in disbelief. In the moment's delay that followed, Steel Mike saw an opportunity. Named after the steel caps on his teeth, he fit the bill as the leader of the Aryan Nations.

He motioned to several of his men to follow him over to the scene of the fight. The Black Domination saw how vulnerable their leader was and ran to protect him while he was unconscious. Steel Mike was not about to be sent to death row for a cheap opportunity to kill an unarmed, unconscious enemy. He knew that the balance of power was more connected to the finely tuned recruiting processes of the prison yard. If the enemy was too weak, he wouldn't be able to pull in the fringe inmates who needed persuading. Instead, he surrounded Scott as the Black Domination grabbed their leader under his arms and feet and struggled to lift him out of harm's way.

"That was some hit, Scott." He was surprised that Steel Mike knew his name, but he didn't respond, deciding it was better to say as little as possible.

"Look, I know about your past, but we can offer you protection."

"I don't need protection."

"Don't be an idiot. You have just dropped one of the leaders of the most powerful black gangs in the American prison system. You need protection."

"I don't care if I die."

"That is a useful attitude inside, but they are not just going to kill you. They are going to make an example of you. They have been known to rip the skin off some of their enemies for way less than what you just did." Although he didn't care if he died, Scott didn't relish the idea of torture.

"What do you want from me?"

"Two things. First, I can see that you are no stranger to weight training. My boys need someone to train them, and it will ensure that you get to use the weights as often as you want without being bothered."

"Sure. What's the second thing?"

"I will tell you later when the time comes. Just know that you owe me one, and I expect you to be available when I need to cash in."

"Listen, Steely Mike, or whatever your name is. I am no one's errand boy." Steel Mike laughed out loud.

"Don't worry, Scrapper. When I need you, it will be for something that my errand boys are not capable of."

Scott thought it was best that he lie low and walked away from the weights. He sat with his back against the wall to provide a much-needed sense of protection from any potential ambush. He knew all the parties in the yard had seen him accept the protection of Steel Mike and the Aryan Nations. He needed time to contemplate his next move. The thought of being skinned alive was gnawing at his subconscious, and he needed a minute to let the adrenaline wear off and allow a less hyped and more balanced view of his new reality to kick in. Just as his thoughts stopped racing and his heart rate started slowing down, he noticed another very large inmate make a beeline for him. He checked his options to avoid another encounter, but he had cornered himself by positioning his back to the wall.

"I saw what just happened."

"Yeah. You and everyone else."

"You really put a target on your back, man."

"I can take care of myself."

"Then why are you sitting over here with your back against the wall?"

"Look, just get lost. I'm not in the mood to talk."

"You need to get saved, my friend."

"I don't need to get saved. I can take care of myself, and besides, if you saw the whole thing, you'd know I'm under Steel Mike's protection."

"Steel Mike cannot protect your soul."

"What's wrong with you? Are you some kind of preacher or something?"

"Yes, sir. That's what they call me anyway. My name is Diesel."

"I hate religion, and I hate God. Get out of my face, preacher."

Diesel ignored his request and launched right into his speech. "I used to be like you. I hated God and church and everything that stood in the way of getting whatever it was I wanted."

"Look, preacher, you and I couldn't be further apart if we tried. You are nothing like me, and I am nothing like you. I have no desire to hear whatever it is you think you need to tell me."

Diesel paused and looked intently into the face of the man standing before him. "No, we are nothing alike now, but we used to be. I was as you are now. I looked at this prison yard with the same blank stare. I had the same fears in my heart and the same anger that drives you to pick up those weights. I know what you are going through, and Jesus is the only solution to your problems."

Anger rose up in Scott. Years of pain and brokenness had hardened his heart to these kind of gospel presentations, but the events of the last hour destabilized his already splintered emotions. He got right up into the face of his proselytizer and grabbed him by the shirt.

"If you ever attempt to tell me about Jesus or God or religion again, I swear it will be the last thing you do." His anger was being fueled by all the bad role models who had let him down, all the people who claimed to be Christians but were no more than con artists. In a moment, all that hate was focused like a laser beam on the stranger who stood in front of him, and all he wanted to do was rip his head from his body so he could never speak another word.

The preacher seemed unmoved by his anger and continued with his appeal. "God loves you, Scott. He died so your sins can be forgiven, and He offers you new life." The guard had seen Scott grab Diesel and knew he needed to intervene.

"Break it up!" said the guard. Scott gripped the preacher's shirt more tightly. Diesel was surprised that he didn't try to draw back.

"I said let him go." Scott slowly loosened his grip until Diesel's shirt returned to its original position. He stared into the eyes of his agitator, looking to read the level of fear he had imparted. Instead, he saw two eyes staring back at him without any fear. In fact, all that Diesel's eyes communicated was genuine concern. For a moment, he almost relinquished his anger, but he reached inside to find a new degree of hate as he voluntarily chose to push away God's messenger and ultimately push away God. The image of his friend Donny having to sentence him to 10 years in prison and the pain he had caused his mother erupted the deep well of hurt inside him. He reinitiated his grip on Diesel's shirt and pulled him close enough so he could whisper in his ear.

"I am going to kill you, preacher. If it is the last thing I do, I am going to kill you. Do you hear me?"

Diesel kept his gaze on Scott, unbroken, as he considered how to respond to this soul in front of him who was bound up by sin. The next words surprised Diesel when they came out of his mouth. "Not unless I kill you first." Scott couldn't believe what he had heard and let go of Diesel's shirt as he tried to process what that meant. There was no animosity in his voice and nothing about his face communicated that he intended to cause any harm, but there was a haunting sincerity about his statement.

Before either man could work out the meaning of the last statement, the guard pulled them apart and they both turned and walked away from each other. As Scott put some distance between him and the preacher, he broke free of the confusion of the last statement the preacher had made and started plotting how he could end the life of the one who was the embodiment of his hatred.

Chapter 57

Scott

Steel Mike shook his head as he listened to the proposal of his new recruit. "You have lost your mind, Scott. As much as I want you to be part of our group, why do you want to kill the preacher?"

"I don't expect you to understand. I have history with his kind, and I can't do my time with him tormenting me day in and day out in the yard. Besides, he threatened to kill me first."

"No way! You're pulling my leg."

"Look, I will do whatever you want me to do if you just get me a one-on-one with the preacher. I don't even need a weapon. I will end him with my bare hands." Fury had found a willing dwelling place in its newest convert. It was boiling just below the surface, and the hope of having its appetite satiated was the only thing keeping him calm.

"None of us like the preacher, and if he threatened you, we can take care of that. But if you follow through with this and get caught, you'll end up on death row."

"Think of me as an asset. If you do this for me, then I belong to you, but if you don't do it, then I don't belong to you. So if I fail or if you refuse to do this, you have lost an asset. Your only option to gain me as an asset is to set this up. If I succeed, you win, but if I fail, you have lost nothing."

"If you succeed, you realize you won't just owe me once? You will owe me as often as I need you."

"Yes," Scott replied, unable to see clearly past his hatred. He would have sold his own mother to get a chance at releasing some of his rage on the one on whom he was projecting his lifetime of pain and hurt.

"Give me a couple of days to set it up."

Across town, an eerily similar conversation was occurring between two parties operating on the other side of the law.

"Why do you want to have a one-on-one meeting with this Scott guy, Smithy?"

"Our paths crossed while I was still on the force, and I need to get some information from him."

"I care about you, Smithy, so I gotta ask. Is this guy a drug dealer?" He knew he could have offended his friend by asking, and before he could get a response, he found himself defending his question. "You kinda went off the deep end recently, and I would feel awful if I found out this guy was just hooking you up with a new supplier or something."

Smith understood his friend's concern, and if he had not already given up on life, he would have been sympathetic to his dilemma. "Trevor, we've been friends for more than a decade. We went through the academy together, and I've been to both your kids' christenings, right?"

"Yeah."

"Have I ever lied to you?"

"No."

"The reason I need to see this guy is because he said some things to me that drove me over the edge, and I need to understand what he meant." Smith was saying words that were truthful, but he was leaving out his true intention in an effort to manipulate his friend. He didn't care that he would get him in trouble or that he may leave him riddled with guilt after he killed Scott. His hatred was all-consuming, and friendships, or anything else for that matter, were simply a means to an end. He could see that Trevor was processing his explanation, and he thought about what else he could say that might lighten his concerns and get the outcome he wanted.

The ever-present figure in the shadows was more than willing to propose a strategy. Smith could have sworn he heard a hissing sound as an idea began to form in his mind.

"Listen, Trevor. I am about to tell you something I have never told another soul. Promise me you will keep this in the utmost confidence?" As

Trevor nodded his agreement, Smith could tell he was about to hit the point of critical mass in gaining his friend's complete trust.

"I was sexually abused."

Trevor's look of shock revealed that he couldn't imagine this decorated former officer who had intimidated the fiercest criminals by his sheer size and strength would be vulnerable to such abuse.

"I was just a young boy when it happened, and I suppressed the memories until I ran into Scott. Cantrell and I were investigating him, and during a one-on-one conversation, he told me he knew I had been abused. I had buried it so deeply at the time that I denied it. It was not until a few days later that I had a flashback of the event. I don't know how to explain it, but it was like I was reliving it, and it drove me over the edge." Smith was losing track of what was partially true and what was a lie, but he didn't care as he saw his friend's compassion overcome his skepticism.

"I don't know what to say, Smithy. I am so sorry. I get it now. I looked up to you for years, and I couldn't work out why you would have gone off the deep end the way you did when it seemed like you had everything going for you."

"I have found a way to cope with it for now, but I know Scott knows more about my abuse. I don't know how, but I'm guessing he knows the guy who abused me, and he told him about it. The problem is that I don't want to talk to him in a crowded room with a bunch of people listening to our conversation. You understand, right?"

What could his friend say? He had never experienced anything that would hurt so much that he would want to kill himself, and he was not about to patronize his friend who had just confided in him his deepest, darkest secret. "I'd be lying if I said I understand any of what you are going through, but I do understand why you would need to keep this private."

Smith knew it was the moment to close the deal. His friend had surrendered any resistance and was willing to help him any way he could. "You know all the guys at Brushy Mountain? All I need is to get about five or ten minutes alone with him. He just has to come into the room right before regular visitation is over and stay in the room. It won't even look suspicious."

"Okay. Okay, Smithy. What are friends for, right? I'm sure I can get you ten minutes alone with him in the visitation room after regular visitation is over. When do you want to do this?"

"As soon as possible, Trevor. Not knowing whatever it is that he knows is eating me up inside, and I just want to move on and get my life back together."

"Okay. I'll reach out to my friend who schedules visitations. He'll put you in the open room where you guys can sit across a table from each other. You'll still have to follow all the other rules, but at least you will be able to look him in the eye and have some privacy."

"Thanks, Trevor. You have no idea how much this means to me. I haven't been able to get Scott's words out of my mind since I, since I, well, you know." This was the truth, but the plan he had concocted would put into place an irreversible set of circumstances that would most likely end in his death by lethal injection or life in prison, and both were worth the opportunity to kill the one the figure in the shadows had convinced him was to blame for the hell that had become his existence.

Chapter 58

Joey, Smith, Scott, and Diesel

Dick looked at his son as he parked the car in the visitor's lot at Brushy Mountain Prison. He felt helpless since he had spent the last decade watching the boy who was so full of life self-destruct before his eyes. Like most men, Dick was a fixer. "Every problem has a solution," he told himself, but he never could identify the problem, and his heart broke watching the son he got back from the dead try to undo the very miracle God had given him. Everything Dick had tried over the last few years was just shots in the dark, and he couldn't help but feel that this was his last chance.

"Are you ready to do this, Joey?"

"You think I would come all the way out here and then just turn around?"

"I was just checking." He waited for his son to respond, but he just pulled the handle on the door and got out without saying another word. Dick felt his heart sink as it had done in his conversations with Joey so many times lately. This time, he reached out to his heavenly Father for help. *Father, I am at a loss to help my son. I believe You love him more than I ever could, and You know everything that's going on inside his heart. Please use Diesel to help him heal from whatever is eating him up. Lord, please save him.*

He could see Joey walk off toward the security checkpoint. Because of the steroids he had taken during his cancer treatments, he had developed the muscularity of a man. He was almost 17 now and was taller and broader than his dad. He looked like he could hold his own, even in a prison, but Dick was still scared that the negative influences of a prison and the testimony of a man he never met might do more harm than good. *No room for second-guessing. This has to work.* He slammed the car door and jogged to catch up with his son.

After the metal detector and pat-down by the security guard, they put their personal effects into a bag and handed them to the guard behind the counter.

"This way." The guard started walking toward a steel security door with thick glass. Joey followed the guard, and Dick got up behind him.

"What are you doing?" Joey's response felt more like a bark than a question.

"I'm going with you." Dick looked genuinely surprised by his son's words, and Joey reeled in anger.

"Look, Dad, this is something I have to do on my own. If it's worth my while meeting with this guy, then I have to do it alone." Now more than ever Dick realized two things. First, this was truly in God's hands, and second, his son, with all his faults, was becoming a man.

"Okay, son. I will be here when you come out." Joey turned, and without another word, he was on the heels of the guard who was holding his security badge next to the card reader with a look of mild annoyance.

Dick waited in the outside room. It felt like an eternity not knowing what was happening on the other side of the wall. Every few minutes, he released a new prayer from his lips like a valve releasing pressure. He watched as one by one the other visitors left, some crying and some having fresh resolve that their loved one would be okay. Finally, he was the last one waiting, and he hoped he would have something to work with when Joey came back through the door.

As he offered up one more prayer, someone came in the door behind him. He didn't bother to look but thought it strange that a new visitor would be arriving when visiting hours were coming to an end. He saw the guard walk behind him to the door and assumed the late arrival would be ushered out. He heard some hushed talk, and then the guard and another man who looked like a wrestler from behind walked by him. As the guard got to the door and swiped his card, the visitor took a look over his shoulder at the lone man in the waiting room, and their eyes locked.

"Officer Smith?" He was shocked by his muscularity and size but more by the empty look in his eyes. The light that hope gives a soul looked like it had been extinguished.

"Pastor Dick?"

Click, Click, Click. The triple lock on the door opened, and the guard held the door for Smith as he tried to process why his old youth pastor would be at this prison at the same time he was. He turned his attention to the guard who was taking the heat for his late visit. He followed as the officer opened the secondary security door and then walked 10 feet to the final security door. A few more feet and he would get access to the man he had been obsessing nonstop about killing for the last month. He tried to shake off the unsettledness of seeing Dick in the waiting room.

"What's he doing here?"

"His son is visiting with one of our inmates. They've been talking for over an hour."

"They can't be here. I had express instructions that this visit must be just me and the other inmate."

"The kid was crying, man, and it was obvious that the inmate was helping him deal with some stuff. The room is plenty big. You can have your meeting on the other side, and they won't hear anything you guys say." Anger rose in Smith as his plan started to unravel right before he could live out his dark fantasy. The figure in the shadows seemed even more disturbed as he saw his nemesis waiting for him in the room as well. Smith was about to unload on the unsuspecting guard when they both heard the door from the inmate side of the room click three times.

"What the hell?" Smith was about to come unglued. In the 10 seconds he had been in the room, he had started to rework his plan to get the kid out of the room before Scott came in. He had his script prepared in his head, and he was meant to be sitting down when Scott arrived. Part of his vengeance was to catch him off guard. He could see the guard walk in ahead of Scott, and then he could see the inmate denims and the bald head.

"Where are his cuffs? He's supposed to be wearing cuffs." It was obvious that Scott had been pumping iron, and Smith knew he could only choke the life out of him if his hands were cuffed.

Scott's gaze was fixed on Diesel as the door opened, but then he saw a teenage kid at the table and heard a familiar voice from the other side of the room.

"Detective Smith, what the hell are you doing here?" His murderous focus equally destabilized by the unexpected dynamics in the room.

"I'm not a detective anymore thanks to you, asshole."

"What on earth are you talking about?" Smith wanted to unleash all his fury on Scott, but he knew he would get only one chance to kill him, and with two guards still in the room, he would have to choose very carefully that moment or he would be carrying this anger for the rest of his life.

Diesel stood up, and the three men still standing in the room, as well as the guards, turned their gaze toward him, surprised by his intrusion.

"You are all here because of me. I requested your presence here today. You may think that you orchestrated your steps, but I asked God to bring you to this moment." Diesel turned to the guards. "You can go." As if under some kind of spell, the guards exited through the doors they came in, and at the final click, an eerie silence fell on the room as the battle royale was put on hold waiting for this conundrum to be revealed. "You are going to want to sit down."

For the first time in his relationship with Smith, the figure in the shadows was void of ideas, and with two very large protectors holding him at bay, he was equally powerless to force any backup plans into effect.

"I don't understand what's going on." Smith's fog of rage and deception was starting to dissipate, and his thoughts seemed to fall under his control for the first time in as long as he could remember. His fog opened the door for Scott to become the aggressor.

"I came here to kill you, Diesel, and that is what's going to happen, so both of you better stay out of my way or, so help me, I will kill all of you." Scott shifted his weight onto his front foot to launch himself into a sprint toward Diesel. His right hand swung back instinctively as his body sought to generate the momentum his brain was saying it needed. As his arm started the movement forward to match his legs, he was jerked backward by his unmoving hand. It felt like his hand was in a vice, and the momentum of the rest of his body caused his feet to come out from underneath him as he fell hard on his back. The chair he landed on crumpled underneath the body-slamming it endured. Scott heard a crack and felt a searing pain in his ribs. He looked at his hand, which was suspended in the air. He was completely confused, but the protector holding him back could hold him in this position for an eternity, if necessary.

For the first time, Diesel looked at the man who wanted nothing more than to kill him. With eyes full of love, he uttered the words that changed the tone of the room. "You all came here to unleash your pain and hate on someone else, but as I told you the other day, Scott, I am here to end your life and theirs, too."

Chapter 59

Joey, Smith, Scott, and Diesel

"What are you talking about? You can't kill us." Scott had unwittingly allied himself with the other two in the room and in doing so triggered Smith's own defense.

"I don't know what you're up to, Diesel, or whatever your name is. I am former law enforcement, and I can have those guards back in here in a second." Smith's grasp on reality was slipping, and he could only hope that the guards were actually observing the events from the visiting room.

"You are wrong, Detective Smith. Where would they come from?" The cryptic question forced a puzzled look on all three faces, and they immediately looked at the doors as if to point to the obvious answer to his ridiculous question. Fear gripped all their hearts simultaneously as the shape and form of the room started to transform. Instead of a large room with two dozen tables and twice as many chairs, they were in a 10 x 8 foot cell with a bunk, toilet, and sink. They had been at least 15 feet apart, but now they could reach out and touch each other if they were able to move. All four men were wearing prison denims.

"I don't understand. Where are we, and why can't we move?" Joey was the first to express his fears, and Diesel looked at him with renewed compassion in his eyes for the broken boy before him.

"Joey, I have spent the last hour explaining to you that the abuse done to you as a little boy broke God's heart and that God did not cause your cancer but was the One who healed you. You are going down a road that has no good outcome. You are going to have to trust me. If you don't *choose* to die, then the pain that awaits you on the other side of death will make all the pain you have suffered in your short life seem insignificant." Joey dropped his head. Somehow, deep within him, he knew the man he met just an hour ago was the only person who ever spoke the truth he so desperately needed to hear.

"I don't think I am ready to die, Diesel, but I don't want to have the things you say happen to me either."

Diesel turned his attention to the two men in front of him. They both tried their best to hide their fears, but they had no way to explain the events of the last few minutes. As they stood shoulder to shoulder, they almost spanned the width of the room. They looked like caged warriors. They were almost identical in size, and veins were popping out of their necks as the fight-or-flight defense instinct was in full fight mode. Smith was about 10 years Scott's junior, but they looked remarkably similar now that they were dressed the same. Although Smith's hair was receding, it still offered the only significant difference in their features.

The figure in the shadows was having a war of his own. His protégé, who was about to complete his activation into full-blown darkness, was slipping from his grasp. The cell was full of an unseen light that prevented him access and broke his control over the mind of his slave. The same protectors who were in the waiting room now stood inside the bars of the cell, blocking his hold on his captive. His voice went from a clear authoritative tone to a high-pitched squeal as he launched obscenities across the room. His curses seemed to melt in the light that was getting brighter and brighter on the other side of the bars. His despair at his loss of influence didn't go unnoticed by the protectors who were enjoying every second of his pain.

Diesel took control of the room once more. "Listen to me now. I may have orchestrated this meeting, but this will only work based on the decisions of your free will. I know that from a young age, just like Joey here, you were all set on an awful path through abuse, and just like Joey, you each suffered from testicular cancer and blamed God for the exceptional pain you suffered. Your paths to adulthood were particularly rocky, but you both made the worst of a bad situation. If we don't do something today, it will mean that Joey will end up worse than both of you." The two men were in complete disbelief as this uneducated, self-proclaimed prison yard preacher unpacked the deepest hurts in their lives. They sought for a response to match their feelings, but both men had only painful stares to offer.

"The same pursuit of pain avoidance and pain numbing that you both have wasted decades pursuing is in store for Joey. It is inevitable. Just like you, Detective Smith, he will seek to find his self-worth in a career of law enforcement, and just like you, due to his inability to have kids, he will be seen as an ideal candidate to go into child abuse investigation. Just like you, it will drive his own pain deeper and deeper until it is unrecognizable as the source of his unhappiness, and no matter what successes he achieves, he will be just as empty as you are. Then, just like you, he will turn to alcohol and drugs to numb the pain that torments him day in and day out. Just like you, he will self-destruct in his career and forsake all reason to end his own life. Just like you, his journey will be orchestrated by an invisible entity who desires only to steal from him, kill him, and utterly destroy everything he was created to be."

Diesel could hear sniffles from the teenager beside him as he heard his future proclaimed in such doomsday accuracy. He shifted his gaze to the older man who still bore a murderous hatred for him.

"Just like you, Scott, he will lose all dignity and self-respect. He will go from friend to stranger, offering lie upon lie to get the means to the next fix, until finally he cannot tell the truth from a lie, and all the relationships that ever meant anything to him will be destroyed by his selfishness. Just like you, he will betray even his mother's love. He will fail to end his own life and stare down the barrel of a ten-year prison sentence seeking death through lethal injection as a way out."

Scott tried to process how he would know anything about his life, never mind the intimate facts he was able to share in such detail.

"I don't care what you know about me, all I want to do is kill you."

"Scott, you are the one person who can kill me. You can stop me from ever becoming who I am today. Without your agreement, I will never continue to be a yard preacher and never have the opportunity to offer you a way out of the hell you are living in." Scott was not expecting to be empowered by his captor.

"Then I choose that you die. I choose that you never exist. I hope you rot in whatever grave your fake reality came from." Diesel looked at him with a knowing compassion and seemed completely unmoved by his hatred.

"Don't choose just yet. I have an offer for you that may outweigh your hatred for me." Diesel looked at the two men, and Smith realized he was waiting on their permission to make the offer.

"What is the offer?"

"Are you really going to listen to this idiot?" Scott turned to stare his fellow captive in the eyes to see if he was legitimately wanting to know what he was being offered.

"I came here to murder you, Scott. Instead, I find myself in a cell with you, and I can't move my body, and all of a sudden, things are starting to make sense in my head. So yes, I do want to listen to what he has to say."

Scott couldn't help but see the irony of the situation. "You came to kill me, and I came to kill him, and Diesel came to kill us all. Who did you come to kill, kid?"

"Myself!" The sobering answer seemed to connect with Scott in a place deep inside that had been dormant for what seemed like a lifetime. Compassion welled up inside him, and for once he responded not for selfish reasons but in genuine concern for another.

"Okay, for the kid, I will listen. For the sake of the kid." Joey seemed surprised by the care of this hardened criminal. Diesel wasted no time in case they changed their minds.

"Each of you has interpreted your pain and suffering as punishment from an uncaring and hateful God. You have filtered everything in your life through self-destruction, and you have been led on your way by willing tutors who were assigned to you from the pit of hell to bring about your demise. The fact that you are even alive today is a result of many miracles. If you could only see the countless times the hand of God, who loves you more than life itself, prevented each of you from entering into the eternal punishment of hell we all deserve."

"If He was so loving, then why did He allow that pain in the first place?" Smith's question was genuine, and Diesel knew it needed to be answered before they could ever understand the offer he was about to make.

"Each of you grew up in church and heard the message of the gospel. The problem is you heard man's sincere but twisted understanding of what was supposed to be the good news. The only way we can have a genuine relationship with God is if we have the freedom to choose that relationship over a legitimate alternative. God made man in His image and gave him the ability to rule over the whole planet as sons and daughters of God without the horrible effects of sin. But we chose self. We chose sin. We chose disobedience, and we chose a master who wants only to destroy everything that bears the image of the one who sentenced him to destruction." All three stared at Diesel like children hearing a story for the first time.

The figure in the shadows was now on his knees as his true identity and motives were being exposed, but there was nothing he could do. His power and rights over the mind and body of Smith were suspended, and the others had all chosen to listen of their own free will. The light coming from Diesel's truthful words and the strong presence of the protectors allowed due to the prayers of Dick in the waiting room meant their minds were free to hear clearly what Diesel had to offer. It was a nightmare scenario playing out. Smith could only watch as the potential for a complete reversal of years of work hinged on the decision that could be made in the light of truth. He screamed murderous threats at Diesel to shut up, but his words couldn't penetrate the dense light filling the room. Diesel continued, unaware of the feeble opposition and confident that God was in control of the events unfolding in the cell.

"Even today, we are created with a free will, and we can choose what to do with that will. The problem is that the free will of other sinful human beings intersects with the worlds of those around them. We have all suffered horrendous harm, but our lives have done the same degree of damage and more to the ones we have loved; it just came in a different form. In a world full of free will and with the hateful, murderous, and destructive influences of an evil slave-driving master, we simply have no hope of ever living a life of fulfillment."

"Then why are we here?" Smith's lifetime of pain taught him to expect only bad outcomes, and he could not see past the last statement he just heard.

"Because I have something to offer you today. There is a way past this existence. There is a way to truly live." He paused as he readied himself to redeliver the message he had used to open this encounter. "However, you must choose to die so you may truly live." For all their self-loathing and extensive attempts to take their own lives, there was a resistance in their hearts to give up their sovereignty and die at someone else's discretion.

"I don't think I can do that." Smith was remembering pieces of Scripture and snippets of sermons that had hung around his memory for years. "Are you saying that God wants us to die so we can live? Doesn't that seem a lot to ask?"

"Let me answer the first part of that question. The very basis of the message of Jesus is an exchange of lives. Yours for His. Your broken, sinful, unproductive life for His powerful, wonderful, overcoming, victorious, devil-destroying, people-rescuing life. He offers redemption. You think that is just a religious word, but it is not. It is the most beautiful word my ears have ever heard, and it means that He is offering to restore your life to the fullness of its original purpose. He is not just offering to take away the punishment of your sins, but remarkably, He is offering to make you sons of God once more. He wants to appoint you as warriors in His battle against the kingdom of darkness so that His Kingdom of light can be established everywhere you set your feet. We can once more be God's agents of His reign here on the earth and then in complete fullness once He comes back again."

Their eyes were as big as saucers, and they expected these strange words to stop making sense, but they understood it all. Smith was in tears. He found it hard to accept that God wanted anything more for him than pain and loss. His heart sought for a reason to hold on to his own sovereignty, but the only thing he had been living for was to kill Scott. In this moment, even that lost its appeal. He looked at the teenage boy across the room from him, and a realization hit him.

"You're Pastor Dick's kid. I met you about five years ago at the diner when your dad dropped you off. I remember now. What happened to you?" Joey looked up for the first time since Diesel started to speak.

"I was doing okay for a while, and then I got cancer. I thought I was going to die, and then somehow, I got better. At first, I thought it was God, but no matter what I did, I still felt guilty, so I presumed it had been God who made me sick in the first place. I knew I could never please Him, and I was afraid I would get sick again or worse. Over time, I guess I couldn't bear that feeling any longer and just got madder and madder at God, blaming Him for making me feel miserable."

Smith turned his attention to Diesel as he could relate perfectly to the pain the young man was feeling. "Are you telling me that if I choose to die right here, right now, that Joey will not have to suffer like we suffered?" Diesel was proud of the step Smith was trying to take, but he knew the equation was not that simple.

"No. Joey will still suffer just like you, but if you don't choose to die, both your life and his will mean nothing and end in darkness and torment forever. If you do choose to die, you will both have the privilege of giving your life for the purposes of the truly good King." At that same moment, Scott realized that the kid was also familiar to him.

"Hey kid, why do I think I know you?" Joey had already recognized Scott but had not felt like he could speak before now.

"I met you on the streets a while back. You were living under a tarp, and you told me not to become like you." The poignancy of the moment hit Scott like a ton of bricks. "You told me you had been just like me when you were younger and that I should not make the choices you made."

"Well, did you listen?"

"For a while, but then the voices in my head started telling me there was nothing I could do to keep from ending up on the streets, and it was then that I just gave in and started getting into trouble." Scott couldn't help feeling that his proclamation of wisdom was turning into a self-fulfilling prophecy. Diesel watched as the three made connections of their pasts, but he held back form telling them the full truth until they were ready.

Scott was the oldest. He bore the deepest scars, and although he could not deny that this kid's story was doing something inside of him, he had years of dark choices to overcome. The pendulum of his heart forced its way against the new feeling he was experiencing.

"I refuse to give my life for a God who is as heartless as He has been to us. He didn't have to create us. He didn't have to give us the miserable existence we have lived. He didn't have to give us choices so some twisted bastard can take advantage of an innocent young boy. He didn't have to make a world with alcohol and drugs and pornography and lying and stealing and murder. It's easy for Him to ask us to die because He botched up His creation. It doesn't cost Him anything for us to die." The last statement had such venom that Diesel wasn't sure he could ever leverage Scott sufficiently out of his pain to see the truth of his situation. He bowed his head and prayed.

"Father, show us the great price you paid for us."

A light from above filled the room, and a scene unfolded before them that filled the whole back wall where the sink and toilet were. It was so real that it looked like they could walk right into the vision before them. All four men looked on in wonder as their minds tried to piece together what was happening in this scene from a time and place that belonged long in the past. The characters were hard to make out at first since it was the dead of night, but they could hear an anxious and painful prayer from a man who kneeled alone in the middle of a garden. Then they saw Jesus up close as He perspired drops of blood while contemplating the cost he would have to pay to offer a way out for humanity. The scene changed as soldiers came, and Judas, his close friend, betrayed Him with a kiss. The four watched a trial for false charges convene during the middle of the night before a biased jury. They saw Him face His accusers with silence as they humiliated and beat Him.

The scene changed once more, and they could see soldiers twist a vine with three-inch flesh-piercing thorns into the shape of a crown and ram it onto His head so the thorns dug into His skull. This beaten and falsely accused God-man voluntarily allowed the soldiers to whip Him with leather straps with metal hooks that ripped strips of flesh off His body with every lash. They could see the crowds mocking Him as He carried His own cross through the streets until He reached the hill where they would execute Him in one of the worst forms of torture ever created by man. They watched in horror as the crowd cried out for His death and the soldiers nailed His hands and feet to the cross. They hoisted Him up so the sheer weight of His own body hanging on the nails caused excruciating pain. They watched as He struggled to breathe, and the crowd taunted Him and jeered. "He saved others, let Him save Himself if He is the Messiah," they heckled. His anguish was palpable, not from the outward torture but from the inward hell He was experiencing. Somehow, they saw the sins of billions of souls poured on Him. The only sinless man to ever live experienced sin for the first time in a magnitude that would rip asunder any soul that was not perfect. They could hear his heart cry out in pain, "Father, Father, why have you forsaken me?" In the midst of all his physical and soulish torment, they could see Jesus switch his attention to those around Him. Instead of the hatred they were experiencing in their own hearts toward the soldiers who crucified Him and the murderous crowd who treated Him so cruelly, they could see the love in the eyes of this extraordinary man on the cross. Then He uttered the words that seemed to unlock the torment hidden in the deepest recesses of their hearts.

"Father, forgive them, for they don't know what they do."

The scene disappeared, and the room dimmed as the four were left to consider the significance of what they had just witnessed. Nothing about this encounter made sense, but somehow, they knew the images they had just seen were not Hollywood's version of what happened. They had just witnessed the historical accounts of the Bible come to life before their eyes. Diesel looked into Scott's eyes, and he could see that Scott finally understood that the true and greatest cost of salvation fell on Jesus.

Chapter 60

Joey, Smith, Scott, and Diesel

"It's time I answer the second part of your question, Detective Smith. You asked if you are being asked to die so Joey may live. It's true that you are being asked to die, but the truth is that I am asking you to die not so Joey may live but so that I may live."

All three looked at him with indignation. Everything he had shared so far had been leading them to a point of self-sacrifice. The older men were both willing to die so what they perceived as an innocent life might be saved. Joey had just hoped he would be offered a way out of the future that Diesel had proclaimed over him. However, the belief that this was all somehow for Diesel's benefit uncovered the remaining selfishness, pride, and self-righteousness that had been hiding in their hearts.

"There is no way I'm dying for you!" Scott's desire to kill Diesel was fueling back up. Smith was adjusting in his heart the wrenching scenes he had just watched and the indignation he now felt at the outrageous request he had just heard.

"Listen, Diesel, I don't know who you are, and that video you just played on whatever new device you have up your sleeve was bizarre, but if you think I'm going to give up my life so you can go on your merry way, you can forget it." Joey watched as Smith rebuffed Diesel's offer and prepared his own speech as he moved from sitting on the bed beside Diesel to the side of the room where the other two were standing. Joey stood as tall as the others, and although he didn't have the muscle mass they had, he was almost as broad.

"I thought you wanted to help me. All you have done is tell me how terrible my life is going to be, and now you want me to give my life for you?"

Diesel looked at the three standing before him and breathed deeply as he thought how best to share the last piece of the truth with them.

"This is not going to be easy for you to take, but you need to know the truth." He paused as he considered the gravity of what he was about to share with them. "You are not here of your own will. I have brought you all to this moment of time because there is something I have to do, and I can't do it without you. Right now, I am sitting in this very bunk making the most important decision of my life. God has spoken to my heart and made me the offer I made you a few moments ago, and for the first time in my life, I finally understand the exchange of His life for mine so my life can be redeemed. I want to accept His offer, but I can't do that without each of you."

Smith's logic training that had served him well in law enforcement jumped in to point out what he thought was obvious. "What has this got to do with us? If you want to accept redemption, then you go ahead and die. Why do you need us?" Diesel sighed, for he knew he could no longer hold the truth from them. "Because you *are* me."

The three of them struggled to process the implication of the four simple words they had just heard. Diesel was not about to hold back now. "Each of you represents a stage of my life, and each of you must agree to die before I can and before we all receive new life." They all looked stunned, and Diesel knew they still needed further explanation. "When the Lord offered me salvation just moments ago on this bunk, I knew I needed to yield everything I had ever done, everyone I had ever hurt, and everyone who had ever hurt me to Him, and I can't do that without each of you. I have repented and am willing to accept His offer, but each of you must do the same or I cannot go through with this. I will never know redemption, and I can never become the preacher of the gospel that I am now."

Smith's brain was still working overtime. Pointing to each man, he said, "So you're trying to tell me that we are all the same person? That Joey will become me, and that I will become Scott?"

Scott jumped on his logic. "And I will become the yard preacher that I came here today to murder?"

Again, Diesel sighed. "Yes, and I am at your mercy. I cannot live until we all die. Scott, the man in the bunk is you in just a few weeks. Your cellmate

Spencer, who keeps reading the Bible and annoying you, will soon affect you in a way you would never expect. You are about to change, and a hunger is going to grow in your heart—a hunger to have what he has, a hunger to live."

Scott tried to internally refute what he was saying, but he knew it was true. He turned toward the bars, grabbed them, and violently shook the metal frame. "No! No! No! It can't be. I can't let go of this pain. I can't forgive that bastard who molested me. I can't believe God is good after all that has happened in my life. I can't ask for forgiveness. I can't, I can't, I can't!" He stared into the hallway and shook his head.

The figure in the shadows who once ruled every aspect of his life reached up in hopes he could regain control of Scott's mind. The protectors could see the bond reforming, and they moved quickly in an attempt to shift the momentum back to the offer Scott was contemplating rejecting. They put their hand on Joey's shoulder and seemed to suggest an action without saying any words. Joey in turn reached over to him and put his hand on Scott's shoulder, turning him away from the antagonist standing outside the cell so he could look him in the face.

"Scott, you told me to not turn out like you. Well, it seems inevitable that I will. If you don't let go, then I have no hope. No hope at all."

"I want to help you, kid, I truly do, but you have no idea what I have gone through." Smith had been facing the wall, processing what choice he would make. He did not want to become Scott, but more importantly, he did not want his life to count for nothing.

"Scott, I came here to kill you because I blamed you for destroying my life. It turns out that I was more right than I knew. Look, I have been through hell, so I know you have, too, plus more than I can imagine. But I don't want my life to be the sum of my and your mistakes. I want it to count for something. If there is any chance I—or we—can repair some of the damage we've done, then I want that. I am willing to die if you are."

Scott turned to face Diesel, ready to mount his defense, when he broke and tears streamed down his face. He tried to gain his composure, but for a long while, the other three watched as years of bitterness and pain flowed out of him. As Scott examined his heart, the only remaining resistance came to the fore.

"I don't want to become you, Diesel. I don't want to become the ridiculed yard preacher, the idiot who goes around telling everyone that God loves them and wants them to go to heaven."

Diesel knew this struggle more than Scott himself, but he fought the urge to mitigate the cost. "Scott, dying means you don't have any rights anymore. Your story is one of going to hell and back. If you will let God save you, then the very foundations of hell will shake and heaven will rejoice. If a self-destructive hellion like you can be saved, then anyone can. The message of how God can save a life like yours is too powerful to keep quiet. If you decide to die today, you will become me, and when we get out of here, I promise you there will be plenty more opportunities to embrace the humiliation of the gospel."

The words hit like a sledgehammer on his pride and at the same time grabbed hold of the one part of him that had come alive when he felt compassion for Joey. He wrestled back and forth internally when, all of a sudden, the brightness returned to the room. The four watched as they saw a form materialize in the shape of a man shrouded in light, far brighter than the sun in the middle of the day. They all knew they were staring at the resurrected Savior whom they had just watched be crucified moments ago. They did not see His lips, but they could hear His words. "Scott, I know your pain. You saw how I have paid the price so you may receive forgiveness and receive my life in place of yours. My holiness in place of your sinfulness. My strength instead of your weakness."

Scott found an honesty that had lain dormant inside him. "Lord, I can't forgive myself. I have shamed my whole family. I was supposed to lead my family after my dad died, but I abandoned my role out of fear and selfishness and pride. All he ever wanted was to help me become the man You wanted me to be, but I have caused him more harm than anyone else could have." Scott dropped to his knees, and the tears flowed again as years of unspoken pain welled up inside of him. The others watched in amazement as they saw the compassion of Jesus for the man who had just rejected Him. Then they realized there was another man standing next to the Savior whose form looked familiar.

"Scott, it's me. It's your dad." Scott looked up in disbelief as he heard the voice of the man he had buried a decade ago.

"Dad, is that you?"

"Yes, son. It is me. Our heavenly Father has allowed me to see you one last time."

With tears flowing down his face, Scott poured out his regrets. "I am so sorry, Dad. I'm sorry that I didn't take care of my brothers. I'm sorry I wasted my life. I'm sorry I betrayed Mom. I'm sorry I dishonored you and all you stood for. I never understood God like you did, and I didn't have the courage or the strength to be like you."

"Son, I was far from perfect when I walked the earth with you. It was my limited understanding of the gospel that gave you the wrong ideas about our amazing Father in heaven. I forgive you for all that you have done, my son, but I, too, need forgiveness for not introducing you to the truth I was too afraid to believe for myself. Son, I love you more than you could ever imagine, but I don't have long, and you have a decision to make. God has presented you with the choice to accept His life in exchange for yours. The man you came here to kill today is the man you were meant to become. I believe in you, my son, and if you choose to die, know that I will be so proud of the man you will become. You will bring the truth of the gospel to others whom I never understood and could never communicate with. I rescued others from hell, but you will show them the full redemption of their lives, a true exchange of their lives for the full life Jesus intends for all who choose Him."

Dick knelt down in front of his son, and Scott embraced him with all that was in him.

"Don't go, Dad. Please don't go. I need you."

"These moments are a supernatural gift, son, and I can't stay any longer, but your heavenly Father will always be there for you." Scott could no longer feel his dad's arms around him, and in a moment, Dick disappeared completely.

Scott slumped to the floor as he unloaded all the pain he had been fighting back. Tears flowed from his eyes, and his nose gushed like a volcano. Smith and Joey were moved by what they had seen and knelt down beside their future self as he weighed his decision and their future in his heart and mind. The forgiveness from his dad gave him the strength he needed to make the radical choice to die. Scott relented, and as he did, the years of pain, guilt, shame, selfishness, pride, vulgarity, depravity, and much more rolled off his tongue. He held nothing back as he sensed the washing of his soul every time he mentioned the next sin that came to his memory. All the way back to childhood, sin after sin unveiled itself, and just as quickly as it was unveiled, it was banished by the cleansing blood of his newly found Savior, never to hold the power of captivity again.

As he rose from the floor, he felt like he was floating, and a sense of relief and, more importantly, true freedom engulfed him. Sometime during the encounter with Jesus, the figure in the shadows had disappeared, and the boundaries of hell had indeed shifted under the power of God's grace.

As Scott opened his eyes, the other versions of himself were gone, and he was alone with his cellmate. Turning to the man he now remembered as the target of his ridicule, he saw him in the light Diesel said he would. The one who had appeared naïve and stupid would now be his source of understanding.

"Spencer, I have no idea what just happened."

Spencer chuckled as he answered his new protégé. "Well, Diesel, I know exactly what happened. You just died to your old way of life, and now you are a brand-new creation. Diesel, for the first time in your life, you are truly *alive!*"

CPSIA information can be obtained
at www.ICGtesting.com
Printed in the USA
FSHW020706170419

9 781632 963260